MisStep

MisStep

Stepping, Book 1

Christopher McMaster

Southern Skies Publications

ISBN: 978-1-99-117162-7 (paperback)

978-1-99-116011-9 (Epub)

www.southernskiespublications.com

Cover art: Vila Design at: www.viladesign.net

First Printing, 2022

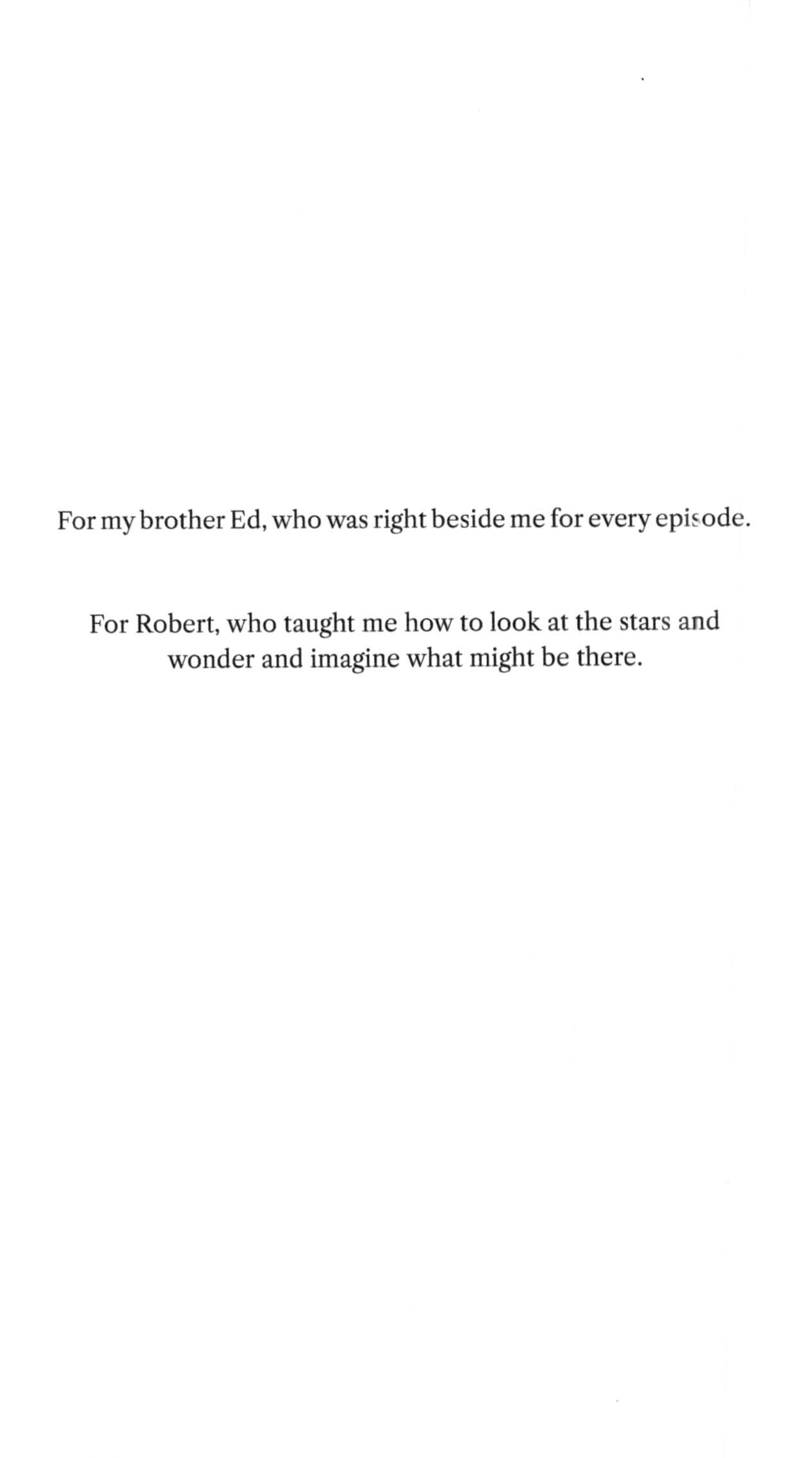

For my brother Ed, who was right beside me for every episode.

For Robert, who taught me how to look at the stars and
wonder and imagine what might be there.

Prologue: Stepping Out

Stepping Out

THE PERSONAL LOG OF CAPTAIN ELIZABETH SHERIDAN

With an introduction by Jimena Ruiz, Secretary General of the United Nations

Introduction

After the exploratory ship *Fortitude* returned to Earth, everything changed. The crew of the *Fortitude* had already taken seven Steps prior to the discovery of planet Kepler 76-e, now known as Shackleton, or more popularly as 'The Shack'. It was so named to reflect our own collective "Shackleton Moment", when the people of Earth wisely decided to turn back, to admit that the prize, while worthy, was out of our reach, and the only way to save humanity was to focus on our planet.

In 1908, Ernest Shackleton's prize was the South Pole. It was a time of exploration, filled with toughened heroes, the celebrities of their day. He could have continued and been remembered as the first man to reach the pole. But he would have died on the return, just as his contemporary, Robert Scott, did a few years later.

Shackleton turned back, and in doing so, he saved his men. Similarly, we turned back, and in doing so, we saved ourselves. The crew of the *Fortitude* was in the depths of space for over sixteen years. Captain Elizabeth Sheridan had no way of knowing that the story of the *Fortitude*, of the disappointment the crew experienced, and the crushing despondency they felt when they decided to turn back, would have impacted humanity the way it did.

Kepler 76-e is the fifth planet orbiting a Sol-like star, located 2089 light-years from Earth. It is situated in the Goldilocks Zone, the habitable area around a star where the temperature is just right—not too hot and not too cold—for water to exist on a planet in liquid form. However, it wasn't merely water that the *Fortitude*, and many other exploratory ships, sought.

They were looking for life. Every planet so far discovered, and this is true to the present day, is devoid of life, even in fossilized form. Many of these planets contain water, both liquid and frozen, but none hold even the most primitive type of life. On our Earth, life first began over 3.5 billion years ago, maybe even over 4 billion years in the past. Not long after our oceans formed, microscopic single-celled organisms emerged, then grew and evolved into the myriad forms of life we celebrate today.

Early theories held that life on Earth might have come from biological matter carried by space dust or meteorites. We no longer believe this to be viable hypothesis. Earth is unique among trillions of planets orbiting billions of stars. Our Milky Way Galaxy, comprising over 200 billion stars, is itself one of perhaps two billion galaxies in the known universe.

And yet, as far as we can find, life is only known on planet Earth. Our home.

While Captain Sheridan and her crew Stepped back to Earth, despairing in what they perceived as their failure, today we see their discovery and voyage differently. Captain Sheridan, in her own words, "gave up." And when the *Fortitude* and its sole surviving crew member returned to Earth, we all, also, gave up. But in giving up, in losing hope that there was a new start or a sanctuary somewhere in the stars, we began to value what we had.

We will still reach out to the stars. We will still study and settle the planets we find, building new homes from bare rock, and mining their rich resources. We will still search for life. But not like before. Through her grief, Captain Sheridan helped us to see that we need to value what we have. The planets that have been, and are still being, discovered can never provide enough to meet humanity's need for air to breathe, land to farm, or oceans to fish. As news of the fate of the *Fortitude* spread around the globe, and especially after the publication of her personal log, Elizabeth Sheridan shocked a generation into action, initiating what would be known as "The Great Clean-Up". During its time, it was called other things, with similar themes: the seventh generation, the waking up, a coming to our senses, taking responsibility, planning for a future. It was a true turning point – a pivotal decision.

I am honored to write the introduction to this reprint of Captain Sheridan's brief log, a record she began to keep only after she and her crew realized that the beautiful green of The Shack one sees from space was only rock. Although she may not have known it at the time, what she penned was a wake-up call. I like to think that she knew, somewhere deep down, that that was what her words would become. She was the leader of the expedition, but also served as ship's doctor. Her deep concern for her crew fills her journal, but so too does her concern for those left behind on Earth. It is nice to believe, if perhaps only a sentimental notion, that that was what motivated her to write them. If you are fortunate to view the original copy of her log kept at the United Nations Museum at Geneva, Switzerland, you will see that she did not date her entries. She seemed to let the pain inside her escape onto the page nearest to her pen at the time. This reproduction of her personal log has tried to stay true to how she wrote it.

Astrogator and astrophysicist Alan Seed was the only crew member of the *Fortitude* to return to Earth. As promised to Captain Sheridan, he shared the story of their exploration as well as her personal log. Their experience was not solitary. In the years immediately after the return of the *Fortitude*, other ships returned with core samples from barren rocky planets. None found the hoped-for sister to our home. Their failure mirrored that of the *Fortitude*, and personal accounts of their crew reflected the despondency felt by Sheridan and her crew. As more ships returned home, their logs were similarly published. But none had the effect of the first by the captain of the *Fortitude*. The return of the others gave it even more power.

We all owe her, and her crew, a great deal of gratitude. While Elizabeth Sheridan, and many of those with her, chose to 'step out' 2000 light-years from home, they will always be with us.

Geneva, Switzerland

THE PERSONAL LOG OF CAPTAIN ELIZABETH SHERIDAN

I instructed the crew to cease geological surveys of the surface of Kepler 76-e. Nate refused. I have to find an opportunity to apologize to him. When I ordered the ground crew up, he said, "No. It's too soon."

I made myself listen to the recording. Then I deleted it from the record.

"It's not too soon," I told him. "It's already too late. It's time to go home."

For me, it is. I didn't quite know it on the bridge speaking to the survey crew at that moment, at least not consciously. But the decision brought relief.

Not to Nate. "No," he said. I could hear his anger; he didn't mask it. "What are you doing, *ordering* me?"

"Yes, Nate," I said. "Return to the ship so we can prep for return to the Ein-Ros[1]."

"No!" he insisted.

"This is an order, Mr Huckins! Return to the ship."

"No. What are you going to do about it?"

---

1. At the time of Captain Sheridan, Donuts were referred to as Ein-Ros, in reference to the Einstein-Rosen bridge the devices created. (Editor)

We reduced ourselves to bickering children. The Captain and First Mate of an interstellar ship throwing tantrums. In hindsight, it's easy to remember that arguing with a child is a no-win situation. The child always wins. When there's no adult involved, it can only go badly.

"Refusing an order is mutiny!" I actually said that.

"Fuck you, Liz. This isn't the military."

I did the only thing I could. I shut up. Dead air filled the comms between us. Finally, I said, "Be careful down there."[2]

I waited for a reply, but none came. They would be back in two cycles; that's all they had supplies for. Forty-eight hours to clean up my mess. From his chair at navigation, Alan stared blankly at me, probably too confused or shocked to register what he just witnessed. At the time I wanted him to intervene, to take over, deem me unfit to continue command. I pleaded with my eyes, but he couldn't or wouldn't translate. Nobody wants to be in my shoes. I don't want to be in my shoes.

***

The survey party returned today. I went to Nate's cabin and stood in front of the door for several minutes, wanting to walk away, wanting to pretend what happened didn't. But I didn't have that kind of out. His door slid open when I knocked. He was standing in the middle of his cabin. I walked towards him, put my arms around him and he started to sob. Our tears soaked the backs of each other's necks. I don't remember going to his bunk, but that is where we stayed, holding each other, crying.

---

2. The official log for this date consists of one line: Survey party continuing work planetside. There is no recorded evidence of this interaction. (Editor)

***

The ship is quiet. Like a coffin. I gave instructions to Alan to plot the most efficient Steps home. It's likely all the crew feels the same way, but it is ultimately my decision. The responsibility is all mine. I am reassured by the lack of opposition. I expected more of a fight. At least an argument. Shouting. Storming out. But they just stared at me, resigned. They are tired of searching for something that none of us believe we will ever find. Nate almost looked sympathetic. They can all blame me.

Alan didn't look up from his work. He leaned over his screen, exploring trajectories, calculating fuel ratios, adjusting computations. Gary secluded himself in 'his' reactor room, prepping for acceleration. I tried to busy myself in the sickbay, tidying already orderly supplies. There's not much I could do. I've been too neat of a ship's doctor. I was tempted to reorder all medicines alphabetically—demerol, dextroamphetamine, diazepam, nitrazepam, temazepam, xylocaine. I put quite a few in their own cabinet and locked it. How will I hide the key from myself? We move numbly. I fear when I can feel again, knowing where the key is. The cannabinoids are now in a glass-doored cabinet that used to house bandages, those with higher THC content to the front so they can be easily seen. Hopefully some will help themselves to this 'first aid.' I lack the ability to help myself. That is a sure sign of depression—having a helpful medicine at hand but not being able to bring myself to use it.

***

I sat on the bridge staring at the planet for hours. The green is the first I have seen, that any of us have seen since we ... left. Why is that such a hard word to write? World after world of barren rock and poison air, of excitement and anticipation giving over to disappointment after disappointment.

Green. Fields of green, wrapping this lonely place. Dark and rich. Swaths of velvet. White clouds swirled in the atmosphere, winds dragging long tails over dark continents. A large spiraling storm formed a brooch on her green gown. If I didn't know how dead it was, I would have thought it so beautiful from here. Maybe it is, but I've seen far too many dead worlds to find beauty in any of them.

When I was a girl, there was a small field outside of town. I made the mistake of returning before leaving, visiting my old home, somehow knowing I would never return. It was gone. Built over. Dead. Dying, like the planet itself. It made me secure in my decision to leave Earth on the *Fortitude*. I would find a new home for all of us, a green place, a healthy place. Our first Step was so exciting. The anticipation, the exhilaration. Eight months building up to discovering nothing but a wind-blown rock. But we carried on. Another year sheltering from solar radiation behind an inner planet or moon while the Ein-Ros faced the star, absorbing and converting photons into the incredible amounts of energy needed. Then a Step, and another discovery. Deeper into the unknown. Another Step, farther than anybody had ever Stepped, and were rewarded with water![3] Dark rivers emerging from underground, flowing into vast alluvial plains and disappearing into fine sands, returning to its subterranean sea. Kristin spent weeks analyzing

---

3. The planet Captain Sheridan is referring to is HAT-P-5b, the colony planet known colloquially as 'Hat Pin'. Its rivers of clear water, underground caverns and resource rich minerals has enabled it to grow into a significant center of mining and settlement. (Editor)

it at the molecular level. But the results were the same. Devoid of any life. So, we kept going.

Green. Green. Green. Green. Green.[4]

I tried to remember what that field smelled like when I was a girl. I must have been sitting, eyes on the screen, for several hours. Alan startled me back to the moment, saying my name. He held out a mug of coffee and a handful of tissues. My cheeks were wet. Snot ran down my chin. I took the tissues and wiped my face. I tried to meet his eyes as I took the drink, but he was looking down. I think he was crying too.

****

Acceleration has increased gravity on the ship to 1.4. It mirrors our mood. The Ein-Ros is three months away. I am so heavy. Weighed down. A leaden hand pushing from the center of my heart, down, down, down. I fear all crew feels the same. It will be at least two weeks until we reach peak velocity and power down the reactor. So. Heavy.

****

The watch system has started to break down. I couldn't sleep, again, so I went to the bridge. Nate was alone. Kristin has not come out of her cabin for several cycles. Our dear astrobiologist. Her primary role was to study new life. She wanted to be the first to see it and study it. First contact, even if through a microscope. Every Step brought a new level of frustration and disappointment. To Kristin, astrobiology wasn't just about an

---

4. This page in Captain Sheridan's original log is bordered in what looks like green pen. (Editor)

evolutionary record, but the future of life in the universe. The future of our life in the universe. But all she found was ... not death ...but the lack of life. The impossibility of life. She tested algae and moss in the atmospheres, samples of the hardiest high-altitude plants from Earth. None survived. She developed an obsession with the rocks, grinding them ever smaller, insisting there was something 'between the molecules'. She'll have lots of time on the trip back to study it. If Dana gives her access to her core samples.

Gary is with the reactor all the time. There's none of his usual humor at the mess table. I don't even know if he's eating. I had to order him to let me in. He looks like he hasn't slept since ... I don't know. He spoke in single words, and only in answer to questions. I gave him a sedative, a sleeping pill. He held it in his hand, looking confused. He caught me glancing at the reactor with a look of worry I didn't have the strength to hide.

"She'll be okay," he said. A hoarse whisper, an actual complete sentence. If he'd listen, I would confine him to sick bay. I'd confine all of us, force sedatives and sleep. But the chain of command seems to have broken down as well.

***

Kristin didn't answer my knocks at her cabin door. I overrode the lock, and when the door slid open, it was empty. Her bed was unmade. The room smelled of an unwashed body. Her papers had been strewn over the floor. Her notebooks toppled from a shelf as if they were thrown. Cynthia lay in the corner among broken glass and spilled soil. Each leaf of her *aspidistra elatior*[5] was sprinkled around her quarters, torn into smaller and smaller pieces. I searched the mess hall, the sickbay, the washroom, but could not find her. I called over ship's comms but got no response. I demanded the bridge answer. Dana eventually reported she was alone there. That she had not seen Kristin. Each answer had to be pulled out of her. I need to go to the reactor room. Gary will not reply.

***

The starboard outer airlock door was open. I wouldn't have noticed if I hadn't stopped to look into the only place I had not yet checked. The airlock is manually controlled from the inside and only operates if the inner door is sealed. From the inside. It could only have been done deliberately, by somebody determined to get out. The alarm would have to have been disengaged, which it was. I checked all the suits. One should be missing, but they are all there, hanging by each of our lockers.

Please, Kristin. Prove me wrong.

***

I assembled all crew in the mess. Kristin's seat was empty.

"Kristin has stepped out," I said. The conversation burned into my memory.

---

5. Aspidistra elatior is the Cast-Iron plant. Astrobiologist and Hydrologist, Kristin Vaughn brought her plant, which she named Cynthia, with her from Earth. She nursed it for the sixteen years she was on the Fortitude. (Editor)

It was something we all knew, but the words had to be spoken aloud. To make it real. We sat as silently as tears ran down our cheeks.

"Like Oates[6]," Dana said. Softly. But we all heard.

"No, Dana," I said. "Not like that. Not like that all. We all feel bad. But stepping out is not saving anybody. Kristin wasn't holding us back. None of you are holding us back. We're not struggling to survive on some godforsaken icefield. We're just trying to get home. We're stronger together." I tried to sound like what I said held truth, but part of me envied Kristin.

The crew stared blankly at me. "Nobody is to be alone until I say. We need to rely on each other until we get through this. We can't be trusted by ourselves."

I was encouraged by the lack of resistance. "Nate and Gary will bunk and work together. Dana, you will partner with Alan."

"Clear?" I asked loudly, summoning an illusion of authority.

"Clear." Murmurs around the table.

"What about you?" Alan asked.

---

6. Lawrence Edward Grace Oates accompanied Robert Falcon Scott on his ill-fated expedition to reach the South Pole. Afflicted with gangrene and frostbite, Captain Oates chose to die rather than be a burden to his companions, and thereby increase their chances of survival. He left his tent to freeze on the ice, saying as he went, "I am just going outside and may be some time." The story of the Terra Nova Expedition was among many of the books in the library of the Fortitude, and crew were quite familiar with their contents. (Editor)

"I'll rely on all of you," I lied. "We'll remember Kristin when we flip for deceleration[7]."

After leaving the mess, I returned to the airlock. *Oh, Kristin.* I closed the outer door and secured the exit.

***

Flip and Decel. Preparations have kept us busy. Moving mass, inspecting the reactor. I assigned both teams to go over it, more to double-check Gary's work. The room is usually spotless, but there are worrying signs. Discarded food packets covered the floor. Glass panels were smudged with dirty fingers. Spilled mass. I had to leave the room before I lost control. Spilled mass! Infused deuterium pellets just lying about the deck! I felt so angry. Alan helped me go out, almost pushed me, and closed the door behind me.

Anger is a symptom of frustration. Frustration is a product of stress, of a lack of understanding. I remember the seminars before leaving. Psychologists speculating on what we might feel after years in space. They had no idea. *Use and develop the tools you can to show patience, acceptance, and trust.* Lucky for them now that they are so far away from me. So far away.

---

7. There is no record in the official log of a ceremony being held for Kristin Vaughn, nor any other member of the crew. Just as Captain Sheridan's personal log became sporadic, with long periods of time elapsing between entries, the official ship's log similarly contained long periods with no entries. Only in the last three months of the return to Earth did astrogator and astrophysicist (and last remaining member of the crew of the Fortitude), Alan Seed, regularly record entries into the ship's log. (Editor)

***

Hat-P-5 grows larger in the viewscreen. We'll be docking with the Ein-Ros and leaving this system soon. Not soon enough. Once docking is complete Alan will go alone to initiate Step. He won't allow any other crew to join him in that inner sanctum. He never has.

***

I have to trust Alan in the control room, at the center of the Ein-Ros, monitoring the quantum computer that is calculating our Step, his only company an AI that speaks in coordinates. Alan has been very withdrawn but speaks with me when I ask. Nate and Gary talk to each other quietly. It's not my imagination that they go silent whenever I am around, or when they notice I am near. I have nobody to talk to.

***

Step. I usually dread the maneuver, the way it seems to stretch my body in all directions at the same time. Regardless, there used to be some anticipation, an excitement. Going farther than anyone has ever gone before. This time we're just trying to go back. Pointless pain. I don't even know what home is anymore. This ship has been my home. The crew, my family. Now the ship is only ... a means to an end? An end none of us wanted? And my crew are like strangers. I don't even know myself anymore.

After the Step, Alan returned to the *Fortitude.* There was no celebration. No traditional drinks. No welcome back. No thanks. We only went backwards for the first time. We will wait behind an inner planet while the Ein-Ros recharges. Alan estimates it will take five months to collect enough power for the next step. He has plotted a four Step route back to Earth, utilizing maximum power to increase the distance of each Step. He has identified several larger G class stars with recorded exoplanets to shelter behind while the Ein-Ros builds up the power it needs. There is a risk the quantum computer can become damaged with the extra demands. But if it means a quicker way back, we all find the risk acceptable.

***

Freefall is making me weak. Floating like a ghost. It doesn't matter. I keep losing track of hours and cycles. We must be nearing time to re-join the Ein-Ros and Step. What will we tell them? That we failed? That nothing is out there? "Sorry guys, we couldn't save you. We're all going to die." I don't want to face that.

***

Nate and Gary are gone. They stepped out together. They hacked the starboard air lock. Gary left a note on the wall of the reactor room, but we can't make any sense of it. Gary probably couldn't either. Lines slanting down the page. The reactor room is a mess. Squiggles of shit smear the walls. Globules of piss float in the air. Both he and Nate must have holed up in there, not even leaving to relieve themselves. I know I should feel more, I should cry or ... anything. But I can't. And to honest, I am glad I don't.

Dana is still talking to herself. She rolls her eyes and lapses into silence, but then snaps out of it and goes back to her conversation. Long babbling monologues that make no sense.

Coaxing her to sick bay I tried to give her a sedative, but she swung her arm and hit me away. I floated to the bulkhead and hit my back on a cabinet. By the time I steadied myself, she was out the door.

***

Alan found Dana drifting in the loading bay, near her core samples.

We used the port airlock to dispose of her body.

***

I had the dream again; at least I think it is a dream. I may not have been asleep. I am not always certain when I am. I was barefoot, walking on green grass. Each cold damp blade tickled the soles of my feet. They were young feet. Or I was young. Yes, I think I am young, a girl, back on Earth, back at home, in the field we used to visit. The sky is the palest blue. It is so beautiful. I breathe the warm, unfiltered air. I walk on. But the grass is becoming rougher. My feet are covered in dust, and the grass is coarse and dry. The sky has lightened, a burnt dirtied blue. I walk on until I come to a stream. There should be water. I know that it once was water. Only now it is a dark sludge. The smell is overpowering. But I walk closer, to the bank and step into the stream. My feet sink into gooey mud, but the mud burns. I step in deeper. The water reaches my knees, and then my thighs. My skin is in agony, burning, blistering, being eaten away. I go deeper still until I am chest deep, then neck deep. It is agony. I exhale slowly and then sink under the surface.[8]

I write this down in the hope it will stop. I can still feel the burning.

****

The ship is on autopilot. It will dock with the Ein-Ros and then Step. Once in the solar system, it will detach, and accelerate towards Earth. Flip and Decel are programmed. Alan has promised to stay with the ship, to tell them what is out there, tell them to care[9]. He said he will do that for me. We sat together in the bridge, his hand resting on mine. We spoke

---

8. Some have tried to find the field that Captain Sheridan describes from her childhood. They maintain that the dreams that plagued her were not from her own subconscious, but visionary glimpses of what would meet her upon return to Earth. The town where she grew up did have several parcels of open land around it before urban sprawl consumed them. The exact location of her childhood 'park' is unknown. A commemorative plaque has been placed near the location of the house where she grew up. The stream she describes was no different from most waterways in and around urban centers at the time. Whether a reflection of subconscious fear, or mystical glimpse into what awaited, it is commonly accepted that the recurring nightmares Captain Sheridan experienced during her last weeks on the Fortitude were a significant factor in her decision to step out. (Editor)

9. Astrogator and astrophysicist Alan Seed honored his promise to Captain Sheridan. He cooperated with the official investigation into the deaths of his crewmates, including handing over all confidential papers, such as the personal log of Elizabeth Sheridan. Three months after his return to Earth he stepped out, in his own fashion, and joined his Captain and crewmates. (Editor)

with our eyes. I heard what he was feeling, and I am certain he heard me. That he understands why I am giving up. His smile was so soft, so gentle. He has been a rock. You know what I mean, Alan.

I am not as ... brave as the rest of my crew. I am going to go to the medicine cabinet in sick bay and numb myself first.[10]

---

10. This is the last entry in Captain Elizabeth Sheridan's personal log. (Editor)

Part 1: First Step

1

Jens woke to a scream that he knew was his own. Not a terror-filled scream. Something more complicated, more confused. Frustrated. Angry. Worried. Lost. He was relieved that the bulkheads were thick. Nobody would have heard outside of his quarters.

The dream was the same. He was at sea, on the scow. Scow, cow. She was cow of ship. Big, fat. *Lugubrious.* She was certainly lugubrious. Skipper hated that word, because he didn't know what it meant, and not knowing made him feel stupid, and if he was honest, *know* that he was stupid. But his ego would never allow that.

Jens once suggested painting doleful cow eyes on the prow. Skipper didn't get the joke. It made him feel stupid, which made him feel angry and spiteful, bringing out the true depth of his character.

It was a glassy sea that day. No wind, no swell. Hot. Nothing to blow the smell of garbage away. Some of the crew wore foam plugs stuffed up their nostrils. Soak the foam in essential oils, vinegar, anything. Jens never bothered, just like Skipper never bothered. It was some sort of macho challenge, or test, or game the skipper played. Oh, how he liked his games. As long as you rolled on your back and presented your belly to the alpha dog, your cruise would be bearable. But show a little initiative, a bit of independent thinking, a trace of a spine, and the games would begin.

The scow scooped up the rare plastics and dumped its harvest into the hold. Scoop. Drop. Scoop. Drop. It was a dying industry, after the gold rush, when only the desperate miners were left. The scow's drones were searching for longer periods, as the doleful cow of a scow drifted farther from land to find its harvest. Earth's clean-up was big business. Garbage was money. And the scarcer the garbage got, the dumber the skipper became. On the new clean green earth these types of jobs at sea were becoming scarce, and when there were two thousand in the line in front of you for every job shoreside, the likes of Jens and Skipper simply did not matter.

"All he wants is loyalty." That was Rogers, a newer crew member. What a strange interaction.

"He doesn't know what that word means." A dangerous moment of honesty. This was memory, not dream.

"Just serve the boat, stay true to mission," Rogers said. "And he'll take us places." Jens looked at him, trying to decide if he was an acolyte, or just naïve.

"He doesn't want loyalty, he wants submission," Jens said. "He's just a bully with a massive insecurity complex. He's not going to take you anywhere."

That was too far, and the look from Rogers told Jens he might as well as said it to the boss himself. Jens felt a weight lift from his shoulders, realizing he finally didn't care anymore. This would be his last voyage, and probably his last pay check for quite a while.

"Jensen, what the fuck do you call this!" Stormy now, swell at four meters, wind gusting at sixty knots. Skipper shouting in his face, spittle mixed with rain. Line was strewn across the deck, coils that weren't secured properly. Jens didn't do it, but it was somebody on his watch, so he was responsible. Probably Rogers, getting back at him for disrespecting his skipper. Even if the toilet blocked up, it was the Watch Captain's fault, and the Watch Captain would clean it up. Skipper would see to that, especially if it happened on Jens' watch.

Jens wouldn't be surprised if the Skipper saved up his turds and emptied himself during Jens' six hours on deck, complete with a few rolls of toilet paper to make sure it would clog and overflow. Jens was actually his most experienced crew member, something that caused even more resentment.

"You're fucking worthless, Jensen! Get this mess secured."

The ship rode the waves, just as it was designed. Jens bent his knees and stood on the deck as if it was at its mooring, perfectly balanced. The sky darkened. A squall. Skipper staggered forward in protest of Jensen's inaction. He grabbed a line for support and shouted in Jen's face.

"Get your worthless ass moving and clean up my deck!"

Jens stood, knees flexed, riding the deck, up, down. Rain drenched them. Jensen squinted his eyes to stop the water from blinding him. Dark, flat face in front of his. Was this dream, or was it memory? Whatever. It was soon going to be light-years away.

One thing Skipper had taught him that he found useful was that the most important thing to have on board any ship, and on your body at all times, was a sharp knife. That nugget of advice came early in their relationship, when Jens was still an obedient little pup.

Sheets of rain. Up. Down. A wave crashed over the railing and Skipper lost his footing, slipped to his knees. But he didn't lose his grasp. He pulled himself upright. Jens' feet seemed bolted to the deck. Another wave smashed over the railing. By the time Skipper steadied himself, Jens had his knife out. The look on his face ... dream, or memory? Whatever it was, it wouldn't go away, an image he could never share with others.

Confusion. Anger. Rage. But not pain, no, not pain. Skipper would never show that. That would show weakness, and he had to show he wasn't weak, even when he was dying and it didn't matter anymore. Jens drove the blade in again. Skipper's eyes widened. His grimace grew more ominous. He drove the blade in a third time. Jens left his knife in Skipper's ribs and grabbed his coat at the shoulders. He dragged his captain to the railing and unceremoniously pushed him over. Jens didn't hear a splash. He didn't even bother to look back. Instead, he turned his attention to the deck and started coiling and securing the loose line.

Jens untangled his hands from the sheets and loosened the straps holding him to his cot. He floated up, pushed off the ceiling and drifted to the door. He pressed a button and it slid open. He pulled himself out and floated into the corridor, propelling himself along the handholds. It was time to wake Herschel and get started.

"Up and at 'em! It's time for work," Jens shouted. He followed that with a few pounds on the metal door.

"I've got two minutes 'til watch. Piss off!"

Jens was still getting used to the lack of discipline. Life on the sea scow ran like a military company. When a superior said jump, you jumped. When one said to tidy the deck, you ... He let that train of thought drift off, just as he did, pushing lightly and floating down the corridor. Jens wasn't even that sure of his rank on this ship. Captain Teal seemed to hold a very loose rein, but Jens was deciding that she was good at the job. And as she saw her crew were competent, she let them do theirs.

Teal wasn't at his job interview. She left all that up to the company man earthside.

"So why do you want to space?" Standard questions. The man interviewing him sat behind a desk large enough to be called a table.

"I want to use my skills where I can, and develop into the best officer I can," Blah blah, et cetera, et cetera.

"You're not applying for an officer's position," the man said.

"I'm only making my goals transparent," Jens answered.

"I don't think very much here is transparent," he said.

"I'm not sure I know ..."

"No, um," he looked at Jens' dossier again. "Mr Jensen. I think you do. Tell me, your skipper lost at sea, an investigation underway, and you want to leave the planet. Clarify."

Sweat formed under Jens' arm and began to trickle down his side. It helped keep him focused. "A man has to eat, and to eat he needs work," he said. "Besides, the pickings are getting slim out there. It's a dying industry."

"True about that," the man replied. "This file tells the story of a rather unpleasant relationship. You didn't like your skipper much, did you?"

"I think that feeling was mutual," Jens answered. "But while we sailed, professionalism overrode petty feelings." Bullshit, Jens thought. The man across the table smelled it.

"Bullshit," the man across from him said.

"Okay," Jens admitted. "He was an insecure little megalomaniac. He didn't like initiative, and if you got too good at your job, he felt threatened. Sure, I didn't like him, but when we were at sea, I worked for him—"

"You thought you could do his job better."

"Yeah, I did," Jens said.

"And he is lost at sea and you skipper the scow home. Funny that," he said.

"If I wanted to skipper the scow I wouldn't be here right now; I'd be applying for his job. You have the reports. As soon as I noticed the skipper was missing, I followed protocol, and we did everything in our power to search ..." *To search for him, after I went to my bunk for four hours to stare at the ceiling, let a lot of nautical miles pass beneath us, before climbing back on deck and sounding the alarm.*

"Yeah, it's all here," the man said, closing the file. "You followed protocol to the letter. Looks neat and tidy. I also have testimonials. I would suggest re-considering some of your references in your next application."

"And I'm sure you can't tell me who they might be," Jens said.

The man opposite pursed his lips and shook his head.

"But you could tell me who gave me a good one. And why I'm sitting here now."

"You know who. He's a good man, and I trust his judgment. But we also have an informal network, and I have to listen to that too."

"It's a small community," Jens said. "That doesn't surprise me. And what does this informal network say of me?"

"It says you have a problem with hierarchy. That doesn't bode well when you're on a ship, light-years from Earth," he said.

"Fair enough. I have a problem with *bad* hierarchy, but not with discipline on a ship," Jens said, realizing his mistake too late.

"Yes, Mr Jensen." He leaned back in the chair and took a long look at Jens. "Working on a space freighter isn't the picnic a garbage scow is. There's no view, for one. You're locked in a lead-lined shoebox for months on end. You'll need to start at the bottom when it comes to piloting and walking. But like I said-- months in a shoebox is plenty of time to train. You're lucky, Mr Jensen," he said.

Jens knew enough to know when to speak and when to keep quiet. He kept quiet.

"We're a little short of competent crew at the moment. We have a ship that lost a couple of crew members quite recently. Something involving law enforcement, and them not being able to leave the planet for a few years. Besides, it seems that Stepping has lost a bit of its luster, and those willing to spend years of their lives transporting settlers and supplies to far-flung rocks are getting hard to come by. And I can tell you, you'll be going *pretty* far. Wipe that smile off your face."

His tone grew hard. "I'm giving you this job because of our mutual acquaintance. He said you were competent, and he said you were trustworthy. My god, you better not prove him wrong. He also said I still owed him one, nothing you need to know about, and giving you this ticket would clear our slate."

He stood up and reached across the table. Jens took his hand and bit down as he squeezed tight.

"I like your Captain. She's good at her job," he said. "Do not give her any grief. If you do, and if you ever set foot earthside again, you won't be walking much farther." He let go of Jens' hand.

"Shuttle leaves 0600 tomorrow. I'm sure you'll be on it," he said. "Go straight to the *Cirrus* and check-in. She's your new home. And close the door behind you."

Jens was strapped into his seat by 0530, watching the door of the shuttle and only starting to relax when it closed for take-off. He felt pushed into the cushions as the craft sped down the runway and took off, banking for its long spiral to launch height of eighty thousand feet. When the time came for the final push into space, he copied those next to him, leaning his head fully against the back of his seat. The force of the thrusters sat on his chest like a fully-grown gorilla, pounding its fists on his temples for good measure. He strained to see out the port, but the shuddering of the shuttle blurred his vision, and it was enough to just keep breathing.

And then the beast ceased its attack. Jens sucked air into his lungs now that they were free of gravity. He felt his body float upwards, held in place by the straps on his seat. He reached for the bag in the pocket on the back of the seat in front of him, opened it quickly and vomited. He folded it closed so that the contents of his stomach wouldn't float around the cabin.

So, this was freefall.

The shuttle adjusted position, and a slight kick to his back signaled a push towards the space hub. Halfway to the destination, the shuttle slowly flipped and kicked again, this time decelerating. Docking was so smooth Jens didn't feel it. He unstrapped when the intercom announced it was okay and tried to show the caution it advised. He hit the ceiling, attempted to correct his flight, and was pushed back into his seat. He held the armrest tightly to stop his momentum and tried again, moving from handhold to handhold, keeping one hand gripped to something not moving.

Icons on the docking bay exit instructed passengers to ensure their feet were facing downward as they entered the port's artificial gravitation. He managed to maintain his balance and stepped onto the moving walkway, letting it carry him into the hub. Here was at least a bit of familiarity. From space the port resembled a bike tire with its rim removed, thin spokes sticking out from a central hub, and at the end of each spoke was a docking bay. The interior of the hub looked like any large airport on earth. Jens studied the monitors until he found the spoke he needed, saw he had several hours to wait, and located a bar next to a large viewport.

Selecting the most expensive single malt whiskey on offer, he ordered a double. He took a sip like a condemned man enjoying his last meal, and gazed down at the most beautiful and rich planet in the known universe. The blue expanse of the Pacific lay below him. He tried not to suppress the emotion he was feeling. He wanted to at least acknowledge it. Loss? Regret? He spent most of the last five years of his life on the water, with an uninterrupted horizon that circled his entire world. The colors of sunrise. Clouds towering in the distance or exploding with blinding light right overhead. *Will I ever feel the water all around my body again?* he thought. *Swim in the sea? Breathe fresh air? Be drowned by rain while on watch?*

It didn't matter. It was too late for regrets. He made his choice, and he burnt his bridge.

Jens lifted his glass and noticed it was empty, as well as that hours had passed as he watched his previous life pass beneath. He made his way down a spoke to his gate where a much smaller shuttle waited to take him to the convoy. Stepping into freefall through the departure gate, he managed to keep his whiskey inside and make his way to a seat. The shuttle detached and a brief blast from the engines propelled them away. Jens watched the convoy grow from a speck of distant light to a collection of eight freighters fixed together for their four-month voyage to the Donut in the Vulcan zone, a mere 0.2 AU's from the sun. Each freighter held a precious cargo: building supplies, seed, fertilizer, panels and solar cells. Everything needed to build a new world. One even carried settlers, who believed a barren and empty rock in a far-flung corner of the galaxy could bring a better future.

As they neared the convoy, Jens tried to see which one was the *Cirrus*, but they all looked the same. He knew it was most likely on the outside of the cluster. One thing was certain, calling the ships 'shoeboxes' was complimentary. They were more like the containers loaded onto the cargo ships that plied the Earth's oceans. Rectangular metal hunks devoid of any individuality or character. The only way to differentiate bow from stern was the fusion reactors that propelled them. Of course, when it came time to decelerate the ship would flip, and the stern become the bow. Was that called 'shunting' back on ancient Earth? In space, there was no up or down, so it probably didn't matter if a ship had a front or back.

He wondered about his new home, a container ship with a nuclear reactor in it. The reactors required fuel to generate power. Matter equals energy. While the other freighters were filled to capacity with essential supplies, the *Cirrus* was full of the mass needed for their reactors. She was essentially a fuel truck. An oil tanker. Or, more honestly, as the fuel was recycled waste infused with radio isotopes, she was a garbage scow.

The irony wasn't lost on Jens.

2

Jens turned at the sound of Herschel's door, gave a slight flick of the wrist and floated back down the corridor.

"Why doesn't she turn on the gravity? This floating is getting old," Herschel said.

"It's probably broken," Jens teased. "Or she's trying to save every bit of power she can until Decel."

And she likes to have fun floating, he added to himself with a smile.

"Besides, it makes lifting easier," he said.

Hershel groaned. "Another delivery?"

"Two actually, our first run to the *Calderón* and then another trip to the *Avarua*." That got his crew mate's attention. "You like it there, don't you? You'll get to see Pani."

"My day just got brighter," Herschel said, floating down the corridor towards the mess hall.

"Just a take away this morning," Jens told him. "We have a ton of shit to shift. Twenty tons, to be precise. And grab me a bag of chow as well!"

Jens made his way to the tender and started readying it for flight. Two months ago, he needed the checklist at hand. It was rote memory now. By the time Herschel arrived, no doubt deliberately late to avoid the chore of prep, the craft was ready. They both looked at the empty hold, and then at each other. Without speaking, they drifted to the nearest cargo bay on the *Cirrus*. The whole of *Cirrus* was a cargo hold, just divided into bays for organization, and on the off-chance that a different type of cargo might be obtained. *Cirrus*, a garbage truck dreaming of becoming a … but cargo was cargo, whatever was inside. Other freighters might look down on a lowly mass transport, but the only real difference was the paycheck, which was … lowly.

Herschel unstrapped a pallet of mass, sixteen sacks, each weighing forty kilograms. He guided it off the deck and carefully maneuvered it to the tender. Jens followed with another pallet. And then another. Zero gravity wasn't merely energy-saving or playful – it made their work a *lot* easier.

"Your turn to drive?" Herschel asked.

"You know it is," Jens replied.

They strapped in and sealed the pilot's compartment.

"Calling bridge, *Little Cloud* is loaded and ready for disembarking. Open bay doors, please," Herschel said over the comms. Jens mouthed a word to him.

"Over," Herschel added.

"Bay doors opening, *Little Cloud*. Have a good run. You boys be safe out there. Bridge out."

"I love her voice. I could listen to it all night," Herschel said.

"Her voice. Right," Jens said. "*Little Cloud* out," he said into the comms, reminding Herschel to close the communication.

The side of the docking bay slid open, exposing the emptiness of space. Jens took the controls in his hands and slowly expelled his breath. A gentle touch of the controls and the tender floated above the deck. A small compensation to steady, followed by a burst from the port thruster and they began to move out of the *Cirrus*.

"Practice makes perfect," Herschel said.

"No," Jens answered, keeping his eyes on the controls. "Practice makes *better*." He knew they both needed a lot more practice.

Starboard thrusters brought them to a halt outside the freighter. He played a bit with the distance, moving far enough away to see the dark hull. A thrust upward and they moved above the convoy, flying over rectangular hunks, tethered three abreast. Three more were tethered below those. With the *Cirrus* and *Ryk* attached underneath, it meant the propulsion of all eight reactors, firing simultaneously, when it came time to Flip and Decel.

"Polarize the screen more, mate. Man, that sun is huge!" Jens said.

"Shades on," Herschel said. "It seems to get brighter the closer we get. Funny that."

"Real comedian, aren't ya?"

"Are you going to practice, or what?" Herschel asked.

Jens laughed. He took the tender to the front of the convoy, moving forward until only empty space was beneath them, and *Little Cloud* led them all. Then he banked sharply and flew to the stern of the convoy, steadying the tender and dropping behind until the dormant reactors of the ships filled their view screen. If they were in this position when the engines fired, they wouldn't even see the flash before it vaporized them. He took the tender back over the convoy, turned it to port, then to starboard. He dipped as close to the top of the nearest freighter as he dared and pulled up sharply before steadying the craft.

"One more time!" Herschel encouraged.

Jens dipped and rose, banked to starboard and made a full three-sixty.

"Better," Herschel said. "Might want to check the paint underneath though. That was pretty close."

"Plenty of room to spare," Jens said. "Let's get rid of this mass, eh? Pani awaits." He pointed to the radio. "Comms."

"Oh, yeah," Herschel said. "*Calderón, Calderón*, this is *Little Cloud* with delivery. Requesting access. Over."

"*Pequeña Nube, reconoció. Apertura de la puerta de la bahía de carga. Terminado.*"

"I guess that means we're in," Jens said.

"Your *comprensión* is improving, *mi amigo*," Herschel said.

Jens took the tender to the opposite side of the convoy, descended past the top freighter and slid into the docking bay of the *Calderón*. They waited as the bay door slid shut and the compartment pressurized. The *Calderón* carried what was probably the most expensive and valuable freight in the convoy, disassembled fliers and high-tech gear for power generation. It made the *Calderón*, next to the *General Xing* with its human cargo, the upper crust of the nascent convoy society. When they finally reached their destination, the *Calderón* crew would unload the fliers in orbit, where technicians among the settlers on the *General Xing* would assemble them to glide to the fledgling colony below.

Herschel struggled out of his seat and opened the tender's door. He jumped onto the deck and landed on his ass.

"You got your gravity," Jens called.

Herschel slowly picked himself up. He walked heavily to the tender's cargo door and opened it.

"Do you want to call them? See where they are?" Herschel asked.

Jens pressed the comms button. "*Calderón*, as soon as you lend a hand we can go," he said.

"*Lo siento, Pequeña Nube. Nos has pillado a la hora de la cena.*"

"What did he say?" Jens asked.

"Something about dinner time," Herschel answered from the rear of the tender.

"You have got to be shitting me," Jens said. "*Calderón*, a little assistance with unloading would be appreciated," he said into the comms. "*Terminado,*" he added.

"*Lo siento, amigos. No queremos comer con las manos sucios.*"

"I hate these guys," Herschel said. "Stuck up Spanish pricks too good for the likes of us."

"They're not Spanish. And what did he say?" Jens asked.

"They're not coming to help. He said it might dirty their hands."

"Shit," Jens said.

"That would be *mierda*," Herschel said.

Jens carefully climbed out of his seat and joined Herschel with the cargo. They wrestled the first bag of mass, recycled plastics shaved into fine slivers and injected with deuterium, out of the hold. Jens tried to heave it onto his shoulder, but his muscles were too unused to manual labor. They each grabbed an end and hauled it to the waiting pallet. Twenty-five bags later their backs were screaming, and their arms were numb, but more pallets waited to be filled. Finally, Jens staggered back to the tender but stopped when he saw Herschel wasn't following. His crewmate was unzipping his flight suit.

"What are you doing?" Jens called.

"Leaving a little scent for those pricks. *Las manos sucios*, indeed!" He had managed to get his own prick out and start to spray the sacks with a fine yellow stream when an alarm sounded and a red light started flashing.

"Fuckers! They're opening the door!" Jens called.

Herschel tried to stop mid-stream and put himself back into his suit. A warm wet feeling down his leg told him he failed. He staggered to the tender, trying to zip up his suit. They closed the doors of the tender and got to their seats before the air in the docking bay hissed out into space.

"Watching us the whole time," Heschel growled.

"Yeah, and no doubt having a good laugh," Jens added.

He piloted the craft out of the *Calderón* and watched the docking bay doors close behind them. The *Avarua* tethered immediately below, so he guided the craft lower.

"You better clean yourself up before you see Pani. You smell like piss," Jens said.

"Stuck up Spanish pricks!" Herschel growled.

"They're Chilean," Jens corrected. "Chilean pricks."

Jens piloted the tender into the *Avarua* docking bay. As soon as the compartment pressurized, several of the crew came in. Jens opened the loading door of the small craft and the laughing men grabbed the sacks, swung them onto their shoulders and took them into their ship. Despite his aching back and sweat-drenched body, their smiles were infectious. Jens afforded himself a small grin. He watched the men in their colorful lava lavas, muscles of their bare backs rippling under the weight of the cargo, and brown skin decorated with tattoo patterns from their homeland. Jens felt lighter, just watching them do the work.

Pani greeted Herschel as he clambered down from the cockpit. "You are my hero!" she said. She spread her heavy arms wide but quickly closed them, holding him back with an outstretched hand.

"But you stink!" she laughed. "Come and get washed up. And get out of that flight suit! Jens, you too," she called. Pani turned around and marched out of the docking bay, her full figure bouncing. Hershel grinned broadly and followed obediently.

"You poor things!" she said. "They filmed you guys, edited it and sent it convoy wide. Did those bags feel heavy to you?"

"Back-breakingly heavy," Herschel said.

"They had the gravity up to 1.3. And the heat. Way up."

"Spanish pricks!" Herschel said.

"Chilean," Jens corrected.

"And you," she said, turning to Herschel, "are a star!" Pani reached over to kiss him, wrinkled her nose and gave his forehead a quick peck before pushing him away. She looked at Jens. "Both of you. You've got quite a fan base already."

Pani laughed as she opened the door to the showers. "Now in you two go. Throw out those flight suits and I'll get them washed."

They filed in obediently, stripped, and tossed out their clothes. When they left the showers, they found lava lavas waiting for each of them. Jens wrapped his around his waist and tied it as best he could. The bright orange pattern made his spacer complexion look even pastier. It didn't take Jens long, locked inside a tin can, to lose his tan. Herschel's thin white legs didn't give any consolation.

Herschel picked up a yellow plastic flower that Pani left on top of his lava lava. He stuck his nose in and breathed in deeply.

"Ah, I love the islands," he said.

"I think you love an Islander," Jens said.

"You are not too wrong there," he said. "Come here, and I'll tie that so it won't fall off." He adjusted Jens' lava lava, and stuck the flower behind his crew mate's ear. "You feel kind of lighter?" Herschel asked.

"Yeah!"

"These Cookies aren't dumb. They turn their gravity down. Makes the work easier. What would you say, 0.7?"

"I'd say it feels better than on the *Calderón*," Jens said.

They left the washroom and walked towards the mess. Jens stood gazing at a poster attached to the bulkhead. Turquoise waters, white sands, blue sky.

"Now that's a nice touch," he said.

"There's no place like home," Herschel said. "Or, at least like their home."

"Not much of that left, though," Jens said.

"Pani says they're recovering well, once the acidification was reversed. That's what was killing the corals. And the fish."

They walked to the mess hall and the door slid back.

"*Kia Orana*!" the crew called. "There they are! Did you use up all of our water?"

Pani grabbed Herschel and pulled him into the room, wrapping him in her thick arms. A large Islander placed a bottle of beer in Jens' hand. He saw the entire crew of eight in the room. Bright plastic flowers decorated the walls. The central table was filled with food: fried bread, potato salad, cooked taro leaves, coconuts. Bottles of beer! Jens took a long sip from the bottle in his hands, closed his eyes and let the amber liquid slip down his throat.

"Thanks, man," he said. "This is the first beer I've had in ... What's the occasion?"

"First Flip!" the Islander said, grasping Jens' hand. He pulled his face close, touched his nose to Jens' and breathed in sharply. "Rua," he said.

"Jens," Jens said. He was pulled around the room to meet the others. Hemi, Rangi, ("the Captain"), Hauora ("just call him Ora, and thank him for the beer"), Ihaka, Kawai Joe, Lisa and Siaki.

Jens took another drink of beer. "But it's not First Flip for another two weeks," he said.

Rua laughed. "No, but it's Herschel's birthday, so we brought it forward."

Jens looked over at Herschel, beer in one hand, Pani in the other, and a grin on his face. Jens raised his bottle, and Herschel nodded.

"He didn't even tell me," Jens said.

Pani disappeared into the galley and returned with a cake complete with candles. On each wick, she had glued paper colored to look like flames. Everybody sang what sounded like Happy Birthday ("*Rā 'ānau ki a koe*!"), Herschel pretended to blow out the candles, and the crew clapped.

Jens finished the last sip of his beer and Captain Rangi placed another in his hand. "You can relax, Jens," she said. "Teal radioed to let you know you didn't have to rush back. She said after that performance on the *Calderón* you could both have the night off."

Jens took a drink of beer. "Was that all she said?"

"Pretty much. Said you'd be pretty busy in the build-up to Flip with mass drops, so enjoy the rest." Rangi looked at Herschel and Pani. "I wouldn't have let you take him away tonight anyway. Those two deserve a bit of a break. You'd have had some mechanical trouble or something with your tender to stop you from leaving. Anything can happen to a ship while the pilot is in the shower." She smiled and raised her bottle, chinking its neck with the neck of the bottle in Jens' hand. "Talk to Hemi tomorrow morning and he'll give you the missing part of your ignition switch."

Jens surveyed the party spread on the table. "How'd you get away with all this extra mass? We're stripped to bare essentials. Nothing but space for fuel and cargo."

"A Captain has her tricks," Rangi said. "Besides, there's only one First Flip on a run. *Here* we celebrate. So, drink up, Jens. Don't live up to your reputation for once."

"My reputation?"

"All work and no play," Rangi said. "Though from what I've heard about you and Teal, I have no idea how you earned it."

"I'm still getting used to a different work arrangement," Jens admitted. "My last ship wasn't as relaxed."

"So I've also heard," Rangi said. "But rumors are like dog shit. Better not to step into them."

"Alright, who's first?" Ora called. "Birthday boy? Yeah, bring me the birthday boy!" Herschel was hustled into a chair by the waiting Islander. "Arm or leg?" he asked.

Herschel looked confused until he saw the needle and ink in Ora's hand.

"Arm or leg?" he asked again.

Herschel looked to Pani, who answered for him. "His thigh. A nice big beautiful pattern," she said. "With a turtle in the middle!"

Ora pulled up Herschel's lava lava, wetted his thigh and shaved a large area. "This is going to hurt you much more than it will hurt me," he said, smiling, as the needle began to hum.

"Your turn next," Rangi said. "It's tradition. Every First Flip deserves a tattoo. Arm or leg? You aren't getting out of this unscathed." She clinked his beer bottle again and took a swig.

"I'd recommend the upper arm, spilling over to the pec. That would suit you."

Herschel guided the tender over the convoy in what was an unconscious reflex. Load the tender, direct it to the target freighter's docking bay, enter and secure the craft, and wait as the ship's crew unloaded the mass for their reactors. Everyone was on edge in anticipation to Flip, checking and re-checking every detail. On each drop, Jens and Herschel unstrapped and tried to help unload, but the crew was always there to shoulder the mass. Even when they tried to help, they were humorously pushed aside and made to watch the others work. Jens shifted restlessly as the others beavered away.

Then out of the loading and back to the *Cirrus*, loading tons of deuterium laced garbage into the tender and delivering it to the waiting freighters.

On the *General Xing*, Herschel and Jens were escorted to the crew mess and treated to a meal of the local fare before they went on a tour of the settler accommodations. The entire area of the cargo hold had transformed into a small town, with sleeping quarters, recreation areas, market spaces and public washrooms. The lack of privacy and space were good practice for what lay ahead on their future colony, most probably sealed inside protective domes for most of their lives. Jens stopped before the carcass of a chicken, hung by its feet and drying in the vented air.

"You see," his guide said, in English that was much better than Jens' Mandarin. "The colonists practise self-sufficiency in the many months to their new home."

"You have chickens on board?" he asked.

"Of course. Livestock travels with us. Humans are not the only settlers on board!"

Jens smiled and nodded at the earnest young woman, trying to imagine the chooks scrabbling around the dead rock of the alien planet the settlers would call home, searching in vain for any native insects. But given enough feed, they would at least start to fertilize the dead soil.

As *Little Cloud* left the *General Xing*, dozens of suited settlers moved about the surface of the freighter checking the couplings in preparation to Flip.

"Nice little pool of labor they have there," Herschel said. "Six hours on and six hours off would be a little less tiring if we could share it with a couple of thousand settlers."

"Nah," Jens said. "You'd be exhausted just training them, let alone making sure they didn't blow up the ship. The biggest problem on the *Xing* is probably fighting off boredom. Two thousand people cooped up in a shoebox for months on end. They've got two more Steps. Months and months of waiting for the Donut to re-power after every Step. At least we're too busy to go stir crazy."

"True," Herschel agreed. "And after mass drops, we get to walk outside and re-check each coupling, overdosing on harmful radiation if we spend too long outside. Really something to wake up to, eh? Even with crews helping unload, I'm wrecked." He scratched the tattoo on his leg under his flight suit.

Herschel piloted the tender to their next drop, the *Ryk*, an experienced German freighter carrying an entirely disassembled hospital in its hold, as well as pharmaceutical 3-D printers. From the outside, it looked the same as any other freighter. Inside was a different story. The level of orderliness and hygiene made the pair from the *Cirrus* feel grubby in the extreme. Both were treated like visiting officers, escorted out of the bay to the *Ryk's* mess hall, where plates of bratwurst waited. By the time they had finished the meal, their tender had been unloaded.

"I can get used to this," Jens said. "Is it just pre-Flip practice?"

"I don't think so," Herschel said. "Maybe more to do with the *Calderón's* little joke and our subsequent fame. Even *they* helped on the last drop. Not to mention the wine." The Captain of the *Calderón* himself greeted the pair on that visit, gifting them each a bottle of Chilean red.

"*Para compartir con tu Pani*," he said to Herschel. *To share with your Pani.* "Maybe you can entice your Captain to share a drop," he said to Jens in accent-free English.

"I had weight restrictions drilled into me before boarding the shuttle, and even threw gear away before take-off, but everybody here seems to have secret stashes."

"I'm not complaining," Herschel said, admiring the label.

As they re-entered the *Cirrus'* docking bay, they watched Baldy and Stephan pilot the *Rain Storm*, their second tender, out to begin the fuel drops of their watch. Six hours on, six hours off, non-stop movement before Flip. The *Cooper* with its Irish crew, filled to the brim with seed stock and fertilizers; the *Plymouth*, machinery to create factories, and the power cells and technology needed to flourish almost five thousand light-years from Earth; the *Sunrise Blossom*, *General Xing's* sister ship, carrying the building materials needed to grow the young colony recently established around the star OGLE TR-56b. The colony was so new that names were still being tried out, some more complimentary than others. Ogre was bandied about, obviously, and probably fitting in light of the planet's conditions, but not very good for attracting colonists or capital. The third Step to the new colony was the longest and riskiest and needed a more attractive name. The colonists on the *Xing* called it *Sukhavati*. Western Paradise. It had a nice ring to it. On their one-way trip, that is exactly what they hoped it would be. They tried not to think about the stark reality awaiting them.

Both Jens and Herschel collapsed onto the hard metal chairs around the mess hall table, too tired to drink the cups of coffee in front of them, but happy to sink into the half gravity now activated on the ship.

"You guys look like zombies," Suzie said. "Why don't you grab your few hours of sleep?"

"Why don't you?" Herschel asked. "Aren't you off watch too?"

"That I am," Suzie said. "But I'm going to clip on and watch the dolphins play at the bow."

"What does that mean?" Jens asked.

"It means a whole six hours of not seeing reactor cores or cleaning engine rooms."

"Are you satisfied with them?" Herschel asked.

"They'll do the job. They're not just the cleanest in the convoy, they're probably some of the strongest. Teal has encouraged us to make some minor improvements. That's why she saved so much of the solar cell. Extra power, just in case."

"Just in case of what?" Jens asked.

"Just in case," Suzie said. "Always good to have a 'just in case' up your sleeve, don't you think? Teal has quite a few cards stashed up hers, in case you haven't noticed."

"Do you want some coffee?" Herschel asked. "Sit down and moan with your shipmates."

"Not for me, maties. Dinner with the Captain tonight, if it is night. Whatever time means anymore," she said. "Jens isn't Teal's only favorite." Suzie blew a kiss and left the mess. The two men gazed exhaustedly after her.

"Shit," Herschel said. "Sorry, man. That's gotta suck."

"Whatever," Jens lied. "Right now, I am too tired to care."

"Don't 'whatever' me, man. That has to hurt. I thought you and Teal had something going."

"Well," Jens said. "I thought so too. But I guess I was wrong."

"That's kind of fucked-up," Herschel said.

"No, it probably isn't," Jens said. "She's free to do what she wants, with whoever she wants. We never exchanged rings or whatever." Jens took a sip of tepid coffee. "She can have anybody over to dinner."

"Knock it off, Jens," Herschel said. "You can say it sucks big donkey dicks if that's how you feel."

"It's okay, really," Jens said. "I don't like it, and I can tell you, I *did* like it while it lasted. There's no doubt about that. Freefall is very fun. But she never said it was anything other than ... whatever it was. It felt good. Like medicine. And, man, I needed some of that medicine. But yeah, now I feel kind of gut-punched—"

"Too right."

"But the *Cirrus*, and Teal, and shit, even you, are a hell of a lot better than where I came from." Jens tried another drink of coffee and spat it back into the cup. "And I'm happy to take that, even if the Captain has another bed warmer. She's still a good captain."

"Agreed," Herschel said. "You have to tell me about your last ship sometime."

"No, I don't have to do that," Jens replied.

"That's what I thought you'd say, but I'm sure you'll slip up sooner or later," Herschel persisted. "We have literally years to spend together."

"If we don't explode in a nuclear flash," Jens said.

"Not worth thinking about. It'd be over before you knew it."

"Bliss," said Jens. "What about your last ship? You've spaced before, but no Steps?"

"I flew maintenance runs between the hubs and Luna. That gets old quick," Herschel said. "And then the *Avarua* was so desperate, Rangi signed her up for this run. Three Steps into the great nothing. Years away delivering shit to no-hopers trying to build a planet. Pani's too good to give up, and I pulled the slender thread I had and got a posting on the *Cirrus* so I could follow her."

"I'm starting to see a pattern," Jens said. "This whole convoy seems to be made up of waifs and strays."

"And people just trying to get a long, long way away," Herschel added. "From whatever they don't want to talk about."

Teal walked slowly over to Jens, indicated to use a private line, and only spoke when she saw him do so.

"I understand Alvarez gave you something. Why don't you bring it to my quarters after hand-over and we can talk."

Jens looked across the hull where Herschel and Ed were checking couplings before Flip. The convoy was swivelling its stern towards the sun. The increasingly large flaming ball was over their shoulders rather than in their faces. Jens could see a vast expanse of stars in the black void. The brightest one was Earth, which was sitting above the pair moving carefully over one of the last of the attachments securing the *Cirrus* to the convoy.

"I might pass out," he said, thinking of the wine stashed under his bunk. "This two on, two off is killing me."

"There'll be plenty of time to rest once the reactors kick in," Teal said. "Was that a yes or no, I can't read your face through your helmet."

"It's a yes," Jens said. "And you'd see a smile."

"Good. I have some glasses." She turned and made her way to the hatch where the First Mate, Lassen, and his watch of Suzie, Stephan and Baldy were no doubt suiting up.

"Time to go in, boys," she said over the team link.

Both crew members stood and turned to face where the command came from, even though the sound was directly in their ears. They took a step in her direction, every movement appearing in slow motion in the vacuum surrounding them. By the time they reached the hatch, the other watch was climbing onto the hull. The initial banter at passing was a casualty of exhaustion. Two hours was almost the maximum exposure to solar radiation. It meant shorter work periods, but also shorter rest. They had all been living on cat-naps for four days.

The watch took off their suits in silence. Herschel looked at Jens through bloodshot eyes framed in dark rings. He made to say something but was too tired to make any sound. Jens stopped long enough in his quarters to fetch the bottle of Chilean wine and splash water over his face in the washroom. He looked at his tired face in the mirror and smiled weakly.

The Captain's door slid open on his first knock. Her hand reached out, grabbed his shirt, and pulled him in. He heard the door slide shut behind him as her open mouth found his. After a long moment, she gently pushed him back.

"Let me see it," she commanded.

Jens handed the bottle over for her inspection. She smiled, gazing at the label. "Very nice. I told him he had to make up for that little stunt with you two. This will do."

Two glasses sat on a small table beside her bed. She pulled the cork, poured a generous amount in each glass, and climbed onto the bed. He had missed this.

"If I drink that, I'll be no use outside," he protested.

"Just as long as you're useful inside," she replied. "But enough is enough. I just radioed Lassen's team to tell them we're finished as soon as his watch is over."

"Thank God for that," Jens said.

"So, come here. Quit being awkward and come to bed." She held out the second glass for him.

He slipped out of his shoes and slid in next to her. He took a long sip and sighed. "This is nice," he said.

"It is," she replied. "It's very nice."

"But?"

"There doesn't have to be a 'but'," she stroked his head with her free hand. "I like crewing with you, and I like sharing my bed with you. I'm being honest about how I roll. Maybe I should have been more explicit about that the first time you came over."

Jens smiled at the memory. "The first time I *floated* over. It wouldn't have changed anything."

"Good," she said, taking a longer drink and running her hand down his chest. "Why don't you take this off and climb under the covers with me? Let me see that tattoo."

Jens responded by handing his glass to her and pulling his clothes off. She gave it back once he was under the sheet, disrobing just as quickly.

"Suzie's rather pretty, don't you think?" she asked.

"She is. Kind of high maintenance, bouncy in a hard work sort of way ..."

"Bouncy isn't necessarily a bad thing. She's very smart too."

"I hope so," Jens said. "She's our Donut Hole."

"I'm tempted to invite both of you over for dinner one night. What do think of that?" she asked.

Jens took a gulp of wine, tilted his head and looked at her.

"Oh!" she said. "That pause tells me everything I needed to know. You have some dark corners, Mr Jensen."

Jens laughed, finished his glass, and set it beside the bed. "I guess I better enjoy you while I have you all to myself," he said before disappearing under the sheet.

The crew sat in their launch chairs, strapped in and waiting. The seconds counted down before Decel, the simultaneous ignition of all the ship's fusion reactors, eight controlled explosions designed to give just enough thrust to slow them to a complete stop within a hundred kilometers of Donut 326-B. Jens was blissfully and ignorantly relaxed until Suzie told him everything that could go wrong with the ST reactors on board, replete with an unhealthy dose of horror stories about things not going right. Like reactors failing and convoys disappearing into a sun.

Jens had learned enough so far to know ST stood for Spherical Tokamak, the type of reactors used for interplanetary transport, all about the fuel they needed, and even how heavy the fuel sacks were at a variety of gravity levels (zero-G being his preference).

"Sliding into the sun is an excruciating death," Suzie explained in her serious and quick manner. "Like slowly cooking to death. You think it would just be a quick burn up, but the distance involved means a gradual increase in temperature until the ship systems finally break down. Most choose to end their own lives before that point. At least that's what the last transmissions from those convoys indicate."

Or reactors implode, a much quicker ending. Crews wouldn't even know what killed them. Or reactors melt down, not as quick and full of wasted hope, as crews from other freighters desperately try to uncouple their ships from the convoy or eject their damaged reactor. And of course, the couplings might fail, splitting the convoy and sending ships spinning into space at increased gravities. ("They found one of those once," Suzie said. "Not a very pretty picture on the inside of the bridge.")

Or ("and you'll really appreciate this one," Suzie added with a smile) the allocation for mass was miscalculated, which would cause a different type of meltdown, and crews try to feed anything they can into the reactor, knowing that without deuterium the mass would be insufficient to resist the star's strong gravitational pull.

"Haven't you heard of the *Stellenbosch*? They fed the reactors everything, even the shirts off their backs. Literally. But it still didn't save them. That's why Teal had you guys delivering not only enough to get to the Donut, but what the ships will need after Step as well. Plus a bit more. The *Stellenbosch* used everything – their food, their beds ... there's a story that they even put a crewmate or two into the mass converter before they all burned.

"We're human so we try everything, right up to the end, even if the end is certain," Suzie said. "And I'm afraid that in those cases, the end is certain. Decel to Donut is the easy part. Wait until we Step!" She slapped Jens on the shoulder. "No, the only way to do any of this is to do it right. It's a very good thing you have me here."

Jens dried his sweaty hands on his flight suit and stared at the screen at the front of the bridge. Red numbers in the bottom right corner continued a countdown which was now measured in seconds. He glanced at Herschel, who was sitting with his eyes closed and his mind probably in a better place. Was he with Pani? Jens watched Teal speak into the comms built into the arm of her chair. Twenty seconds. Ten seconds. Five seconds. When the red numbers displayed two zeros, he felt a familiar gorilla place itself on his chest and go to work. He exhaled when he realized he was holding his breath.

Jens heard Baldy whoop, and Stephan join him. Herschel continued to sit calmly with his eyes closed. Suzie looked intently at the monitor extended from her chair, her mouth moving as she spoke silently to herself. After several minutes she nodded to Teal and smiled.

"Decel successfully initiated," she announced formally. She unstrapped herself and carefully stood. "Four weeks to Donut. Might as well get up and get used to the new G, 1.35 if Suzie's calculations are right," she said. She walked past all their chairs, patting a few shoulders on her way out.

"And they always are," Suzie said. "Hey Jens, how do you like your new job?" she asked.

He ignored her and unstrapped, standing up and feeling like he was back on the *Calderón* lifting mass.

4

By the time Decel stopped and zero-G returned, Jens was too tired to care. He ignored the announcement over comms, a polite warning to hold onto something, closed his eyes and tried to sleep just like every other 'night'. He sighed as he began to float above his bunk, exhaling as if it was his last breath. Four weeks of increased gravity had exhausted him to an extent he hadn't imagined was possible. He carried forty-kilogram sacks of mass as part of his job, but under Decel he carried that on his body the entire time the thrusters were on.

His door slid open. Two muscular legs, floating at eye level, filled his view.

"We're here, man," Herschel said. "Donut time."

"Piss off," Jens answered. "I've got another two minutes." He pushed off the ceiling of his quarters and righted himself by the door. For the first time in what felt like a very long time, he smiled.

"God, this feels good," he said. He had been through rough patches before, jobs and places he was happy were in his past, but increased gravity was a burden he found very hard to carry. The cushioning of his bunk after initial Decel felt like sleeping on rock. Moving around the ship felt like a workout at the gym; only there was no shower at the end of this one, no rest from the oppressive weight. Every moment until Donut was a workout. Legs. Arms. Abdomen. Now he floated beside his crewmate, relieved.

"You like that shit, don't you?" he asked.

"It's like going to the gym, every moment of the day, without the hassle of going to the gym," Herschel said.

"You used to have the skinniest legs," Jens said. "Dude. They were like toothpicks. I thought you had some kind of disability or something. Toothpicks! Now you look like ... I don't know what you look like."

"Jealous is what *you* look like," Herschel answered. "Come on. Take a look at this thing."

They drifted to a viewscreen that provided a glimpse outside. The screen was tinted to obscure the sun, which filled the entire field of vision. It heaved and pulsed, the heart at the center of the solar system. Flares erupted, shown in the filter screen as orange fingers poking and retracting. In the center of the chaos was a circular disk. Jens and Herschel looked at its dark side. The panels facing the sun were arrayed to capture the maximum amount of power required for the Step.

"Looks like a black circle," Jens said, "against an incredibly huge headache." He pushed against the wall and floated towards the back of the room.

"Come on, man," Herschel said. "You have to be excited about this shit." He pushed away from the display and grabbed Jens' shirt as an anchor. "It's a Donut! It's a fucking Donut!" he said. "And we're gonna ride it across the galaxy!"

He pushed off Jens and slowly glided to the far wall, grabbing a stanchion and stopping his momentum. "We're going to travel a thousand light-years from Earth. And then again, and then again. Come on. You have to admit you're excited," he said.

Jens looked at Herschel and smiled. He felt his muscles relax for what felt like the first time in ... well, the four weeks since Decel. They were at the Donut!

"Yeah!" Herschel said. "Now that's what I'm talking about! Fucking Donut!"

"Fucking Donut!" Jens agreed.

They floated out of the observation lounge and towards the bridge. The door was open and they slipped in. Lassen was intently working at his monitor, in sole control of guiding the freighter into its docking bay once the convoy detached. Teal was unstrapped, but holding onto the arms of her chair to stay in position. The black disk loomed large in the polarized screen. Jens saw Suzie busy at her monitor. As soon as the *Cirrus* was docked, she would join the other Donut Holes at the central hub of the Donut checking the calculations of the quantum computer. Even though the computer was far beyond the understanding of a single human mind, even the minds of the twenty-four Donut Holes from the freighters attached to the outer ring, every Step was second-guessed, double-checked, and re-confirmed.

Rumor had it that this was just an orgy by the sun, that once the computer did its computing, there was nothing else for Donut Holes to do but drink and screw until the Step was initiated. Jens dismissed those stories as below deck bullshit. He knew Suzie well enough to know that the calculations were far too serious for a party. In the last few days of Decel, she was always at her monitor. Checking. And re-checking. Her obsession gave the crew a sense of reassurance.

Jens floated over to her station and gave her a kiss on the head. He breathed in the scent of her hair.

"Go away, Jens," she said. "This is too important."

"I know," he said. "I just want you to know we're all here with you."

"Great," she said. "Now go away."

Jens pushed away from her chair and she added without looking up, "Thanks. I really appreciate it."

Teal noticed the intruders for the first time and shooed them away. "Above your pay grade, boys," she said. "Might as well hang in the mess room until we detach. While you're there, bring us some coffee."

"Latte!" Suzie called.

"Just black and strong," Lassen said.

"Like your women, eh?" Herschel finished, but nobody paid attention.

"You know what I want, Jens," Teal said without taking her eyes off the screen.

Herschel and Jens drifted down the corridor to the mess.

"I have no idea what she wants," Jens muttered. "I know what she enjoys because she enjoys everything, but I have no idea what she actually wants."

"You sound like a wonderful lover," Herschel said.

"No," Jens said. "You don't understand."

"Whatever," Herschel said. "I'm going to start calling you 'Superfly'. You seem to have a knack for getting tangled up in spider webs."

"That's a big help," Jens said.

"So you're after help? You're beyond help. I'm trying to be a good example here. One woman, no games, keep it simple." Herschel looked at Jens and tried to show a bit of understanding, but couldn't pull it off. "Just give her a cappuccino. Can't go wrong with that."

Jens floated into the bridge with a tray of coffee balanced in one hand. Suzie grabbed his leg as he drifted by gazing at the view screen projected onto the wall. It imitated a window, something the freighter did not actually have. Cameras placed around the hull were their only eyes. He watched the other freighters drift away from the *Cirrus*, towards the Donut. Suzie grabbed the tray before Jens might upend it and send cups of coffee floating about the area.

"We detached," he said. "That was smooth."

He grabbed the nearest seat and stared as the rectangular black shapes slowly approached their docking bay on the Donut. Sixteen freighters already sat in their bays, awaiting the last convoy to secure before Step. Lassen worked the thrusters on the *Cirrus* to guide the hulk into her bay, not taking his eyes off his monitor. The backdrop of the entire screen was the intense expanse of the sun, swirling orange storms of plasma, eruptions of flares, thousands upon thousands of fusion explosions both hypnotizing and terrifying.

The Donut gave some shielding from the intense light. The side facing the sun was arrayed with solar collectors, harvesting the photons emitted by the star. It had been orbiting in the Vulcan zone for eight months, gathering the power needed to Step. At two and a half kilometers across, it offered almost five square kilometers of arrays to harvest photons twenty-four hours a day, every day of the week, for the time taken to charge.

Jens spotted the hub in the center of the Donut, housing the quantum. The Donut Holes, the astrogators, like Suzie, would all be in the hub soon to oversee the final equation and initiate the maneuver: folding space so precisely as to emerge zero point two astronomical units from a star over one thousand light-years away.

Suzie had tried to explain one evening, but Jens couldn't quite get it. He blamed the painkillers Teal supplied him with, to numb the grinding he felt in each joint as the increased gravity began to wear him down. Lying in bed with Suzie was bearable, but increasingly uncomfortable.

The outer ring of the Donut housed kilometers of conductors, Suzie explained, in which plasma heated to over one hundred million degrees Celsius flowed, kept in balance through the immense power generated by the photons continually bombarding the receiving arrays.

"Just think of it as a big round solar panel, if that helps," she finally said. "With a big huge fusion reactor wrapped around it."

The power generated was so great that it could create a gravity well deep enough to bend space and time until two locations light-years apart would almost touch. The point of closest contact was called the Step Point.

"It's simple. The easiest way to get from Point A to Point B is to put them in the same place," she said. She lifted the bedsheet that covered them. "Point A is here," she said, pinching a piece above her. "And Point B is here," she added, pinching a piece above Jens. She pulled the two pieces together until her hands touched. "See? Speed isn't involved, so no Einsteinian problems with approaching the speed of light, where you could never actually get to the speed of light. No matter how fast we tried to go," Suzie said. "According to Einstein, time would slow down for us. The faster the speed, the slower our clock. Not that we would notice. The bottom line is that we never go as fast as light."

"Relativity," Jens said.

"So, you're not as dumb as everybody says!" Suzie teased.

"Ah, well, it's the only word I know associated with Einstein."

"When we Step, we're not trying to move fast across space. The Donut barely moves a few hundred meters. Point A and Point B," she said, remembering the sheet in her hands. "We don't travel across space. We fold it together. The Donut creates a gravity well that creates a fold in space, bringing the two points together. The quantum computer gives the precise measure, and I'm talking precise, to put us right next to where we want to go. We Step over, and when the well is collapsed," she spread the sheet out again, "we're hundreds of light-years away from where we started."

Suzie didn't have to tell him what might happen if a calculation was not exact, but, of course, she did. Stepping into a sun. Stepping into a solid object. Stepping into nothing, so far from a star that power would never be regained and everything would simply run down and freeze. "Donuts, and all the ships attached to their ring, have disappeared in the past."

The first Steps were small, to the closest stars. Alpha Centauri, Bernard's Star, Wolf 359, Sirius, Tau Ceti. As the technology, and the size, of the Donuts increased, Steps grew longer. One hundred, two hundred, a thousand light-years.

And at every Step, they found the same thing. Barren, lifeless rocks orbiting the distant stars.

Jens squinted at the outer ring and saw the freighters arranged, spaced out around the nearly eight-kilometer circumference. Each had arrived within the previous week, spending the least time possible bathed in solar radiation. The rectangular lead-coated ships were very functional. They offered protection from the unseen storm outside. It was that storm that allowed Stepping, once the engineers and mathematicians caught up with the theoretical physicists—but it also killed anything staying too close for too long a time.

Why is space so dangerous? Jens thought. *And why is that thing called a Donut when it looks like everything that isn't a donut?*

"Hey, why is that called a donut when it looks like everything that *isn't* a donut?" he asked.

"I think it's to make it less scary," Suzie answered. "Donuts taste good. They're comfort food. And, also, because donuts are really, really bad for you," she added. "It's the perfect name."

As soon as the *Cirrus* docked onto the outer ring of the Donut, Suzie disappeared into the Hole. As they had come closer to the Donut, Suzie had grown more withdrawn, spending every waking moment analyzing data. She was trained in what could go wrong, and she always expected that it would. Her only job at this time in the journey, along with the other Donut Holes, was to make sure nothing would.

Donut Holes were a special breed. Burn out rates, as well as suicides, were high. Jens hoped the rumors about the party were true, even knowing they weren't. He could see Suzie needed a break, before she broke.

At Step, Teal floated in front of the door to the bridge, blocking access. The crew floated in the corridor, forming a line. Jens and Herschel floated close but Ed stopped them.

"End of the line, newbies," he said. He spun slowly and faced them. "Who signed on last?" he asked.

"I did," Jens answered.

"Then get behind Herschel," he said. "And shut up and take this serious."

Teal reached out and touched the first crew member in line. She pulled him close, looked deeply into his eyes, and kissed him fully on the lips. Pushing him away again, she said, "May you Step well, Lassen. May your trip be fruitful." She reached into a pocket and withdrew a white pill the size of a small mint. Lassen opened his mouth and she placed it on his tongue.

"Go, Lassen, and see the stars," she said, completing the surreal communion.

Lassen drifted by her and to his seat. She grabbed Baldy by the shoulder, never losing eye contact, pulled him close, and kissed him on the lips. "May you Step well, Baldy. May your trip be fruitful," she said. She reached into her pocket and withdrew another white pill, placing it in the waiting mouth.

"Go, Baldy, and see the stars," she said, and Baldy entered the bridge.

"Does every ship do this?" Jens whispered.

"Who cares?" Ed said. "And shut up."

Jens watched silently as the ceremony was repeated with Stephan, and then with Ed. Teal pulled Herschel close and kissed him.

"Herschel. Thank you for joining us. Today you Step. May you Step well." She pulled Herschel through the door and positioned him against the bulkhead before reaching out and pulling Jens close. Her eyes bored into his, and just at the point of discomfort, she kissed him. Their tongues danced for a moment and she moved her face back.

"Jens. My dear little runaway. Today you will run far. May you Step well," she said, moving aside and letting him into the bridge.

They both looked at her expectantly and she smiled. She reached into her pocket, withdrew a small white pill, and placed it into her mouth.

"On First Step, you don't trip," she said. "You experience every moment of it, so you'll remember every moment of it. Now take your seats." Teal pushed off the wall and gracefully floated to her chair.

Jens and Herschel drifted to their seats and strapped in. Around them, the crew leaned back in their seats, eyes closed and smiling. Jens looked at his palms and wiped the sweat on the legs of his flight suit. Herschel clutched the end of each armrest, knuckles showing white. He stared forward, eyes wide, refusing to meet Jen's gaze.

Jens looked at Suzie's empty chair and relaxed. Whatever was going to happen was totally out of his control. It wasn't a pleasant feeling, nor a place he ever liked being, but sometimes it was unavoidable. Just like before Decel, red numbers at the bottom of the view screen counted down. The viewscreen filled with the heaving and pulsing energy of the sun, dimmed to burnt orange.

"Hey buddy," he said to Herschel. "Have a good Step." But Herschel continued to stare at the screen and clutch the armrests of his chair.

The red numbers slowly counted down. Three digits became two, two became one, and soon nothing but zeros remained. Jens waited for a shutter, or a sound, or ... something to happen. Instead, he looked over at Herschel. Herschel was still staring forward, gripping his chair. Only he seemed to be farther away, stretching away. His chair wasn't moving. He wasn't moving. And yet he was growing distant.

Jens' eyes shifted to the ceiling of the bridge and he saw that it, too, was receding. But it wasn't just the ceiling. His entire skull was following it, stretching away from his body, taking his chest and shoulders with it. He glanced down and saw his legs receding with the floor, stretching in the opposite direction. He was rubber being stretched. He could feel the tension increasing as head and feet grew farther apart.

Just when he thought he would tear in two, he began to slowly spin. Head became feet and feet became head, became feet, became head. A flashing light made perception of up or down impossible. Jens raised a hand to his eyes and tried to focus on it, but it bent backward, flattened sideways, shrank until he had to squint, so he closed his eyes again and felt himself spin faster. He opened his eyes and clutched the armrests of his chair. He grasped for a memory, something that offered assurance, but his mind was pulled in the opposite direction of his body.

Jens was blinded by an impossibly white light. He closed his eyes and the light was replaced with darkness. He sat in absolute blackness, breathing deeply. The previous roar in his head was replaced by silence. Without opening his eyes, Jens moved a hand to his leg, touching solid flesh. He lowered his other hand, resting it on the opposite thigh. His breathing became calmer. He inhaled deeply, deliberately, held his breath a moment, and then exhaled slowly.

Jens opened his eyes and saw a huge burnt orange image fill the viewing screen, storms of plasma, endless thermonuclear explosions. The red numbers on the bottom of the screen continued to display zeros.

"Welcome to HAT-P-5," Teal announced.

The crew began to shift in their seats, lazily stretching and opening their eyes. Baldy and Ed rose from their seats.

"Thanks, Captain," they said, drifting towards the exit.

Stephan rose and followed, nodding to Teal.

"That was a Step, boys," she said to Herschel and Jens. "Now you know what it's like to travel one thousand light-years."

They both continued to sit, staring at her.

"Come along," she said, rising. "Two hours rest. As soon as our perky Donut Hole returns, we'll have a little celebration for her. Then we'll be detaching and reforming the convoy."

She drifted past them and through the doorway. Lassen stopped at their chairs and lifted them out, pointing them towards the exit before floating out.

"Fucking Donut," Herschel said. "I don't ever want to Step again."

"I'm afraid we don't have too much choice in that," Jens said, pushing himself towards the door.

5

When Suzie arrived in the mess hall the crew stood and applauded. She took a bow and sat at the head of the table. Teal pulled the cork out of a bottle of single malt whiskey and poured her a shot. The crew raised theirs.

"To our Donut Hole!" Teal said.

"Our Donut Hole!" the others agreed and each emptied their glass.

"How was the party?" Stephan asked as he refilled their glasses.

"You would have liked it, Stephan. So many sweaty men in one place," she said.

Ed slapped Stephan on the back. "She has your number. I'll have to be careful around you."

"How did you boys like Step?" Suzie asked.

Jens and Herschel grimaced, and the others laughed.

"It's like that in the Hole. Every time," she said. "Next Step you get communion, so quit looking so worried."

"That's if they deserve it," Teal said. She sipped her whiskey. "Herschel, I've had a request from the *Avarua*. It seems they'd like your help over the next couple months." She winked at him as the smile on his face grew larger. "You'll need to be back here once the convoy settles in behind little Hat Pin. We'll be starting fuel runs again, and it'll be just as flat out as before First Step."

"Yes, Ma'am!" Herschel said.

"I thought you'd like that. Give my love to Pani," Teal said. "And Jens, I've got an assignment for you too. I'll brief you as soon as these drunkards finish."

Lassen finished his drink and rose from his seat. He nodded to Suzie. "My lady," he said. "I give you my thanks." He floated from the table. "But I have a ship to detach and pilot towards a re-forming convoy, and must take my leave."

Suzie waved the back of her hand towards him. "Away then," she said, "do your duty. I have an empty glass that needs attention," she told the table.

Her glass was quickly filled as Stephan and Baldy joined Lassen in the bridge.

"Herschel," Teal said. "why don't you go pack what you need? We'll shuttle you over as soon as we've formed the convoy. Ed, can you see he has some nice treats to take over? Rangi likes your muffins."

When the room was clear Teal refilled Jens' glass. He shifted in his seat, watched by the two women.

"The *Sunrise Blossom* will be joining the convoy travelling to Hat Pin. They have a special delivery. Once they make their drop, they'll pick up some new cargo and rejoin us before our return to the Donut. It's an eight-month round trip," Teal said.

Jens took a sip of whiskey and waited.

"We have a stake in the cargo, and I need to make sure the transaction goes smoothly. The *Sunrise* has an upstanding crew, but temptation is temptation. I need to make sure they're not tempted, and that we're not cheated, so we need a presence there. You. Here, let me refill that," she said, pouring more whiskey in his glass.

"Why me?" Jens asked.

"You're the most expendable. And you have a reputation. It's one of the reasons I hired you. You know what that is, don't you?" she asked. "Your reputation?"

"All work and no play?" Jens said. "At least that's what Rangi told me."

Teal and Suzie laughed. Jens blushed, thinking about what Rangi may have actually meant.

"Yeah, that's right," Teal said. "I want you to go, watch the goods, and make sure we get paid the right amount. You'll also meet my contact in the colony. Mr Smith."

"The right amount. Mr Smith," Jens repeated.

"Bright lad," Teal said. "Mr Smith has arranged a consignment for us. You'll deliver our payment to him, and bring back that consignment. Smith will show you what it is for."

"A consignment," Jens said. "What aren't you telling me?"

"Come with me," Teal said. "It's time you knew. And you'll have to know if you want to come back alive. Four months on board and he doesn't even have a clue," she said to Suzie. "*That* is a hand-picked crew!"

Suzie pushed lightly off her chair and stopped him before he left the mess, giving him a long whiskey flavored kiss. "Finally going to lose your virginity," she said. "See me later!" she whispered in his ear. She pushed him gently, and he floated after Teal.

Teal flowed effortlessly down a corridor, stopped herself at a hatch and floated down into the hold. Jens followed the soles of her feet past the stored and disassembled reactors and into the compartments holding sacks of fuel. The sacks rose up the walls of the hold. Jens knew the area well. He and Herschel had hardly made a dent in the supply, which only reminded Jens of all the work they faced in preparation for the next Steps.

"There's not a lot of money in a convoy fuel supply," Teal said over her shoulder. "That's why nobody wants it. We make a little extra transporting reactor parts. Nobody wants that either because of the radiation risk. *Space* is a radiation risk. They travel towards stars emitting enormous amounts, thinking they're safe in the radiation-shielded boxes they're living in, and they worry about reactor parts."

Teal drifted into an adjoining room, one he and Herschel hadn't needed to work in yet. She slowed herself to a stop and faced Jens.

"But we got into this for money, right?" she asked. "Out here we have to get creative with ways of making it, and of making all this worth our while."

She pushed off a stack of fuel and made her way to the corner of the hold. She came to a rest at a pallet of fuel.

"What do you see, Jens?" she asked.

"Work," he said.

"What kind of work?"

"Backbreaking work, when the gravity is on," he said.

"You need to learn how to be more observant," she said. "And I'm not just talking about what's in the hold. You need to see what's going on in a ship, especially when you're on the *Sunrise*." She pulled a sack off the top of the pile and with a light push sent it floating to Jens.

"Open it," she said. "Take a look."

Jens looked doubtful.

"It's not fuel, Jens. Open it."

Jens pulled the zip along the top of the sack and opened it carefully. He tentatively looked inside, glanced at Teal, and reached in his hand. When he pulled it out, he held white pills. He opened his palm and let them drift free.

"Careful," Teal said. "You'll make a mess."

"Drugs?" he asked. "Really?"

"We prefer to call them 'high demand commodities'," Teal said. "It's all about supply and demand out here. There's a demand that we supply. And the products we supply are in particularly high demand, which means we make an awful lot of money."

Jens looked into the sack again before sealing it. "Shit," he said.

"It's very good shit. Good quality, I mean. Those colonists live extremely hard lives. They deserve good quality. And on these outer runs, they expect you to show up with a few luxuries. But all this is just a means to an end. The end is what you're meeting Mr Smith about. He'll explain more. And then you'll see what we're doing is beyond mere money."

"Why wait until now to show me this?" he asked.

"Timing," Teal said. "When you first came aboard, all you could do was look over your shoulder. You needed time to realize you have no alternative. And now that realization has dawned, you need to know because you have an important job to do. I need you to take your place as a partner with the rest of the crew."

"What if I don't want to? What if I turn you in?"

"You won't do that, Jens," she said. "We both know you won't, and that you can't. There's no way you can go back. You have no life to go back to. And you've found something you've been looking a long time for."

"What's that?" he asked.

"Family, Jens. And friendship." She drifted close to him, stopping her momentum with a hand on his shoulder. "Soon, you'll even have a cause. And I know you enough by now to know that you like it here and that at this moment you're relieved that life is a little more complicated than hauling sacks of fuel."

She raised a hand and gently touched his face, pleased that he didn't pull back or flinch. She moved closer and kissed him.

"We're not always going to Step, Jens," she said. "We're going to set up an operation, and then retire in comfort. That's the long-term plan. And I'm happy you're part of it."

"What choice do I have?" he asked.

"You always have a choice," she said. "You might feel backed into a corner or even trapped, but ultimately it's up to you what you do. It always is."

He knew she was right, about choice and about himself. He slipped an arm around her waist and pulled her close, meeting her mouth with his. He worked the zip in her flight suit and slipped it off her body while she removed his. The sacks of high demand goods cushioned their flight as they slowly ricocheted from wall to wall.

After they were back in their flight suits, Teal held Jens' arm.

"Herschel doesn't know anything," she said. "And I want it to stay that way until he returns from the *Avarua*. Okay? Can you keep this from him until then?"

"Why?" Jens asked. "Doesn't he have a right to know what he's gotten himself into?"

"He has every right," Teal said. "But the timing has to be right, and he has to be ready. Let him enjoy his time with Pani. When he returns, we'll explain why his pay check is going to be higher than he expected."

"Higher, that is," she added, "if you do your job on Hat Pin."

Jens grabbed Herschel by the arm, the closest he could get to a hug in freefall. He kept his tongue, just as Teal had asked, and hoped his friend would understand when they met again in eight months.

"Give Pani my love," Jens told him. "And tell Ora the tat healed beautifully and I have some ideas for another."

"Take care, man," Herschel said. "You're going to walk on another planet! I'm jealous."

"You're going to wake up next to a wonderful woman every day for the next four months. Don't pretend to be jealous." Jens patted Herschel's chest, tightening his grip on his arm so his friend wouldn't drift backward. Herschel smiled, nodded for goodbye and floated up the corridor towards crew quarters.

Jens pushed his bag across the flight deck and watched it drift towards the tender. He saw right away that his aim was off. Too high by a meter. He shoved off the wall to retrieve it. By the time he got back to the doorway, Lassen and Baldy were waiting. Lassen Jens expected. He was going to pilot him to the *Sunrise*. Baldy didn't strike Jens as the type that went for sentimental send-offs. Jens grabbed a handhold and stopped his momentum.

"There he is," Baldy said. "The man with the mission."

"With no idea what he's walking into," Lassen added.

"Do you know what kind of ship the *Sunrise* is?" Baldy asked.

"A freighter?" Jens said.

"That's the kind attitude you'll need," Lassen said. "Chinese freighter, to be precise."

"Have you ever heard of the Triads?" Baldy asked.

"You can't work in garbage without knowing about the Triads," Lassen said. "Or prostitution, smuggling, money laundering, hacking ... they have their fingers in everything."

They smiled and looked at Jens.

"You're telling me the *Sunrise* is a Triad ship?" Jens asked.

"I'm not telling you anything," Lassen said. "I just hope you live up to Teal's expectations. My bank account hopes you do too. How's your Mandarin?"

"Passable."

"As in not a word, eh?" Baldy said. "Ever heard the word *lingchi*?"

"The look on his face says 'no'," Lassen said.

"*Lingchi*," Baldy explained, "is one of the Triad's favorites. The lingering death."

"Slow slicing," Lassen added.

"Yeah. You're not killed outright, see? They just cut bits off of you, a little at a time. It can go on for days. Days and days," Baldy said. "They seem to like sharp instruments. Like meat cleavers. Those are quick. Fingers, toes, arms. Leave you hopping about for the rest of your days, if you're lucky."

"Ears. Nose." Lassen said.

"Private parts," Baldy added. "Nothing is safe."

Baldy reached into a pocket and took out a knife. Letting go of a handhold he used his other hand to take it out of its leather sheath. He took it carefully by the blade and handed it to Jens. Jens took the handle, admiring the steel.

"Teal wants you to take this with you," Baldy said. "She said to make sure the crew on the *Sunrise* know you have it. Something to do with your reputation, she seemed to imply. Stories get around fast out here. There's not much else in the way of entertainment. Maybe you guys can play with your knives together."

"You'll have enough months to do that," Lassen said.

Jens sheathed the blade and put it in his flight suit.

"Don't fuck up, Jens," Baldy said. He turned his body and pushed himself up the corridor.

"Sentimental, after all," Jens said.

"What was that?" Lassen asked.

"Nothing."

"Let's prep the tender and get you over there." Lassen pushed off and drifted to the tender. Jens looked up the corridor, half-hoping Suzie, or Teal, might show up to see him off. But he knew they wouldn't. They took care of their goodbyes last night.

6

Lassen piloted the tender out of the *Cirrus* and towards the Hat Pin convoy. This convoy formed a cube, three deep and three wide, characterless and ugly. The *Sunrise* took a top corner, with her added thrust helping to shave a week off the journey to the colony. After their business was complete, she would return alone to the two convoys sheltering behind Hat-P-3a, while the Donut finished re-charging for the second Step. P-3a was a Mercury sized planet, a barren and baked rock, but an effective shield from solar radiation. There the two remaining convoys waited for the Donut to repower.

Midway to the *Sunrise* Lassen swivelled the tender around and decelerated. With a few slight adjustments, he slid into their docking bay and landed gently.

"Take care, Jens," he said, the first words he had spoken since leaving the *Cirrus*. "We'll see you in eight months."

"Not staying for a coffee?" Jens asked.

"I've been here too long already," he said. "Get out of my tender."

Jens laughed, grabbed his bag, and opened the door. He tossed his bag to the deck and followed it down. He heard the door seal shut behind him. A young man in a black suit stood by the door to the corridor. Jens picked up his bag and walked towards him. The young man smiled as Jens approached.

"Welcome," he said, bowing. "Welcome to the *Sunrise Blossom*. What a treat! We're looking forward to having you!

I'm Louie," he said, taking Jens' bag. "Follow me, the rest of the crew are dying to meet you."

Louie walked a few meters down the corridor but suddenly stopped. "Are you okay in that flight suit, or do you want something nicer to wear? I'm sure we have something that will fit you. And if what you like doesn't, our tailor will fix it."

"You have a tailor?" Jens asked.

"It's one of his jobs," Louie said. "But you have to have a few skills up your sleeve in space. We all have specialties. With you on board we all get to use them! You're going to very busy. Now, your clothes?"

"I'm fine," Jens said.

"You'll change your mind, or Zhang might get offended. He's probably already got a whole wardrobe planned." Louie said. "Come on then. They're waiting in the mess hall."

"What's your specialty?" Jens asked.

"Languages!" Louie replied over his shoulder. "You'll be fluent in Mandarin by the time I finish with you."

Jens stood to attention, or his best simulation, as soon as he entered the mess. He started to address the Captain but was cut off.

"Jens, welcome aboard!" he said. "I am Captain Wan Huang. But please, call me Wan." He strode forward and grasped Jens' hand, shaking it firmly. "Come in and meet the crew," he beckoned.

Jens shook hands as each man came forward, told him their name, and extended a hand. Jens repeated each name several times to himself, glancing from face to face. Louie ushered him to a seat where a bowl of soup waited.

"It is wonton," the man who introduced himself as Yuan said. "I made it myself. I can teach you to cook."

"You know what wonton spells backward?" asked Genjo. "No? It spells 'not now'! Save yourself, push it away! We have much to talk about."

"Let the man eat," said Wan. "Sit down, everyone. Jens, enjoy your meal."

The crew took their seats around the table, watching Jens.

"So, you are our new crewmate for the next eight months! We have heard a lot about you. Your captain is most talkative. Let us hope it is only talk, eh, lads?"

The men around the table laughed.

"Hat Pin is far away, which leaves a great deal of time to fill. We will keep you busy, so do not worry," Wan said. "Or rather, I should say you will keep us busy." The men around the table laughed again. "Please, eat your soup," Wan added.

"We all have our hobbies on the *Sunrise Blossom*. You will give us the opportunity to use them! Your day will be full, but you will sleep well!"

Jens looked around the table. He felt decidedly under-dressed in his coveralls, the only type of garment he had worn since boarding the *Cirrus*. Each man wore a suit, individually tailored for size and taste. He stared perhaps a little too long at the man opposite who wore an orange three-piece with a blindingly white shirt. Zhao.

"Give me your knife," Zhao said.

"My knife?" Jens asked.

Zhao shook his head and laughed. "The knife in the sheath you have tucked into your front left pocket. Take it out."

Jens slowly reached into his pocket and took it out, setting it down on the table in front of him.

"Be careful, Captain! He has a knife!" Zhao said. Laughter around the table again.

"Take it out of its sheath." All humor had left Zhao's voice.

Jens withdrew the knife, exposing the sharp blade.

"Hold it, as you would use it."

Jens gripped the handle.

"You see Captain, I told you about those stories. Utter bullshit. But I'm sure I can teach him." Zhao seemed to be sizing Jens up with his eyes. "Give me the knife," he said.

Jens turned the knife around and handed it across the table, handle forward. Zhao took it, balanced on his hand, held the blade up and studied its edge, before handing it back to Jens.

"Not bad quality, but not very useful," he said.

"Zhao will teach you about blades. He is rather good with them. I advise you to pay attention to everything he shows," Wan said. "Zhang will teach you how to use hands—"

"And feet," the tailor added.

"And probably parts of your body you did not even know were weapons," Wan said. He pointed down the table. "Louie will teach you to speak. Do you think you can do that, Louie?"

"He'll be passing for a local before next Step." More laughter with added pounds on the table.

"You will help Yuan at meals and learn what he does. When he thinks you are ready, you will take over mid-watch meals." Yuan looked pleased, smiling at his new assistant.

"Genjo, what is your intention with this man?" the Captain asked.

"He must be schooled in the arts," Genjo pronounced. "Poetry and painting."

"Wu Pen is our First Mate." Wan indicated to a tall thin man with a neatly trimmed goatee. "I suspect Captain Teal has kept you busy loading and delivering sacks of fuels. I have to believe you have more potential than that. When you are working with Wu-Pen, you will be his shadow. He will be your mentor. He will explain how a freighter operates."

Wu-Pen nodded at Jens, who returned the gesture.

"And Jie?" Jens asked, looking at a man wearing green trousers and a green waistcoat, his bare arm displaying a tattoo of a dragon flying through a cloud.

"Jie is our Donut Hole," Wan said. "There is little that you would be able to understand."

"I will guide him through our library," Jie said.

"Very well," Wan agreed, nodding. "Jens, you have just lost two hours of your rest period. Wu-Pen will give you your rota.

Louie can show you to your quarters. We will accelerate to Hat Pin soon, but there is still much to do. Finish your soup, unpack your gear, and then it is time to start earning your room and board."

Jens nodded.

"You will certainly earn it," Wan added. "And Zhang, see that he has something decent to wear."

Jens woke and put on his suit, fine woollen trousers and jacket. Zhang decided that charcoal grey was his color, so his suit was charcoal grey. He put on a pressed cotton shirt and adjusted his dark grey tie in the mirror. He slid open the door to the corridor and walked to the dojo. While the *Cirrus* maximized every spare room for cargo, legitimate or contraband, the *Sunrise* seemed to have room to spare. A dojo, a library, an armory, a gym. Jens had never seen the cargo hold and was increasingly curious as to what it held.

First on the day's schedule, martial arts. Enter the dojo, change into a charcoal grey linen tangzhuang, a Tang suit, loose trousers, and jacket, bow to Zhang and begin.

"First you learn how to breathe," Zhang said. "Then you learn how to relax. Then you will learn how to stand. Maybe then I can teach you how to move."

Jens placed his feet flat on the deck, shoulder-width apart. He bent his knees, slumped his shoulders, bent his elbows a little outward, fingertips neither stretched nor clenched, palms down. Head erect, chest depressed, allowing his *ch'i* to sink to his navel. *Ch'i*, life force, energy flow, that permeates everything and links everything. *Ch'i* is the breath and the blood. Each must flow smoothly. *Ch'i* is power. To direct *ch'i* is to exercise great power. Every session in the dojo began with the *Tai Ch'i* sequence.

He closed his eyes and breathed low in his abdomen. He inhaled through his nose and extended his arms upward, exhaling as he bent his elbows and brought them downward.

"Tilt your coccyx," he heard Zhang say. "And quit thinking so much. Empty yourself. Feel the *ch'i*."

Jens opened his eyes and focused on his breath, shifted his weight to the left leg, bent his knee, relaxed his left side. He turned slowly, raising his right hand, palm down, and turned his left palm up, holding an imaginary ball. He shifted his weight to his right foot, taking a small step with his left. Bending his left knee, he shifted his weight back to his right, raised his left hand parallel with his chest and lowered his right hand beside his right thigh. Grasp Sparrow's Tail, Zhang called it. Every session Zhang added a posture until Jens would be able to enter, complete the sequence, and begin training.

"Ready stance," Zhang said.

The first time Jens took the stance, Zhang pushed his shoulder and he fell to the deck. He tried again, once more easily toppling over. Jens decided that the increased gravity of acceleration made the deck harder, but was determined to stop experiencing it.

"Good," Zhang finally said, a rare compliment. Every session, he practiced what he previously learned, and learned a bit more. Every part of his body was sore, yet every part was becoming more effective.

"From now on, before you come into my dojo, I want you to prepare yourself in your room," Zhang said. "Meditate for twenty minutes so that your mind is focused and you do not waste my time."

"Yes, Sensei," Jens answered.

"And practise every opportunity you have. Now leave, do not keep Jie waiting."

Jens bowed, washed in the adjoining shower, changed back into his suit, and walked to the library.

Jie was sitting in a leather chair, surrounded by bookshelves. Jens thought the only thing missing was a fireplace, but fire was an enemy in space. One of the many enemies. He sat in the chair opposite Jie and waited. Jie always made him wait, made him sit, and let the energy of the dojo settle down. "Zhang may tell you to use *ch'i*," Jie had said. "But this space is for understanding it."

So, Jens used the library under the guidance of the *Sunrise's* Donut Hole.

"Lao Tse would argue that our true self knows how to live. When we live according to our nature, we don't need anyone else to dictate our path for us. We know all we need to know from the inside out. Read," Jie commanded.

"The more rules, the less freedom. The less freedom, the less happiness. The less happiness, the more crime. The more crime, the more rules."

Jie laughed. "That is a very profound truth, but do you understand it?"

Jens tried to reconcile story and text. "You are a Triad ship. You are part of the reason we have rules, because of your crime. Wearing fancy suits doesn't change that!" he finally blurted out.

Jie laughed again. "The rules you talk about, who made them?" he demanded. "The rules you, yourself, live by, even kill by, who makes them?"

"We have rules to stop us from living like animals," Jens said. "To stop the strong from preying on the weak."

"And who are you, Jens?" Jie asked. "Are you the strong, or are you the weak? Are you more than an animal that kills?"

"I—," Jens tried.

"No," Jie continued. "You are neither strong nor weak. You are neither prey nor predator. At this moment you are only Jens. You are not governed by hate, or lust, or ambition when you maintain balance. You are merely in this moment. Stay in this moment. Now read."

"Knowing others is intelligence; knowing yourself is true wisdom. Mastering others is strength; mastering yourself is true power," Jens read.

"It is very clear, is it not?" Jie asked. "Know thy self. All religions say this. Continue."

"Simplicity, patience, compassion. These three are your greatest treasures. Simple in actions and thoughts, you return to the source of being. Patient with both friends and enemies, you accord with the way things are. Compassionate toward yourself, you reconcile all beings in the world."

"Do you understand the words?" Jie asked.

"I think so," Jens answered.

"Go on."

"There is no going on," Jens said. "At least that is what I keep reading." He stood and selected another text from the shelf. He enjoyed holding paper in his hands. He savored the smell and feel of each book. Although the digital library was exponentially larger, it was not electric text he reached for. He reached for Jie's collection of old earth-bound books.

"Close your mouth," he read. "Block off your senses, blunt your sharpness, untie your knots, soften your glare, settle your dust. This is the primal identity." Jens flexed his arm, stretching a bruised muscle. "Be in the moment, is that all this says?"

"It says, *be* the moment," Jie said. "There is only this moment. You can be in it, and experience the power of the present, which is where all power resides. Or you can continue to daydream through it, and waste your power. Your power is in the present moment, and only you can choose to embrace it. If you know yourself, and are honest with that self."

Jens shifted in his chair, opened his mouth, and then closed it, waiting.

"This isn't a therapy session, Jens," Jie said. "It is about philosophy and outlook. Maybe there is no difference. Maybe it's all the same." He shook his head. "What you're reading about is illusion and ... about the Way. I don't want to say it is about reality. I don't know what that is. But I know you intuit the truth. Misery arises from illusory wants. Happiness comes from knowing true needs. Use the time here to recognize those. Be able to articulate what it is you truly need. In doing so, you will discover who you really are."

"Maintain your defense, and you will not get hurt," Zhao said again. Jens tried to ignore the pain in his arm where the bamboo stick had just struck. He stepped back, trying to take a defensive stance, but his bruised thigh was slow to respond. He was rewarded with another strike, this time across his exposed quadricep muscle.

"If you are too weak or damaged to retreat, what should you do?" Zhao circled to Jens' left.

"Advance!" Jens said through gritted teeth.

"Then why do you retreat?" Zhao asked, swinging the staff quickly and hitting the back of Jens' leg.

Jens lunged forward, dipped his shoulder and rolled, swinging his bamboo staff low to the ground at the same time. Zhao sensed the feint, jumped up, and the staff sailed under the soles of his feet. Jens continued the roll. Gaining his feet, he let the momentum carry him around. His staff becoming a leg, he swung it around as if executing a roundhouse kick. Zhao grunted as the wood connected with his ribs. He grabbed it and pulled forward. Jens released it and Zhao stumbled back.

"Good," Zhao said before Jens started to follow with his hands. Both men stood panting, bodies weighed down by the heavier gravity of Decel. Jens bowed.

"Tomorrow you start with blades. It is time you learned how to use one properly. Now go, or you will be late for your language lesson."

"Ni lianxi le ma?" Louie asked. Have you practised?

"Dan wo mei shijian lianxi," Jens said. I don't have time to practise.

"Zhe bu shi da an," Louie said. That is not an answer.

"Wo shi shi kan," Jens said. I try.

"Bu yao yong yingyu qu xiang. Yao xue hui zi ran yun yong." Louie spoke each word slowly, facing Jens. Don't think in English. You need to learn to apply it naturally.

"Wo zhi dao le, lao shi," Jens heard the advice, as well as the rebuke. I understand, Teacher.

Jens started to write with the tip of his brush pen. He paused it at the right, lifted it off the paper and turned it back. He enhanced the stroke to the lower left, turned it back again and traced a horizontal to the upper right. He lifted and paused it, letting it rest back to the middle of the stroke, adjusted its tip and stopped.

"Good. You are starting to use your own style. But stay true to form. It is a delicate balance." Genjo stood behind Jens, watching over his shoulder. "I think the more you learn about the concept, the less it looks like a child's painting."

Jens finished a stroke and slowly lifted his pen. Like everything he was learning, sequence and order were vital. He lowered the tip of the brush pen, pressed it, and turned it back.

"Rice cooking," he said.

"Indeed, it is." Genjo placed a fatherly hand on Jens' shoulder. "Explain to me your rice cooking."

"Here is the steam," Jens said, indicating to the top of the picture. "It is vapor. I like to think of it as breath on a cold morning. Breath that is seen is a visual representation of the life force. And here below is the rice, the food or the offering. Rice sustains life. Life cannot exist without breath. Rice is not eaten cold. Together the two represent the vital energy. The nature of things."

"*Ch'i* arises from four elements," Genjo said. "The air that you breathe, the very biochemical character of your physical body, the essence of the food you eat, and what you have inherited from your parents. All must be in balance. Contemplate that balance as you use your pen. Now begin again."

"Xie xie, lao shi." Thank you, Teacher.

7

"Jens, a couple of gifts for you." Wu Pen approached with an object wrapped in cloth. He unfolded it and withdrew a knife. "This is from Wan, on behalf of all of us."

Jens studied the blade. It was so sharp he felt that if he looked for too long, it would cut his eyes. From what Zhao taught him, he correctly identified it as Japanese. The cutting edge, hardened on the point. The pattern to the ridgeline indicating its maker. Jens would have to research that pattern when he returned to the *Cirrus*.

"Here is a sheath to hold it," Wu Pen said. "Wear it on your calf, under your pant leg. Let everybody know you have it, but be discreet."

Jens reverently slid the blade into the sheath. When he finished strapping it onto his leg, Wu Pen handed him another weapon.

"Put this in your jacket pocket. Make sure it is easy to reach." He handed over a hand-sized sounder, a simple six-shooter, okay in a quick fight, but useless in anything else. At close quarters the shock wave emitted would rupture internal organs and kill. Across a room, it would only stun. Hopefully, that would be enough.

Jens felt the weight of it in his hand, familiarizing himself with the weapon's balance, just as Zhao had taught him. He checked the clip, saw that it was full. He examined the chamber. He switched the safety off and back on to ensure it was not jammed before putting it into his right pocket.

"Preparations. Tell me," Wu Pen said.

"Wan is on the bridge with the orbital watch. That would be Zhao, operating the docking bay doors and Louie on comms."

"*That would be?*"

"Apologies, First Mate," Jens said. "I created the roster. Wan, Zhao and Louie are on the bridge."

"And?"

"Computations are being checked for return to the convoy sheltering behind Hat-P-3a. Reactors serviced and fueled. Extra fuel laid in to account for any miscalculation in deceleration."

"Jie does not make miscalculations," Wu Pen said.

"I felt it a wise precaution."

"Very well. What is the English? Better safe than sorry. What else?"

"Cargo drop prepared for successful conclusion of negotiations planet side. Landing site coordinates programmed into drop boxes. Voice activation set to your command."

"And?"

"The tender load is secured, and the reactor is fueled. Emergency fuel stowed and secured."

"It's not a tender," Wu Pen corrected.

"Apologies, First Mate. The *flier* is prepared for descent, and secret compartments are secured. No inspection will detect the spaces."

"How do you know?"

"I checked them myself," Jens said.

"Don't you trust my crew?" Wu Pen asked.

"Impeccably. But—"

"There is nothing wrong with being thorough," Wu Pen said. "But be careful how that may be perceived by your crew. They will respect you if you trust in their abilities, not if you second guess them. Doubt sows dissension. Now stand down, Acting First Mate Jensen. You are relieved."

Jens *was* relieved. Shadowing the First Mate had turned into being the First Mate, which meant knowing where everybody and everything was on the ship at all times, as well as seeing that both ship and crew ran efficiently all of the time.

"You are once again a deckhand from the freighter *Cirrus*, under the command of Captain Sandra Teal, a name that has kept you alive to this date, and will hopefully continue to do so below."

After months of travelling under such a grueling training regime, Jens felt that an illicit drug deal on an underground colony over a thousand light-years from Earth looked almost like a vacation and a welcome rest.

"Business is business," Jens remembered Yuan repeating yet again, during mess-duty-slash-business-lessons. "Ultimately, it is only a transaction, as old as humans. Supply and demand. Whatever is supplied and whatever the demand is based on. And business is ultimately based on trust. Sure, that trust is often based on fear. The fear of getting cheated. No!" Yuan said, interrupting his own lecture. "Add what cooks fastest last. Why do I have to tell you that? Where was I?"

"Fear," Jens stirred the wok in front of him, stir-frying the strips of freeze-dried pork.

"Yes – trust," Yuan said. "Like any currency, it must be backed by something. Otherwise, it is worthless. Money used to be backed by precious metals, like silver and gold. Later it was backed by a guarantee, which is fine if people trust the guarantee, and the guarantee can be honored. Look where that got us, eh? Trust in *our* business is backed by fear, which is backed by force. Simply the threat of force, implied or applied, is enough. We trust that when we enter their den, they will not simply kill us. Why? The threat of force, causing an element of fear. Not just from us. They don't need to fear who we are, but who backs us."

"The Triads?"

"Who told you that?" Yuan laughed. "See – an implied threat, real or imaginary. I remember your first day here, walking into the mess with your big scared rabbit eyes. Where did those eyes go?" Yuan mused. "Never mind. Planet side, there will be no rabbit eyes. Hard eyes looking at each other. Let them know you carry a weapon, a blade or a gun, or both. They will do the same. Trust is achieved in the balance of fear and force. We make our deal, you meet your contact and conduct Teal's business, and we leave."

"But the *Sunrise* is backed by a Triad?"

"Such an old-fashioned name. But of course, it is," Yuan said. "That is why we can trust them. They fear us."

"But don't they have their own ..."

"What? Mafia? Gang? Syndicate? Sure, they do, but ours is older. Listen to how you say it. The name alone has force, even if all the Triads have turned into Consortia, corporate enterprises, owning ships, employing accountants, and paying taxes. We are merely part of a Consortium. Triads don't exist anymore."

"And it doesn't matter what we sell?" Jens asked.

"Should it? I admit it should. That's why we don't sell arms, at least certain types of arms. And we especially don't sell to politicos, as tempting and as profitable as that is."

"What's the difference between guns and drugs?"

"Listen to yourself! Still so shaped by the values of your place of birth. But I suppose it's a question you had to ask, because you're in it up to your neck, even if you can't see how deeply yet." Yuan looked at Jens with something akin to sympathy, even somewhat fatherly affection. "What we trade is closer to entertainment. Drugs – what a word! Some are legally sanctioned, like those that numb pain. Those drugs are sanctioned because powerful Consortia make a *literal* killing from it. Other drugs are contraband, depending on your time and place. Like alcohol on Ceti-4. Stupidity. We supply a need people have, a demand for some escape. A colony or authority says the people shouldn't have it? Fuck them, and fuck their patronizing laws."

Yuan wiped his hands on his apron. "And the technology – that is simply supplying another demand, the demand for access. Most of what we trade is a way around walls. Firewalls. Again, patronizing authorities deciding who can see or say what. Now turn off the heat and serve the crew."

"You sound like an anarchist," Jens said, lifting the wok off the stove.

"Every spacer is an anarchist," Yuan said. "Including you."

The flier left the docking bay and propelled itself away from the *Sunrise.* The ship looked small and lonely, orbiting by itself. Jens saw another freighter from the convoy unloading supplies, tenders from the ship pushing cargo towards the planet, a 'cargo drop' in the literal sense, plunging to the surface, saved only by parachutes and balloons that would bounce their scorched containers into the drop zone for ground crews to collect.

The flier leaving the ship showed the path they would take to the surface of the brown planet below them. Farther away several larger fliers were beginning to assemble in orbit, their only flight being to deliver colonists to the surface.

They sliced through the atmosphere in a gradual spiraling descent, each slow circle bringing the barren surface closer. Jens couldn't see what attracted anybody to leave Earth for what lay below. A dust storm turned the surface into a blurry smudge. Black shadows on the horizon slowly showed themselves to be rocky mountains. To the south stretched an endless and lifeless desert of sand and stone. The only thing it had that made the Donuts come was an atmosphere. Even if it was thinner than Earth's was at sixty thousand feet, it was still something to work in, maybe even work with.

Wu Pen slowed the descent whenever the flier's wings began to glow, the thin atmosphere providing more than enough friction to cook them in their seats if the speed wasn't controlled. He was in no hurry. He adjusted the wings, and pulled the nose up.

"How about some drinks, Jens?" Wu Pen said. "Might as well enjoy the ride down." He nudged Jens' arm. "You've got plenty of time to watch the scenery. On the rocks, please."

Jens unstrapped from his seat and walked to the back of the flier, returning with three glasses of whiskey.

"Over there, see?" Wu Pen pointed out the window.

Jens scanned the horizon but shook his head.

"There – looks like a pile of dirt or rocks."

"Yeah, okay," Jens said.

"Laika. That's all you'll see of the place out here. The rest is down below."

"It's a dog of place," Yuan said, laughing at his own joke. "Laika, get it? The first dog in space."

"I didn't think that was the name," Jens said.

"It's the local name, so it's the only name that matters."

Jens sipped his drink, watching the surface become clearer as the flier continued to spiral. The closer they got, the more they saw signs of human habitation. Slag heaps, open pits, smoke and steam escaping from vents. Even the reactors blended into the rock. Everything was a shade of brown. He searched his memory for any comparison, something to help him understand the vast wasteland under him. Nothing came to mind.

"Millions of people, all living underground like moles," Yuan said. "Not even a dog deserves that."

"They get what they came for," Wu Pen said.

"Which is?" Jens asked.

"Money. There's a lot of cash in this rock. All they have to is dig it out, process it, and sell to Earthers. Or they feed and clothe those that dig. Or service in any other way. Every gold rush is the same. Only this gold has a long time before it runs out. Look below you. There's nothing but rocks." Wu Pen breathed out slowly. "Cargo holds of money," he finished.

"And freedom," Yuan added.

"Money and freedom," Wu Pen agreed. "And nowhere to use either. That's where we come in." Wu Pen handed him an empty glass. "That's it for relaxation. Game faces soon. Prepare yourselves. Remember your instructions."

By the time Jens returned to his seat, a long landing strip scarred the surface in front of them. Wu Pen touched down, hardly noticeable in the low gravity. He folded the wings upright, taxied off the main runway and followed a side route that ended at an entrance in the rock face. He guided the flier in and waited as others joined them. The wide door behind them closed and the one in front slid open, revealing an expansive hangar. Wu Pen parked in their allotted bay and powered down.

No one spoke as each man adjusted their suit and tucked weapons into pockets. Jens opened the door and extended the steps. He climbed down and stood.

"What are you waiting for?" Yuan asked.

"I don't know. Customs or border control or something."

"Yeah, right. Welcome to Hat Pin." He slapped Jens on the shoulder. "Come. Our business partners are waiting."

Wu Pen strode ahead, and the other two fell in behind. They entered the nearest compartment of a waiting train and sat. It moved forward with a slight jolt and was swallowed by the rock. Lights flickered as they sped through a tunnel. It stopped several times, each station the same. Finally, at another station carved into the stone, Wu Pen stood and exited the car.

Jens followed. A walkway led to a wide viewing platform. Jens stopped at the edge.

"Fuck me," he said.

The lights of the underground city made the vast cavern glow, reflected off the roof that towered over a kilometer above. Glassed-over openings bored through the ceiling let in additional light, which was reflected off mirrors to give a semblance of a circadian rhythm to the day. Every and any opening to the surface was sealed, and filters circulated the atmosphere within. A river of black and lifeless water wound through the city, the primary reason for the settlement's location – that and the ready access to minerals.

Hover pods darted above the buildings. All three placed a hand on a weapon when one landed nearby. A door opened and a man in a black suit stepped out.

"Dimitri," Yuan said. "Good to see you again!" He walked forward and offered his hand. Dimitri shook it.

"Yuan, always a pleasure," he said. "Wu Pen," he added, nodding towards the other. "Welcome back. And this is the new man? Jensen, isn't it?"

"Yes, he is a representative of Captain Teal's," Yuan said.

Jens couldn't decide if Dimitri smiled or smirked. He indicated to the hover pod and they got in. The door closed and it gently lifted, flying over the city just above roof level. Most buildings were two or three-story prefabs, but some ambitious stone structures rose from the city center. Electric cars moved about the streets below.

"We'll meet at the Pistolety," Dimitri said.

"Good choice," Yuan agreed. "A very open environment. Jensen will be meeting a contact after we conclude our business."

"Mr Smith can wait, he is not going anywhere," Dimitri looked at Jens, his eyes lingering at the bulge in his jacket pocket before moving down to his ankle.

Jens let his own gaze move to the city below, trying for nonchalance. Yuan was taking the lead, that was clear; just as were Jens' instructions to follow.

The hover pod settled on the pad in front of a stone building with Cyrillic letter on it. The door opened and they followed Dimitri into the bar, where at a table set against a wall two others sat waiting. A slight woman in a blue dress sat next to a hulk of a man. Her white skin was offset by her jet black hair. His skin was covered in tattoos, decorating the one hand resting on the table and climbing up his neck.

Yin and yang, Jens thought.

Yuan approached the table.

"Natasha, I am very pleased to see you," he said. He slowly pulled out a chair and sat. Wu Pen and Jens followed.

"Your visits are always welcome, Yuan," the woman said, remaining seated. "Will you be spending any time to take in the pleasures of our fine city?"

"Unfortunately, we are only here for business. We only have a small window of time to re-join the convoy," he said. "I am unfamiliar with your colleague."

"This is a friend of the family," Natasha said. "Vladimir is very interested in business."

"Well, Vladimir." Yuan's tone shifted from silk to steel as he looked at the man. "We do not do business with weapons pointed at us under a table."

Lines from a book that Jie made Jens study came to mind. It was a book about war that was applied to business.

"We come in good faith, and yet you try to intimidate us," Yuan said. "It must be a big gun for those fat fingers to fit around it."

If your opponent is of choleric temper, seek to irritate him. Pretend to be weak, that he may grow arrogant, Sun Tzu wrote over twenty-five hundred years ago. Jens watched Vladimir for a response. The big man's lip twitched. His jaw tightened.

At a glance from Natasha, Vladimir placed his other hand on the table. It was also covered in ink, as well as bruises on his knuckles. As far as Jens could tell, the woman was the only one at the table not armed, though he wouldn't bet on that. Trust backed by force. Force backed by deception. Jens smiled, watching the actors play their parts. This was more than *yin* and *yang*, more than working with *ch'i,* energy. This was manipulating it.

All warfare is based on deception, Sun Tzu wrote.

"If you have no time to visit, let us at least eat." Natasha shot a glance at a waiter, and he brought plates to the table.

"Wonderful," Yuan said. "Pistolety make the best cavy in Hat Pin!" he added to Jens.

The smell made Jens' mouth water. Boiled potatoes were piled beside the thin strips of barbequed meat. Dark green spinach added a third color. It was their first fresh vegetables in months.

"Fresh greens," Yuan said, admiring his plate.

"Do you grow them underground?" Jens asked Natasha, exploring the protocol of the table, gambling that by speaking he wouldn't cause offense. He was pleased when she answered.

"There are greenhouses lit by the reflected sun. The mirrors increase not only the light but also the heat," she said. "The cavy aren't so fussy. They thrive anywhere. Perfect little livestock. They, too, are very fresh," she said.

Jens took a bite and chewed slowly, savoring the flavor. "Cavy sounds familiar," he said. "But I can't remember what they are."

"Guinea pig," said Yuan. "Perfect for stir fry. We should have a colony on the *Sunrise*!"

Jens cut another bite and put it in his mouth. He smiled at the thought of furry rodents scurrying about the freighter, or floating about in the library in zero gravity.

"I am told you were a sailor recently on Earth," Natasha said to Jens. "Do you miss the sea? Wide open horizons, with the air and sun touching you?"

Was she genuinely interested, or was this some maneuver? *When the position is such that neither side will gain by making the first move, it is called temporizing the ground.* Okay, Jens thought.

"I do miss that," he admitted. "But I enjoy the room onboard the *Sunrise*, and the *Cirrus*. On the scow, the quarters were rather cramped, and the deck was very small."

"And you can't fall over the side of a freighter and be lost at sea," Vladimir said.

Irritate him? Pretend to be weak? "No," Jens said. "But you can get sucked out of an airlock." Vladimir was a big man, but if he had spent his life on Hat Pin, he would be weaker. Training at higher gravity would give Jens an advantage should anything turn physical.

In all fighting, Sun Tzu advised, *the direct method may be used for joining battle, but indirect methods will be needed in order to secure victory.* Jens smirked inwardly.

"It is called vented." Wu Pen spoke his first words since entering Pistolety. He had spent the meal tracking movement in the bar, watching Vladimir's hands and ensuring that they were visible at all times.

"Apologies, First Mate," Jens said. "You can get vented," he said to Vladimir.

"I've never seen the ocean," Natasha said, ignoring the posturing of the men. "To be surrounded by water in all directions! It is hard to imagine."

"My favorite time was the early morning, the dawn, with the sun rising out of the ocean." Jens ignored the stare from Vladimir.

"Describe it," Natasha said.

"Every sunrise is different – the colors, orange, purple, pink. A type of peach, I never learned the name of it, but it always reminded me of birth or death. Beginning or ending. Even the grey, what would otherwise be considered dull, becomes a spectrum. But what is always special is that every color, every sunrise, is so ... ephemeral."

Natasha looked at Jens, waiting.

"It's a time of the day before anything happens. It might be a cool and colorful respite before the glare and heat that will come later. Or a bit of peace and quiet before a hectic watch. They are all moments to savor."

"You have brought us a romantic," Natasha told Yuan. "Thank you, Jensen. But now to our business, which unfortunately lacks romance." As if on cue, waiters cleared away the plates. When one cleared the table, another appeared with glasses and a bottle of clear liquid. He filled each glass.

"A toast," Natasha said, raising hers. "With our best vodka, our finest batch. To the continuation of a fruitful relationship."

"Agreed," Yuan said. They downed their drinks, and a waiter refilled their glasses. "You see, Jensen, dinner is the sunrise before the deal. A respite before whatever might happen will happen."

"I have your share worked out and ready for transfer." Natasha wrote on a napkin. She slid the paper across the table to Yuan.

He glanced at the number. "It looks a little less than I expected. Twenty percent less. It seems we brought twenty percent less cargo." Yuan set his glass down. "We can dispatch that from orbit once transfer is complete. The fragiles on the flier we can negotiate."

Vladimir set his drink down and placed both hands flat on the table. Jens and Wu Pen did the same.

"Maybe the fragiles are already unloaded," Vladimir said.

"We would have heard if that was the case," Yuan said.

"How could you hear unloading from here?"

"Everybody would have heard," Yuan said. He picked up his glass and took another sip. "An explosion that would probably have ripped a hole in the hanger. Any retinas scanned that were not ours would detonate—"

"You come here with a bomb on your ship!" Vladimir moved a hand towards the edge of the table, matched by Wu Pen's.

"Do you need to make any calls? Let anybody know?" Yuan asked Natasha.

"No," she said. "I think they all heard you. Stand down," she said to the air. "And you too, boys. Calm yourselves." Gone was the sweetness Jens heard earlier. She wrote on another napkin and pushed it towards Yuan.

Yuan smiled and nodded. Natasha raised a hand and snapped her fingers. A waiter approached cautiously, slowly reached into his waistcoat, and withdrew a small disc. He handed it to Natasha, who handed it over to Yuan.

"You can check the payment," she said. "all the codes are on the disc."

Yuan pocketed the disc. "I am sure there is no need," he said. "And I think business is going to be very good between us for a very long and prosperous time." He finished his vodka and held out his glass. Dimitri refilled it. "You can tell your men to unload the flier now," Yuan said. He tilted his head and spoke into his comms. "Wan, it is time to dispatch the cargo to the landing zone." Yuan downed his drink in one fluid motion, placing it carefully in front of him on the table. "I do enjoy your vodka."

"You will find a case in your flier," Natasha said, sweetness returning to her voice.

All six stood. "As always, my dear Natasha, we part as very satisfied colleagues. I wish you health and fortune."

"And to you, Yuan," she said. "Mr Jensen, it was delightful to meet you. May you enjoy your next sunrise."

"Thank you," Jens answered.

The three left the bar and walked to the waiting hover pod.

"Your pod is there," Yuan said, indicating a solitary one-seat vehicle nearby. "It will be programmed to your contact's location. We will see you back at the hangar at 1800 hours, *Sunrise* time. Sunrise time – that is appropriate." He laughed as he entered the pod with Wu Pen.

The door closed as soon as Jens strapped himself into the seat. He heard the propellers above him begin to whirl and felt the craft lift off the ground. It flew low over some nearby prefabs and dipped lower to enter a two-lane passageway. The pod hummed above the lane until the tunnel opened into another vast cavern. The lights of hundreds of buildings illuminated the subterranean space. Sunlight reflected from mirrors gave the illusion of day, but that light was beginning to fade. It was three am *Sunrise* time, but here the people were leaving work or preparing for dinner.

Time lost all meaning in space, useful only for keeping watches, for scheduling work. Maybe it meant as little to the miners on this dark colony.

Jens watched a prefab draw close as the hover pod descended. Each building looked the same—square panels of flexi-steel fitted together to form walls and ceilings. The pod came to a stop in front of just such a building. A large sliding door formed its entrance. The door was slightly ajar, opened wide enough to admit a person. A man stood by the opening, in light brown tactical pants and a thermal shirt. His greying temples indicated middle age, but his physique urged caution. Jens touched the sounder in his pocket.

The door of the pod lifted upward, and Jens stepped out.

"Mr Smith, I presume," Jens said.

"Mr Jensen." Smith smiled and extended a hand. "Welcome. Thank you for meeting me here. Not too many off-worlders get this far into Laika."

Jens shook his hand.

"Of course, we like it that way. It's better for business, with fewer noses sniffing around. Which is why we're here." Smith pushed the door and it slipped open farther. "Please, come in."

Jens tried to place Smith's accent. It definitely wasn't Russian.

"You're from Earth," he finally said.

"Originally," Smith said. "Minneapolis, Minnesota. Do you know it?"

"No."

"There's a big beautiful river running through it called the Mississippi."

"I've heard of that," Jens said.

"But even there they'd ask where I was from," Smith said. "I've lived in too many lands and in too many languages. You pick up accents without even knowing. You even start sounding like the ship you're in before long."

"I probably already do," Jens said.

"You do. *Are they treating you well on the Sunrise?*" he said in Mandarin.

"*Yes, they are,*" Jens answered. "*I am their captive pupil.*"

"*I am sure they have a lot to teach.*"

"*You have no idea.*"

"*Oh, I might.*"

Smith led Jens across an empty warehouse floor and into a smaller office. He gestured to a metal table with two chairs. Smith took a bag of light brown soil out of his pocket before sitting down. He opened the top and took a pinch out, sprinkling it on the table.

"You don't know what this is, do you?" he asked.

"No," Jens said. "It looks like dirt."

"What exactly did Teal tell you?"

"She told me I was to meet a Mr Smith to pick up a consignment."

"But she didn't say anything else? You are a very trusting person, Mr Jensen." Smith ran his finger through the dust on the table.

"It didn't seem like I had much choice," Jens said.

"That's where you're wrong, Mr Jensen," Smith dusted his hands and sat back. "*You came down with Yuan. He is teaching you business, correct?*"

"*He tells me I am a slow learner. He calls me the village idiot.*"

"*That is no doubt a compliment, coming from him.* Business. I have no doubt combat, as well. Weapons. At least sounders and knives, eh? Hand to hand?"

"Language. Art. Philosophy."

"Interesting. Navigation?"

"Very basic. Ship management, mostly."

"What did you do for Teal on the *Cirrus*?" Smith asked.

"Delivered sacks of fuel," Jens said.

Smith laughed hard. "Carrying water and chopping wood. Okay, Jensen. Let me tell you how this works." Smith pointed to the bag of dirt. "But first, Teal gave you something to deliver?"

Jens nodded. He pinched his eyelid with two fingers and lifted it. With two fingers from his other hand, he touched his eye, carefully removing a clear lens. Smith reached out a hand, palm up, where Jens placed the lens carefully. Smith examined the micro disc briefly before taking it and putting it in a small envelope.

"You're right about this," he said, indicating the bag on the table. "It is dirt, if dirt is just ground rock. We have a lot of rock on Hat Pin. Some of it is very valuable. Varieties are still being discovered." He opened the bag and passed it to Jens. "Go on, touch it- — smell it, taste it. It's what you bought."

Jens took a pinch out and brought it to his nose. "Smells like dirt."

Smith laughed again. "By itself, that's all it is. It's from a mineral called pyrosmium. Our operation here mines it and grinds it. All very top of the board, legitimate mining operation. Go ahead and taste it."

Jens touched a finger to his tongue. Smith laughed. "Taste like dirt?" he asked. "As I said, by itself, that's all it is. But it's what's between the molecules that counts. And when you combine it with Shackleton salts—"

"Our next Step," Jens said.

"Exactly. Combined with Shackleton salts and another chemical made from minerals from a colony planet somewhere else along the chain, and you get something very powerful called GLR." Jens' face showed that he wasn't familiar with the acronym. Smith reached into his pocket and took out another, smaller bag, this one containing white mint shaped pills. "You've seen these, though?" he asked.

"Yeah! Teal handed them out at Step," Jens said, remembering the surreal communion ceremony.

"So, you understand," Smith said, but then paused at the look on Jens' face. "Wait! She didn't give you one?"

"No. Teal told us first-timers had to Step on their own."

"That's harsh." Smith laughed again. "Your captain certainly has peculiar methods, though no doubt effective. I mean, look at you." Smith put the pill back in the bag and handed it to Jens. "When you get a chance, take one. And when you do, well— All I will tell you is to be *open* to the experience. Set aside all preconceptions or expectations, as much as that is possible. Don't do it when you have to drive. GLR stands for God's Living Room. The chemists that cooked it up couldn't find a better name. There isn't a better name. You'll understand why after you take it."

"So, it's just a drug?" Jens asked.

"No, it's not 'just a drug'. It's *the* drug. It doesn't take you away from reality. It takes you to reality. And what's beyond reality. It helps you understand the universe and our little place in it. I can tell you about the experience, but all you'd hear is words. Blah, blah, blah. Have you ever heard of DMT?"

"Heard of it."

"DMT – dimethyltryptamine. Called the 'spirit molecule'. It's a chemical that occurs in many plants and animals. We release large quantities of it in our brains when we're born and when we die. Dimethyltryptamine is an indole alkaloid derived from the shikimate pathway ... sorry, I'm a chemist. Long story short, when it is synthesized, what you get is a quick trip to meet god, for lack of a better term. One quick trip, and your life, and your perspective on reality, is fundamentally changed. That's why it's still illegal in many places, on and off Earth.

"What we've managed to do with GLR is not just a quick visit, but a leisurely stay. One pill and you sit and relax in God's living room. And I'm using that word merely as a blanket description of the great What Is. You know I'm not talking here about any religion with books or rules or even names. It's pure energy, the energy of the entire cosmos, outside of and independent of time. With GLR, you have time to be immersed. But out here, on these lifeless rocks, there are no plants or animals with the molecules needed to make DMT, no dimethyltryptamine. Until we found it in the rocks, between the molecules, and made it. It's as if all of humanity's searching for another home has, in a way, actually produced a way to get home."

Smith folded his hands on the table and smiled. "That's what you're now part of, Mr Jensen. It's a very human drive, as old as our species. We've been ingesting substances since forever to take us beyond this mundane plane we seem trapped in. It's what the shamans would do to help them commune with the gods. Mushrooms, mescaline, ayahuasca.

"Ayahuasca was made from a combination of plants. Somehow the people of the Amazon took the vine from one plant, and brewed it with parts of others in a very specific way, and made a brown liquid that took the user to another dimension. They say that the plants spoke to their ancestors, told them what to pick, how to prepare it, how to take it. I can understand that. There are some in the lab, and you might meet some on Shackleton, that say the rocks spoke to us, unconsciously, or at some higher level, guiding us here and there around the stars to these planets. Told us how to prepare the minerals. As if what we find in living creatures on Earth lives somehow in the rocks out here. These white pills aren't just for the shaman or the healer. They're going to make every single person a shaman and a healer.

"Crazy talk, huh Mr Jensen?" Mr Smith asked. He didn't wait for an answer.

"You're here to collect processed pyrosmium. It's probably already loaded on to your flier. You'll drop it off at Shackleton where it's going to be processed into GLR. On your way back through that system, the *Cirrus* will collect the finished product, and when you return to Earth, well, we'll all probably be called prophets. No doubt about it, we will. And we'll become very rich."

"The *Sunrise* ..."

"Probably knows. Possibly not. Could be working *for* Teal. It wouldn't surprise me. Or the other way around. Doesn't matter to us. But it's probably wise not to talk too much about it." Smith closed the bag of pyrosmium and put it in his pocket. "I would advise you to talk to Teal when you get back to the *Cirrus*. You are no longer a deckhand or just a member of the crew. You shouldn't settle for anything less than partner."

"She said it was time I became one. I didn't know what to do at the time."

Smith rose and led Jens out of the office and through the empty warehouse. At the hover pod, he shook Jens' hand.

"What you do is entirely up to you. Whatever your role, you're going to be a very popular and rich man."

Part 2:
Second Step

9

Jens opened his eyes. Flashing red light filled his quarters. No sound. Silence meant one of two things: either the comms were broken, or the *Sunrise* was being boarded. Jens knew the comms were not broken. The silent alarm would only be going off in crew quarters. A whisper designed to wake those caught by surprise. There were many surprises in the dark of space, especially for solitary and sparsely crewed freighters. It was why they traveled in convoys. Getting into Hat Pin, making their trade, picking up cargo, cargo whose value Jens now appreciated more ... Did business go smoothly because they were never meant to get away?

Such thoughts were useless. Jens sat up, slipped into pants, reached under his mattress, and grabbed the sounder stashed there. He strapped the knife to his thigh. He put on soft-soled shoes and crept to the door. Ninety seconds had passed since he woke.

Jens switched the door to manual so it couldn't be opened from the outside. He breathed in slowly, calming his mind, and slid it open several inches. He listened. He slid it open wider, just enough to squeeze through to the empty corridor. Jens held the sounder in his hand as he moved forward. If the *Sunrise* was being boarded, the bridge and the reactor would be targeted. The brain center and the power. Jens headed for the center of the ship. From there, his options increased – a fight to regain control of one of those places, escape out of a lateral airlock, or override the computer system by hacking into the mainframe. Just like a human body, commands went from the brain to the feet. Sever the spine and the body became immobilized.

Jens increased his pace, stopping at every corner to listen. He turned one, two, three corners, making his way to the mess room at the center of the ship. Turning the fourth corner, he faced three men at the opposite end. He took inventory at a glance as he fell to one knee. Average size. Three handheld weapons. Sounders. Baton strapped to one leg. Knives in sheaths on each man. Black tactical pants. Black shirts. Black masks were covering their faces. No high caliber projectile weapons. No gear for spacing. They didn't want to just to raid the ship, they wanted to take it, undamaged.

Just then the gravity cut out. Jens tapped the deck when he felt the gravity fail, rose up, pushed off the ceiling and returned to the deck. *Ill-considered haste can be better than ingenious but lengthy operations*, Sun Tzu again. *Energy may be likened to the bending of a crossbow. Decision, to the releasing of a trigger.* Jens bent his legs, kicked, and propelled himself towards the three intruders. He turned his sounder around in his hand. It was useless in zero gravity, probably breaking a wrist or tearing muscles with its recoil, and accuracy would be accidental at best.

Jens swung his gun at the head of the man to his right, turned in the air and delivered a hammer blow to where he hoped was the ear of the man in the center. The impact of his fist to the other's skull sent Jens sailing sidelong into the wall. He bounced off and pushed against the ceiling, rounding the corner from where the three men came. Pushing off the wall, he flew down the length of the empty corridor. Turning in the air to control his impact against the approaching bulkhead, he hit it feet first, pushed off and sailed down the next corridor.

As the distant wall come closer it was replaced by deck racing up to meet him. Jens landed on his face and chest, continuing his momentum forward as the ship's gravity came back on. He twisted his body and rolled to a stop, eyes focused on where he had just come from. Seconds passed. Nobody pursued—yet. A boarding party wouldn't let crew run free on a ship they were taking over. They would come after him.

Jens inhaled and regained his feet. He staggered down the corridor. Gravity was back on *and* increased. He felt as if he carried bags of fuel on each shoulder. The mess was near, and if he were to join up with any other of the *Sunrise* crew, it would be near there, just as the emergency plan instructed.

Jens listened before entering the mess. He pulled out his knife and stepped through the door into the empty room.

"You must not want to live long," Zhao said from the galley entrance.

"There are three, probably not far behind." Jens pointed at the knife Zhao held by the blade, ready to throw. "The balance is all off on that. Are there other weapons?"

"That's why I practise with it, and I don't miss," Zhao said.

"Are there any other crew?"

"Genjo and Louie. They'll be back soon. They're scouting aft. And they have sounders."

"Good," Jens said. "Genjo's a hacker. He'll know where we can—"

"Jens!" Louie said as he and Genjo entered.

"Well?" Jens asked.

"Huh? Oh, clear to the aft on this deck. But we didn't go below."

"That means you'll go forward, they won't expect it, and you'll buy us time," Jens said.

"Why is he giving orders?" Genjo looked at Zhao.

"He is Acting First Mate," Zhao said. "He is the ranking officer."

Jens ignored the interaction. "Zhao, you and Louie work your way forward to the bridge. Just buy time and distraction.

They're armed with sounders and knives. Genjo, give Zhao your sounder."

Genjo pulled his sounder out of a pocket and let Zhao take it from his hand.

"Don't advance to the bridge, just delay, and then fall back to the chute leading to the deck below. Hold the entrance for as long as you can, then drop down and continue to hold. Clear?" Jens instructed, not expecting an answer. "Give us as much time as you can. Go!" Zhao and Louie left the mess and worked their way up the corridor Jens had just come down.

"With me," he said to Genjo, walking out without waiting.

As Jens reached the chute the gravity cut and he flailed for a handrail. He pulled himself to the chute and floated down feet first, gripping the ladder by one hand and working his way down. The gravity kicked in again, and his hand tightened, catching him before he fell the remaining two meters. His foot found a rung and his other hand gripped a handhold. A grunt from above told him Genjo had halted his own descent and wasn't going to fall on top of him.

Jens' grip began to loosen as gravity increased. He climbed down as quickly as he could before his own weight would drag him down. At the last rung, they lost gravity again. Jens took advantage of the loss and finished his descent. He pushed across the corridor and towards a central panel. Before he got to it, the gravity once again threw him to the ground.

Genjo hit the deck with a thud.

"Get over here," Jens said, picking himself up.

Genjo lifted himself to his knee, grabbed a handhold, and stood. He limped towards the panel.

"This is it, isn't it?" Jens asked. "We can do it from here, right?"

"You want to disable the *Sunrise*?"

"I want to disable the *raiders*," Jens said. "And take control of the ship from here."

Genjo grinned. "Get the panel off."

Jens worked the clasps and removed the cover, revealing tight coils of clear fiber around the ship's central wireless hub.

"Stand close and brace me so I won't move if the gravity cuts again," Genjo said.

He opened a small pouch he wore around his neck. Jens had always assumed it was some sort of talisman, but he withdrew a fine screwdriver and blade. Gravity cut and he pulled his hands back quickly. Jens tightened his grip.

"This is precise work, Mr Jensen," Genjo said. "Do not let me move."

Gravity cut back in, but Genjo didn't stop. As the weight increased, he gritted his teeth and continued.

"We have access to the reactor," Genjo said. "What is your wish?"

"Cut power to the bow and seal all bulkheads. Leave the reactor. Let them know we control it, and can destroy it."

"Done," Genjo said. "They now know where we are."

"That was expected. Can you seal off the bridge?"

"One step ahead," Genjo reported. "Whoever is in there, they're not coming out."

"And life support?"

"You want it turned off?" Genjo asked.

"No," Jens answered. "I don't want to be a killer, not if I don't have to. But make them feel us."

"We have to flip and decelerate soon, or it will be too late."

"Just follow orders."

"Done," Genjo said. "Heat and thin air should send a message."

"Give them another, also," Jens said. "Instructions to leave the ship. Three minutes to vacate. Then clear them a path as soon as they acknowledge."

"And if they don't?"

"Make their air even thinner."

"I can't hold them much longer!" Louie shouted down the corridor.

"Where's Zhao?" demanded Jens.

"Sounder got him. He's still above. Unconscious, but alive, I think," Louie said.

Louie jumped down the chute, firing his sounder up as he dropped. He ducked beside a bulkhead as sounder vibrations ricocheted against the deck and walls. He fired blindly upward, sending vibrations of his own.

"They're trapped in our segment." Jens stated the obvious. "Okay, reduce air in the bridge, and the reactor room if they're there. All of it. Then cut gravity, but hold onto the deck." Jens shouted down the corridor, "Louie, hold onto the deck."

They felt all weight leave them.

"Wait a moment ... wait ..." Jens said. "When I get to Louie, return gravity, make it at least three. I want those guys to hit the deck hard. Wait until I say, then normalize at zero point eight." He pushed off, close to the floor and sailed towards his crewmate at the chute.

Genjo watched Jens, then made adjustments at the control panel. He exhaled when hit by the increased gravity. Jens and Louie heard the sound of bodies hitting the deck at force. One was the unconscious Zhoa, no doubt, but there was nothing that could be done about that. Jens called back to Genjo to weaken the gravity and rushed up the chute with Louie.

"Attention, crew of the *Sunrise Blossom*," the ship-wide comms announced before they could reach the deck above. "This is Captain Wan Huang. Stand down immediately. I repeat, stand down immediately. Put any weapons in your possession on the deck at your feet. Report to the mess. Now. Captain Wan, out."

"Son of a bitch," Louie muttered.

"You heard the man, up you go." Jens swung to the side to let Louie pass. He patted Louie on the leg as he climbed past. "You did well, Louie." Louie handed Jens his sounder. "I'll be up after Genjo. Wait at the top," Jens said.

Genjo waited at the entrance to the chute. Jens extended his hand and Genjo took it. "Thank you, Genjo. Maybe you were right about the action needed, and I showed weakness, thinking I was being honorable."

"You did what you thought right," Genjo said. "And it was honorable. But we don't know how stupid it may have been, yet." Genjo set down his galley knife, reached into his belt and took out three small throwing blades, bent and took a dagger from a sheath tied to his calf. Jens smiled, watching, but frowned when he had to take out his Japanese blade and set it on the deck.

"After you," Jens said.

Wan was waiting in the mess with Wu Pen. Three men in black sat around the table, their masks off: Yuan, Jie, and Zhang. Jie's ear was a deep red and had swelled to almost double in size. Zhang wore a bandage around his head, stained red with his own blood. Both Yuan and Jie had arms in slings. Zhao lay on the floor, still unconscious from the sounder blast he had received. Jens took off his shirt, rolled it up, and placed it under Zhao's head. Genjo and Louie took their place at the table. Jens stood, legs apart and hands clasped behind his back.

"Report," Wan said.

"I am dead," Wu Pen said.

"That is true, as you should be," Wan said. "Who boards a ship without bringing an emergency oxygen supply? Boarding party?"

"We secured the bridge, then sought to subdue the crew," Yuan said.

"Hmm." Wan looked at the men in black. "The bridge was lost. It was rendered useless. And looking at your sorry state, I do not think the crew was subdued. Were you actually boarding a ship ... well, I think you know what would have happened."

"True, Captain," Yuan said. "His actions were unpredictable, yet thoughtful."

"As I see," Wan said. "You must always be prepared for actions that may appear erratic. They are often the only option left to an opponent."

"Yes, sir," Yuan said.

"Crew?"

"He was decisive and clear," Louie said. "Very confident. I'm sure he wasn't, but he didn't let it show."

"He dealt with dissension and exerted his authority," Genjo added. "He knew our skills and deployed them as effectively as possible."

"I would ask Zhao to report, but he is unable to answer at the moment." Wan turned to Jens. "You had control of the ship. That was a smart move. But could you have kept it?" he asked.

"I believe so, sir," Jens answered, realizing that he was the focus of each report. "Were we to have reached the deck above we would have disabled the boarding party and continued to the bridge."

"Where you would have regained control and purged the ship of any remaining boarders, without hesitation, I would hope." Wan smiled for the first time. "Well done, all of you," he said. "Yuan, if you will get the meal you prepared before our drill? Let us eat, and then all crew will take mandatory rest. I do not want to see any of you for twelve hours. Jens and I will take a double watch."

"At ease, Jens," he added. "You passed. Now clean up what is left of your face, change your clothes, and have something to eat."

Jens touched his swollen cheek and winced, looked at the battered crew and allowed himself to smile only after turning around and walking to the washroom.

"You didn't know that was a drill, did you?" Wan asked when they were alone on the bridge.

Jens took a drink of coffee before answering. "No."

The crew had all gone to their quarters after the brief meal, Yuan retiring only after he had prepared enough food for Wan and Jens to last them the long watch. He made a large thermos of coffee for Jens, knowing he preferred that over tea.

"Wu Pen asked me to review all emergency procedures last week," Jens said. "Hull breach, fire, reactor meltdown, mutiny, epidemic, catastrophic power failure, boarding. It is a long list."

"It certainly is."

"I played each out in my mind, as a sort of rehearsal. But when I woke up, I wasn't thinking about that at all. I just acted. I could have killed Zhang, or Jie."

"That would have been unfortunate, but it would have been accidental," Wan said.

"I could have killed everybody," Jens said.

"I would have overridden any, well, *fatal* decisions you might have made." Wan worked the controls on the arm of his chair, and the viewscreen came to life. Hat-P-5 filled a corner of the screen. HAT-P-3a, with the convoy sheltering behind it, appeared as a large star.

"But you did not," Wan added. "I am very pleased with your performance. You showed discipline and composure. When you are in command, you need those qualities. Every decision, deliberate or instinctive, must be based on training, not emotion. Emotion, such as fear, panic, or anger, interferes with judgment. These cause mistakes. You know that. I must commend my crew for training you well."

Jens nodded.

"But what you also displayed was character. That was not from my crew. It is in you." Wan poured a cup of tea from the thermos Yuan prepared. "When it is time, which will be quite soon, you will be in charge of Flip and Decel," Wan said. "Wu Pen will supervise, but only as an observer. He will only intervene if there is a need."

"*Xix xie ni, Chuanzhang.*" Jens replied. Thank you, Captain.

"Once the maneuver is complete, I would like to readjust your training regime. More time for individual study," Wan said. "That means you will need to decide which teacher you will disappoint. Two teachers, as I would like to work with you for the remainder of your time with us."

I would like. Such a polite way to issue commands, Jens thought. But he appreciated it. He allowed himself to relax and smile, gazing at the projected image of the star in front of them. *I would like*, Jens thought. *What would I like?* He liked the compliment Wan offered, the recognition of effort, and even skill. To be encouraged in excelling. It was a shame that some found that threatening. It seemed the logical thing for a leader to want, but Jens knew from experience that not all leaders did.

What I would like, Jens thought, *is for my coffee to turn to whiskey and the bridge into a sandy beach*. But the sea was a lifetime away, and there was no drinking on watch, even such a long one.

So, Wan wanted to teach leadership. Lesson one, let a tired and battered crew rest, especially if you were the one who wore them down

10

"What kind of captain do you aspire to be, Mr Jensen?" Wan asked. His tutorials were mostly conversations, taking place in his private quarters. "You must have seen a few examples."

Jens' eyes looked left, to an image in his memory. "If you asked me that a year ago, I would have told what type I didn't want to be."

"Well?"

"It's a role that can bring out the worst kind of ego," Jens said. "I have found sailing an exercise in... well, after hours with Jie in the library I would say an exercise in egolessness. It was about something bigger than one personality, caring for something that kept us all afloat, kept us alive."

"That is a nice way to put it," Wan agreed. "How do you reconcile egolessness and authority?"

"How do you?"

"What are the five cardinal virtues, Mr Jensen?"

"Humanity, uprightness of mind, self-respect and self-control, wisdom, and sincerity or good faith," Jens said.

"Straight from the book," Wan said. "What does it mean to you?"

"Being honest to yourself and your crew," Jens said. "Trustworthy. Trusted. Although it hasn't been tested, and I don't think it needs to be, I know that you would be the last to leave the ship in an evac, and the first to lead an attack. That type of leadership makes for a loyal crew."

"Leadership styles vary," Wan continued. "Do you prefer vertical, or horizontal?"

Jens stifled a grin. Teal's style was horizontal. He enjoyed some aspects of that. But he appreciated a clear chain of command and knowing where his place was in that. And he had seen vertical styles turn ugly in the wrong hands.

He could have talked about Bligh and the *Bounty*. A superb leader in a crisis, a monster the rest of the time. That led to a mutiny, to Fletcher Christian casting his captain and a couple of handfuls of his supporters adrift in a launch. The small ship had drifted in a vast emptiness, captained by a strutting little dictator who threatened, rebuked, accused, humiliated. Jens used to privately think that Skipper was Bligh reincarnate; only more spiteful, more frustrated in his own limitations. But that was unfair to Bligh, unhinged and deserving of mutiny as he was.

A year ago, he would have said Christian's mistake was to let his captain live. He winced, remembering that he probably had said that, out loud, and his words were sitting in a police file. Jens looked down at his hands. He opened his right, studying his empty palm, staring at wasn't there.

"That dichotomy is too simple," he said. "Without trust or respect, both styles can become a disaster."

"Agreed."

"And crew need to know where they stand, not just that you stand with them."

Wan poured two glasses of Laika vodka and handed one to Jens. "Here is one for you: A good captain looks lazy."

"*Looks*," Jens repeated. "A leader is best," he quoted, "when people barely know he exists. Of a good leader, who talks little, when his work is done, his aim fulfilled, they will say, 'We did this ourselves.'"

"Lao Tse. Indeed." Wan sipped his drink, staring deeply into the clear liquid. "I think it is the water. That lifeless under-ground river in Laika adds a unique purity," he said. "With a good First Mate and a good crew, that is how you might look. But those that work with you will know better. Finding them, a good crew – that comes from judging character, and from training them well."

Wan pointed a finger from his free hand at Jens. "Here is another thought about style. A question. If I died suddenly, at this moment, would the *Sunshine Blossom* not only continue in its mission, but *succeed* in it?"

"Yes," Jens said. "It would. Wu Pen would step up and lead."

"He would probably make you his First Mate, as well. You had very little hesitation in your answer. Am I that dispensable?" Wan asked.

"You are not dispensable. It's just that you are not ... indispensable," Jens said.

"No leader should be indispensable. If they are in that position, they have not trained their crew properly, and they put their ship at risk," Wan agreed. "At worst, the ship will be able to limp home, but even that would be a poor reflection on leadership."

Jens leaned back in his seat. "The *Sunrise* would not limp."

"No. It would not." Wan set his empty glass down, signaling that the session was coming to a close. "You have several words on which to meditate. Respect. Trust. Ego. Is there more?" Wan asked.

"Yes, I think there is," Jens answered. "It's ... humility."

"Good," Wan said. "And what do you mean by that word?"

"To be able to let others take the lead, take the credit," Jens tried.

"It is more than that," Wan said. "You must delve deeper not only into its meaning but its implication, especially regards your ego. Humility is the path to self-knowledge. It allows you to search yourself, to go beyond your defenses, to find your fatal flaw."

Jens painted the words with Genjo, two characters. *Si di*. Fatal Flaw.

"Find your flaws, Mr Jensen, and eradicate them," Wan said. "It is the best we can do, as leaders, and as human beings."

Jens thought returning to the *Cirrus* would be a homecoming, but he had spent more time on the *Sunshine* than he had his own ship. After a few days, he stopped wearing his tailored clothes and got back into his flight suit.

Not much had changed, but a lot was different. Teal's hair was a minor detail. Her shoulder-length waves were shaved to a number two. It was Suzie's idea, probably to pre-empt competition from Stephan, though she would know there was nothing she could do to stop her Captain from having whomever she wanted over for dinner. If that was the reason, it was a dumb move from somebody who was supposed to be intelligent. Jens found the buzz cut sexy.

Teal invited Jens for dinner and thanked him for his delivery and pick up at Hat Pin. Her excitement at the consignment he had brought back brightened her eyes in a way that exceeded even her ecstasy in orgasm—though months alone had taught him to suppress memories of *that* kind of pleasure. She even made it seem as if she missed him, and maybe she had. The calligraphy he gave her hung on the bulkhead behind her bed. Water. It was a simple picture; Genjo thought it one of his best. The highest good is to be like water, the Taoists say. Water conforms to whatever it meets, and yet always seeks its own level. In whatever form, it maintains its own character. Nothing is softer than water, yet it can overcome the hardest rock.

Teal loved listening to the explanation. But Jens chose it for her because water is also a mystery. It has hidden depths. It can sweep away whole towns, whole lives, without thought or planning. It can be dark and cold. Mysterious. Jens buried his secrets in its depths, consciously and unconsciously. What secrets of Teal's are drifting below the surface? What or who did she see in the depths of sleep? Jens had no idea. How much did he know about his Captain and her plans, for the ship and for him? He looked away from the painting and buried his face in her neck, pushing those thoughts away. At least until he was alone.

Herschel wanted to talk about leadership, but not like Jens. They had plenty of opportunity on the final fuel runs as they neared the Donut. Tenders from the *Avarua* and *Cooper* helped, stocking the convoy with extra provisions for the *Cirrus* to carry on its trek to Shackleton with its precious undeclared cargo. The other freighters may have grumbled about the new workload, but none voiced it loudly, and no one pried into Teal's stated reasons for the trip.

"How's Pani?" Jens started to tiptoe around the real topic with small talk.

"She's really good," he said.

Silence sat between them as Jens piloted the tender over the convoy.

"You've really changed," Herschel finally said. Jens waited. "I can still see Jens, but ... not the deckhand I used to work with. What happened over there?"

"Nothing," Jens tried. "I—"

"I mean, when we delivered to the *Xing* you waded in like a local boss. I'm surprised you didn't wear your gangster suit." Herschel swiveled his seat to face Jens. "They taught you the language on the *Sunrise*?"

"Eight months on a Chinese ship and you're going to pick up some of the lingo." Jens fired the forward thrusters to slow the tender and brought it down towards the deck of the freighter beneath them.

"No, you did more than pick up a few words. You picked up a lot of things."

"You had a good time on the *Xing*. You can't deny that," Jens said.

"True," Herschel said. "But not as good as you. That flight officer was positively fawning over you. I never thought I would ever have cause to use that word. *Fawning*. Huge crush."

As soon as the tender was secure and the deck sealed, a half dozen settlers appeared and started to unload the fuel shipment. Jens took advantage of the break to explore the *Xing*, dragging Herschel along. He wanted to experience what they referred to as the village square, the large open deck space, where a semblance of normal life tried to continue. His last visit was much too brief – he breathed in the smells of dried meats and cooking vegetables, and let his ear adjust to a less formal Mandarin.

"Ah, the smell of fresh food!" Herschel's nose was trying to escape but had nowhere to run.

"Look at these!" Jens said, pulling Herschel along by the sleeve of his flight suit.

"*These look so good*!" he said to a woman selling meats. Skinned and smoked cavy carcasses hung on display.

"*Mr Jensen, welcome*!" she returned. She pulled a strip of meat off and handed it to him. "*Please, you taste it.*"

Jensen accepted the gift and stuck it in his mouth. He smiled his approval. The woman handed Herschel a strip. Herschel hesitated.

"Come on, Herschel, don't offend the lady. Eat," Jens said.

Herschel put the meat into his mouth, nodding as he chewed.

"It's cavy," Jens said. "I had some on Hat Pin. Good, huh?"

Herschel swallowed but didn't answer.

"Guinea pig. More like Space pig. They grow them on the ship. Amazing. They have to be nearly self-sufficient for the two years to *Sukhavati*. Let's wade in and check out their veggies," Jens said. "Maybe we can find something to bring back. Cook folks a traditional meal."

"That's okay," Herschel said.

"No? Come here then," Jens dragged him farther into the sounds and smells, depositing him at a makeshift café, a piece of canvas hung on poles covering a workspace; the only thing setting it apart from other stalls were several small tables with chairs around them.

"*Tea for my friend, please,*" Jens called.

"*Our pleasure, Mr Jensen!*" a balding, middle-aged man answered. He set a pot and glass cup in front Herschel. "*Would you like diajin?*" Herschel looked at Jens.

"*Yes, he would. Thank you very much.*" Jens bowed before disappearing in the stalls.

Herschel tasted the rice cake set in front of him. He smiled at the man, the limit of his Mandarin. He poured a glass of the hot liquid, took a sip. As he set it down, he noticed a small pair of eyes watching him. He broke off a piece of the rice cake and offered it. The small boy's hands moved quickly, and the cake disappeared into his mouth. He smiled back at Herschel. The boy reached slowly out and touched Herschel's arm, moving his finger in the thick hair of his forearm.

"I must look like a bear to you," Herschel said.

The boy looked confused. "A bear," Herschel repeated. He lifted his arms and made paws of his hands. "Grrrr, grrrrr," he said.

The boy jumped back and hid behind a counter. Herschel waited, and a small head peeked out. Herschel raised his hands again. "Grrrrrrrr," he growled.

The stallholders near him laughed. One called the boy over and handed him small blueberries. "*Feed the bear. He is hungry! Hurry before he eats you!*"

The boy gripped them tightly in his palm. He took a step towards Herschel. He growled, and the boy stopped. Herschel turned a paw over and opened his hand. The boy ran forward, put a sticky berry in his hand, and darted back.

"Grrr!" Herschel growled. He popped the berry in his mouth and grinned at the boy. "Yum yum!" he said, patting his tummy.

The boy, gently pushed from behind, walked slowly forward, berry held in outstretched fingers. He crept closer.

When he was within reach, Herschel lowered his hand and opened his mouth. The boy worked up his courage, put a berry in the bear's mouth, and ran back behind the counter.

Herschel could hear Jens' laughter among those around him. Jens clapped him on the shoulder, but a voice cut in before he could say anything.

"*Mr Jensen! Mr Jensen*!" an insistent female voice said. Jens looked to his side and saw a young woman wearing the crisp white shirt of the crew, complete with gold braided epaulets on her shoulders and gold buttons down the front of a shirt that was tucked into white pants. A small white hat with a black bill covered her jet-black hair.

"*Mr Jensen! I am so glad I found you!*" she said. "*I am to show you around.*"

"What does she want?" Herschel asked.

"Fran Lu," Jens said. "It's a pleasure to see you again."

"*And you, Mr Jensen,*" she said. "*I am asked by Captain Hui Yin to show you the General Xing. I am not—*"

"*It is okay,*" Jens said. "*May we speak English, so my crew-mate may benefit?*"

"Yes, certainly," she said in a thick accent. "I can speak good English. I can practise," she said.

Jens waited. "So sorry. Introductions. I am Fran Lu, third mate on the *General Xing,*" she said. "I oversee settler areas and our farming systems. I can show you these if you like?"

"I would like that very much," Jens said. "This is my crew-mate, Mr Folkes." Herschel bowed slightly to Fran Lu. "And we, um, we redistribute fuel supplies in the convoy."

"You are modest, Mr Jensen," she said. "Shall we see the area?" Fran Lu asked.

"Lead on," Jens said.

Fran Lu led the pair to a chute that descended to the level below. She opened a door and guided them down to tanks growing nutrient dense seaweed. Another door led to row upon row of Okinawa and perineal spinach, each rooted in a small pot that carried a handful of soil. "The other rooms contain more plants – amaranth, quinoa, all adapted to lower light, such as the conditions on *Sukhavati*."

She led them farther into the bowels of the ship, and into a musty-smelling storage area. She gave them each a respirator to put on before entering.

"This is the grow room," she said. "Our mycologists are very pleased and proud of their success. To them, this is the most important room on the entire ship. And they are not very wrong."

Jens and Herschel looked at row upon row of fungi, tables filled with shapes and colors. Domes broke through the soil. Others stretched towards the lights placed above them, lights shielded to produce a dappled glow beneath. Other tables contained fin-like mushrooms growing off what looked like refuse from the market. Rows of hessian sacks hung from lines suspended above the room. Large earlike mushrooms grew from holes in the sacks.

"This table contains mycelium," Fran Lu said. "This fine white gauze-like hair will mature into what we see as mushrooms when they are ready to reproduce. It is called a flush. Then we harvest the goodness and encourage them to flush again."

"You must really like mushrooms," Jens said.

"It is not about liking, Mr Jensen," she said. "It is about carbon. They are food and medicine, but first of all, they provide carbon. They are vital in creating soils, the first building block in a balanced ecosystem."

"Terraforming," Herschel said.

"Yes, exactly," she agreed. "Terraforming from the ground up. It is a gradual process. The settlers are planning for their great-great-grandchildren. They will only survive if they think that way. But I bore with explanation. Come, try this, it is good raw, and very good food." Fran Lu broke off some of the ears protruding from a hanging sack. "It is, what is the word? Oyster mushroom. Very healthy." She watched as they ate the fungi.

"I can show you our animals if it pleases you," Fran Lu said.

"I would like that very much," Jens answered. Fran Lu walked beside him, her sleeve brushing his. He turned and smiled at Herschel.

"Can we see the cavy room, um, I'm not sure what that's called ... ranch?" he said to Fran Lu.

"Yes, indeed." Fran Lu smiled. "You can meet the *Rancher*," she said. "I must warn you about the smell. It is something you get used to. At least that is what the ranchers say."

"I thought the grow room had a strong odor," Herschel said.

"That was nothing," Fran Lu answered, smiling. "But you will wear respirators. It will protect you from the ammonia in the air, which is still strong despite the ventilation."

Fran Lu led them down another level and through an airtight door. As soon as its seal was broken, a wave of acrid, warm air hit them. "It is the smell of the animals. Here, wear these."

She handed them another respirator to cover their noses and mouths, filtering the worst of the stench. From a waist-high barrier, they looked across a deck strewn with what appeared to be large boulders; these proved, at closer inspection, to be artificial mounds. Small brown animals climbed over them. Over a dozen workers could be seen walking amongst them, spreading grasses, cleaning the floor, carrying squealing handfuls.

Fran Lu stepped over the barrier and grabbed an animal, lifting it by the fur behind its neck. It hung limp like a kitten. She handed it to Herschel.

"These are kerodon. Rock cavy. They are very tough and will do well on *Sukhavati*. Many rocks there," she said. "As you see, the settlers are always very busy preparing for their new life. This cavy is a good choice, I think. They do not need much space, and they breed rapidly. That one is almost fully grown. Almost half a kilo, ready for eating."

"And they taste very good, eh, Mr Folkes?" Jens added. "Just like chicken."

"Oh, much better than chicken," Fran Lu said. "Now I show you the chickens!"

Herschel handed the cavy to Jens who stroked its head before setting it down on the other side of the barrier.

"So, what's the plan? What are you part of?"

"Teal explained the deal," Jens said. "Pick up ingredients, drop off ingredients, pick up finished products, sell to Earth. And become very wealthy, if you're to believe everybody involved."

"Yeah, about that," Herschel said. "How long did you know what *Cirrus* really was?"

"Teal showed me the cargo about a day before you went to the *Avarua*."

"And you kept it to yourself." It was a judgment more than a question.

"Teal ordered me to, said she wanted to tell you at the right time." Jens tried not to sound defensive, but it wasn't working.

"Teal," Herschel said it with a sigh. "Yeah, she told me the grand plan, if I could believe it. She almost sounded like a missionary. Don't you ever wonder about the two crew before us, the ones rotting in prison on Earth? Ever think about what might happen to us, especially if we don't want to join in?"

"Yes, I have," Jens said.

"Pani and I talked about our future. This can fuck that up. I'm not a smuggler or a drug dealer. I signed up for honest work. I thought that's what you wanted as well."

"What I wanted was to get away from Earth," Jens said.

"Well, I guess you got that. I know I don't exactly trust Teal. And to be with honest with you, I'm not sure if I trust that whatever I'm saying now isn't going straight to her ear."

"It isn't. I'm still me. And you're probably right not to trust her."

"That sounds odd coming from you. You two are rather close."

"She's really good at—"

"Stop right there. I do not want to hear," Herschel said.

"What I was trying to say is, she's good at separating the bridge from the bedroom."

"After this contract Pani and I are ... this has gotten too fucked up. I don't even know if they'd let me go. Maybe I know too much. And now Pani too." Herschel turned his seat back to the tinted view screen.

"I know how you feel," Jens tried.

"Do you? You seem to be in your element."

"I mean, I haven't felt like I've had a choice in anything since I set foot on board the *Cirrus*." *Since I threw Skipper over the railing in the middle of the Pacific Ocean with a knife in his chest.* "No, I don't think they'd stop you from walking if that's what you wanted to do. You'd probably be given a hefty severance package to see you off, set you guys up." Jens tried to make eye contact, but Herschel continued to look forward.

"That's a couple of years away from now anyway," Herschel said.

"The drop at the Shack should bring in a little nest egg—"

"I don't want to talk about it. Let's just shift fuel."

And pretend everything is normal when it isn't, and you're the only person in this part of the galaxy I trust. No, my friend, I'm not going to let it lie. "Are you definite about not going to the Shack, about staying with the convoy?" Jens asked.

"It'll mean eight months with Pani," Herschel said. "I'll oversee the fueling until you guys get back. I guess that's a promotion."

"Sure," Jens said. "But I thought you were already fuel overseer, or whatever that role was." He lifted the tender and thrust forward to their next drop.

"I thought that was you," Herschel said.

"No," Jens said, "I think it was you who was in charge. Hey, look, it's the *Calderón*. They seem to be much nicer these days."

"Your friends might have something to do with that," Herschel said. "Or maybe it's you."

"Either way, the wine is always appreciated," Jens said. "They probably have a role in all this too. God only knows."

"Teal only knows."

"And probably Wan." Jens piloted the tender into the loading bay, eased it to the deck and opened the hatches once the air returned. "At next Step, when you take communion ... That's what they're so excited about, and what they want to take back to Earth. Let's talk about it again after that."

"Have you taken it?" Herschel asked.

"No," Jens admitted. "The contact on Hat Pin gave me a bag, but I haven't opened it yet."

"*Buenas tardes, Caballeros,*" Enrique called through the open hatch. "*Señor Folkes, y Señor Jensen. Siempre es un placer.* We'll get this out of the tender so you can finish your drops. Unless you have time for a stop?"

"*Lo siento,*" Herschel replied. "*Tenemos mucho trabajo, y no podemos quedarnos.*"

"*Muy bien, Señor Folkes. Tu español es muy bueno,*" he said. "Let me get you some *empanadas* to take. We made extra tonight."

"*Gracias,*" Jens called back. "It'd be nice to stop for a while," he said after Enrique left with a sack on his shoulder.

"Like I said, too much work," Herschel said. "And I don't want to hang out with these guys."

"Come on, Herschel, they said they were sorry."

"Just pilot the tender, Jens," Herschel said.

11

Jens looked at the white pills in his hand. He picked one up between his thumb and forefinger and raised it to his mouth. He hesitated.

"Jens, report to the bridge please," Teal said over the ship's comms.

Jens looked at the pill between his fingers, shrugged, and put it back in the bag. The third try wasn't the trick. He sealed the bag and put it in a pocket.

Teal sat in her chair, watching the polarized screen. Hat-P-5 filled the view. She had increased magnification and watched the solar winds whipping up the photosphere, plasma arcing over the surface in bubbling eruptions. She tore her eyes away and smiled at Jens as he came in.

"You got a very special invitation," she said.

"To what?"

"To the Donut," she said. "Jie has asked if I would grant you permission to join him in the Hole. Permission granted."

Jens tilted his head.

"That's a pretty special offer," Teal said. "Those Donut Holes don't usually let deckhands invade their space. Was he teaching you astrophysics?"

"No," Jens said, finding his tongue. "Philosophy, mostly."

"Curious," Teal said. "I've never been. He said to tell you to dress properly. Wear your bad dude duds, I guess. You look nice in them."

She faced towards the screen, watching the plasma at play. In actuality, she was facing away from the star, as the ship was nearing the end of its deceleration. They were coming in 'ass first', as the approach was technically known.

"Join me for a while." She beckoned to the chair next to hers, used by Lassen when both Captain and First Mate were on the bridge. "This puts it all into perspective. We're so *tiny*."

He touched her hand gently as he sat. They gazed at the screen like an old couple sitting in front of the fireplace, watching flames dance over logs. After several minutes, Teal looked at Jens. "Do me a favor, will you? Talk to Suzie about it. You'd be going down with her. Just make sure she's alright with it. You know how she can get about her work."

"Yeah, I know," Jens said. "Thanks."

"Thanks? For what?" Teal asked. "Sending you into the breach. Better go see her now, get it over with," she added with a flick of her hand. "Take a few hours, in case things go better than I think they might."

Jens painted *Jing Qi Shen* for Suzie. He spent hours deciding what to choose for her, and even longer pondering the meaning. It comprised three characters, each carrying multiple definitions. *Jing*, in reference to men, was sperm. In women, it can translate to 'hormones,' but for both male and female includes the entire endocrine system, the biochemical character of the body. Not just sweat, but your very genetic chemistry. *Qi*, the life energy, life essence. *Shen*, spiritual energy. *Shen* is developed through self-cultivation.

Jens explained the painting to Suzie as the importance of balance, the need to care for body, mind, and soul. To him, it was a talisman, a plea, for her to step outside her mind and feel more often. He didn't tell her that. He thought she was getting a little better at that balance. She had set the frame on a shelf above the small table in her quarters.

"Into the Hole?" Suzie asked. "Are you serious?" Jens nodded his head, which made Suzie shake hers.

"Those guys must have a lot of pull with the Consortium," she said. "You don't even know who owns these, do you?"

"The Donuts?"

"Yes, the Donuts." She shook her head again. "Sometimes I wonder how you've survived this long."

Jens turned his palms up and shrugged.

"There's no telling who makes up a Consortium, but they're the real power behind the curtain. That Captain Wan might even be a stockholder."

Jens kept quiet. He felt it the wisest course of action at the moment.

"Nobody just visits a Hole," she added.

"Are you cool with it? I could talk to Jie—"

"You'll do no such thing!" Suzie said. "You might get some glares from some of the other astrogators, but they'll keep quiet. I still can't figure out if you're as blind as you make out. You put on this act, or maybe it isn't an act. Both are worrying."

"What kind of act is that?" Jens asked.

"Like you're just a leaf floating down life's stream."

"Feels like it sometimes," Jens said.

"I don't know if I buy it. Has Teal shared her grand plan yet?"

"About GLR? Yeah. The contact on Hat Pin explained it too."

"Mr Smith, mystery man," Suzie said. "No, doofus, the *grand* plan? Expansion of operations. She hasn't, has she?" Suzie punched him in the arm. "Blank look means 'no,' and it means you haven't even figured it out. They think this is going to be such a big thing, they're going to create another convoy. More ships."

Suzie stared at Jens, who still looked blankly back.

"Jesus, Jens. More ships, meaning more captains. Why do you think they've been training you so hard?"

"I have wondered about that—"

"You're amazing. Is that your motto for life? 'Just roll with it'?"

Jens looked at his hands, resting in his lap. "Sometimes that's the only option available," he said.

"Oh, and now I upset you." Suzie placed a hand on Jens' arm. "I'm sorry," she said. "It's just that you roll in here, to this ship, and you're given everything on a silver platter. The Captain. Your own ship. I get a little jealous sometimes." She ran her fingers through his hair. "I'm happy for you. You land on your feet. I'll start calling you 'Cat Man'." She rubbed his head. "There's that smile that makes me wet."

Jens smile grew. Her other hand rested on his crotch.

"Wait a minute," he said. "This drug of theirs. Have you ever taken communion?"

"I'm not Catholic," Suzie said.

"It's what Teal hands out before a Step. At least she did at First Step. She didn't let me or Herschel have one," Jens said.

"I'm in the Hole. Definitely no drugs there."

"So, you never took it?" Jens asked.

Suzie shook her head.

Jens took the bag of pills out of his pocket and showed her. "Do you want to? See what all this fuss is about? Mr Smith gave me these. Said it would change humanity or something like that." He tried to look reassuring. "Teal gave us a few hours."

Suzie stared at the bag, and the faintest smile played across her face. She raised her eyes to Jens' and gave a small nod.

Suzie held the pill in her open palm. "Just pop in the mouth and swallow?"

"That's the general idea," Jens said. "Make yourself comfortable and just wait. It didn't look like it took very long to kick in when the guys on the bridge took it."

"They're tripping the light fantastic while I'm in the Hole being pulled across space."

"Yeah. That wasn't very pleasant," Jens said. "But now's your chance."

"I don't see you taking one," she said.

"Okay, let's do it then. Mr Smith said to be open. Whatever that means."

"Be open," Suzie repeated.

Jens leaned back against the bulkhead; his legs folded under him on the squab. Suzie did the same. He smiled at her, pinched the pill between finger and thumb and put it on his tongue. He swallowed. Suzie copied his actions, sticking her tongue out at him when she finished swallowing. They both closed their eyes and waited.

They didn't have to wait too long.

Jens felt himself sinking into the bed as if his body was becoming denser than lead. Time followed suit, slowing until the clock made no sense at all. Now, then, was, will be, any linear handrail he previously held vanished in his grasp. Thousands of years, or mere milliseconds, may have passed, or were passing.

Jens let go. He sat in a moment, and then another, which was part of the same moment. He felt a tingling throughout his body, starting in the extremities, his hands, and feet, which slowly spread up his limbs and into his torso, into the core of his being. He felt his very cells vibrating, cells that once identified him as a separate entity, that made up a self. They began to move apart and then to dissolve. The vibration that dissolved his body filled his ears, first with a loud ringing, but even that sound broke apart until only a faint hum remained, a universal chant consisting of one all-powerful syllable. The universe was singing.

He became the observer. He could see but was indifferent to his existence. Ego disappeared with form, and yet he continued to exist, merely witnessing. He, or what was left of 'him', gazed into a kaleidoscope of color and shape. Patterns within patterns shifted, moved, and danced, visuals almost painful in their naked beauty. He looked past the geometric shapes, into the openness in which they swirled, as if the universe were a great hall with a glittering honeycombed ceiling of every color imaginable.

He reached up with his mind and struck the dome, knowing it would crack, that it would shatter, that it was mere illusion, just as he knew everything he may have previously seen or thought or experienced was a dream. And the dome fell away, into an expanse that consumed him. Jens let himself be consumed. In that moment, which lasted thousands of years, lifetime after lifetime, and a mere blink of an eye, he became that infinite space, fading into everything that was, is, and is yet to be. Becoming mere energy. Raw love.

Finally, Jens slowly opened his eyes. Suzie was looking at him, tears streaming down her cheeks. He touched his own face and pulled back moist fingers. He reached over and stroked her face with the back of his hand. He pulled her close and they held each other, crying out of both sadness and joy.

I am as much a part of you, he thought, *as you are of you.*

And he knew she realized the same. They held each other, trying to keep their experiences close, fearing they would soon begin to fade like a dream in the morning. But the memory of what they touched would remain, as much as their minds could understand, while a more linear time would allow them to process the experience.

Their hands explored the physical form, a reassurance of their solidity as much as an expression of energy and love. Slipping out of their flight suits, they slipped into each other, another brief taste of unity. When they finished, they lay beside each other, silently gazing at the blackness behind their eyelids.

Teal straightened Jens' silk tie. It didn't need straightening. She adjusted the perfect knot around his neck.

"You look really nice," she said. "Enjoy the ride." She leaned in and kissed him on the lips, a rare display of affection outside of her quarters.

Suzie took his hand, another rare display, taking him to the inner room of the docking bay. They stepped into their pressure suits, checked each other's connections, and joined Lassen in the tender. Lassen's helmet sat in the seat next to him.

"Welcome aboard," he said. "My favorite Donut Hole plus one." He spoke into the comms. "*Little Cloud* ready to depart."

"See you soon, *Little Cloud*," Stephan answered from the bridge.

Lassen piloted the tender out of the docking bay door. The glare of HAT-P-5 obliterated the blackness of space. Even with the view screen at full tint, Jens squinted his eyes. Lassen turned the tender away from the star and flew behind the Donut. All sixteen freighters were docked in preparation for Step. The eight empty bays left from the Hat Pin convoy made the Donut look like it was missing teeth. The tender crept up the side of the massive disc, hovering above the 'bow' landing pad. Lassen set it down gently and put on his helmet.

"I'm going to vent air before letting you out," he said. Jens and Suzie nodded even though Lassen couldn't see through their tinted faceplates. "Give me a thumb or something," Lassen said. "You can speak as well."

"Sorry," Suzie said. "We're good to go."

"Good to go," Jens affirmed.

"Venting air," Lassen said. "Okay guys, opening your door. Have a good Step."

The door beside Jens and Suzie opened, and they stepped out onto the surface of the Donut. Suzie gave Lassen a wave and headed towards a doorway at the end of the landing pad. Jens followed. At the door, they looked up to see the tender flying overhead on its way back to the *Cirrus*. Suzie opened the door, closing it behind Jens. They stood in a small anteroom facing another door. A red light above the door flashed several times and turned green. Suzie opened the door, and Jens followed into another, larger room.

As soon as she closed and sealed the door behind them Suzie took her helmet off. "Hang it in one of the empty lockers," she told Jens as soon his helmet was off. He watched as she shucked off her pressure suit and hung it in a locker with her name above it. He got out of his and hung it in a locker previously used by an astrogator from the Hat Pin convoy.

"Your pretty suit got creased up," she said, stroking his jacket. He leaned down and kissed her. The annoying little mathematician was starting to grow on him.

"Stop that," she said, pushing away from him. "Come on, time to go down to the Hole."

She led him to another door, which opened into a circular elevator. They entered and strapped themselves into seats.

"Down," she said. The door closed, and the room started to descend.

"This will take a few minutes," Suzie said. "As soon as we arrive, you don't exist to me, okay?" She reached over and patted his leg. "Nothing personal, but there is nothing personal in the Hole. Nobody will talk to you, or each other, unless it's about the numbers."

"Okay," he said.

"And don't call anybody a Donut Hole, not that you'll be talking to anybody," she added.

"I call you a Donut Hole all the time."

"Not in here, you don't. We're astrogators."

"Okay," Jens said again.

"It gets really grueling. Step lasts forever. Time doesn't mean quite the same thing," she said.

"Like GLR?"

"Nothing like GLR," she said. "Nothing is like that."

The elevator settled to a stop. Suzie quickly unstrapped and kissed the still restrained Jens. "See you on the other side," she said. Then added: "Open door."

The door slid open, and she left the elevator. Jens unstrapped and followed. The Hole was a large circular room. A circular table sat in the middle, surrounded by twenty-four seats. Jens could recognize the Donut Holes from the *Sukhavati* convoy. Anton from the *Ryk*, Lena McGee from the *Cooper*, Ma Yun from the *General Xing*, Luciana from the *Calderón*, Chuck Young from the *Plymouth*, Kawai Joe from the *Avarua*. Jie, in his tailored suit, was the only one to look up from his screen and acknowledge Jens.

He got up and greeted Jens, still standing near the elevator door. Jie grabbed Jens by the shoulders and pulled him close in a strong hug. "*Good to see you, my friend,*" Jie whispered in Jens' ear. "*I am so happy you are here,*" he said. "*Come.*" He took Jens to the wall, the farthest they could get from the central table.

"*It is a privilege,*" Jens said.

"*You will just observe, but you will see what happens in a Hole,*" Jie explained. "*Touch nothing and speak to no one, understand?*"

"*Understood,*" Jens answered.

"*There are quarters for rest behind our seats.*" Jens followed Jie's eyes to the eight doors along the wall. "*Each room has three bunks. Use the one behind you if you need. If an astrogator is resting there, say nothing. Their mind is in complete focus. You must not cause any distraction.*"

"*To a mind that is still, the whole universe surrenders,*" Jens said.

"*I am pleased you are still reading. But we don't want the whole universe, merely to move through it.*" Jie shifted to English. "The journey of a thousand light-years begins with a single Step. Now take an empty seat." Jie turned away and sat back in his seat. Soon he was staring intently at the screen in the table in front of him.

Jens sat at the table. He quickly saw that the 'table' was a large monitor. He reverently placed a hand on it, realizing for the first time that he was sitting at the quantum computer that utilized the power of a star to fold time and space. Directly in front of him was a smaller display. Numbers and symbols played across it. He recognized a few – a pitchfork which represented wave function, m for mass, square root, pi. Jens stopped trying to read. The symbols and their combinations made an incomprehensible dancing alphabet to his untrained eyes.

He could read the red numbers in the bottom right corner of the monitor, just as he saw on the viewscreen on the bridge of the *Cirrus*. Count down.

"Making adjustment," a Donut Hole at the table said. McGee.

"Concur," answered another. Suzie.

An intense silence returned to the room, interrupted by minor adjustments called and negotiated around the table. Jens sat back and waited, watching the astrogators move their fingers over their screens like witches concocting potions, working with the most powerful and mysterious witch of all, the quantum computer deep in the heart of the Donut. The hours continued to pass.

Finally, the red numbers on the corner of his screen reduced to two digits. Fifty-nine. Fifty-eight. Fifty-seven. Each of the sixteen astrogators lifted their hands from the table and rested them on their laps. Heads relaxed against the back of their chairs, eyes closed. Jens kept his open, watching as the red numbers counted down.

At zero, the numbers blinked and moved around the bottom of the screen, inching their way left and then right. The zero itself looked flatter. Jens started to feel the same way, as if his body were squeezed between two huge fingers, or as if the entire mass was condensing, and yet at the same time becoming somehow larger and heavier, so heavy that even his vision was being compressed. Jens tried to keep his eyes open, tried to focus on the monitor in front of him, but what he saw became too heavy for his vision to hold.

The light, his dense thoughts managed. *The light is too heavy ...*

Jens closed his eyes. It didn't help. His body seemed to fold into itself, collapsing into a denser and denser collection of cells; until, if unchecked, it would become its own black hole.

Jens tried to scream, but he couldn't move his mouth—the sound was too heavy to escape. With the thought that sound had mass came the realization that thought, too, brought its own mass. Panicked thoughts rolled out of his mind like boulders, filling his very core, a space threatening to be over-loaded, dragging his whole being under the ... *under the what?* his mind asked.

He tried to focus on the blackness behind his mind, an empty field of no thought, no being. He brought back the sensation he felt in Suzie's quarters, trying to relax into the feeling or image or memory of nothingness and of totality. He ignored the ever-increasing solidity of his body, losing himself in a formless world. Time flowed like cold molasses. Jens gave up hoping that it would soon be over. He knew it never would.

"We're here." A hand gently shook his shoulder. He opened his eyes and saw Jie looking down. "Welcome to Kepler-76."

Jie sat in the seat next to him. "We will assess the Step data a while more, but you get some rest. You will need it. Take a bunk. Sleep. You will feel much better for it."

Jie stood and guided Jens by the hand, out of his seat and into the rest quarters behind the chairs. He took Jens to the nearest bunk and helped him lie down. Jens was asleep before his head was on the cushion.

Jens woke to a scream that he knew was his own. His eyes flicked open. Across from him, he could see Suzie sleeping.

A Donut Hole from the Shackleton convoy slept in another bunk. A dim orange glow lit the room. A restful light. He shifted quietly in his cot, wriggling his fingers, moving his feet, reassuring himself that he still had limbs. After a few moments, he let himself drift back into dream, where he was sinking deeper and deeper under the waves, a knife protruding from his chest.

"Wake up." A familiar voice. Suzie. "Wake up," she repeated. "Time to go home."

Jens tested his limbs again before sitting up.

"You look terrible, Jens," Suzie said. "Even that suit doesn't hide it."

"That *was* terrible. How can you stand it?"

"It has its upsides—"

"Fuck me," Jens said.

"Later," Suzie replied. "You didn't even have to work. What are you moaning about?"

"I don't even know why you need to correct a quantum computer."

"She's not as smart as she thinks," Suzie said. "Without us, she'd be at least twenty thousand kilometers out, or maybe even worse. She's way too focused on the energy conversion."

"Twenty thousand kilometers? You stay down here for that?" Jens asked.

"You always need a human back up, Jens," Jie said from behind him.

"Always," Suzie agreed.

"*Xiexie, zheshiwoderongxing.*" Jens said.

"He says it was a privilege," Jie said to Suzie. "So, Mr Jensen. You would like to also observe on our next Step?"

"Ah, well ..."

Jie and Suzie laughed. "Don't worry, my friend," Jie said. "Once is more than enough, I can assure you." He stood back. "You really must take care of your clothes, Mr Jensen. Zhang would be very displeased with how you treat his work."

"Can we go now?" Jens asked.

"Yes." Jie failed at hiding his smile. "You two will come with me. A tender from the *Sunshine* is waiting above. We'll take you back to the *Cirrus*."

The three turned away from the blinding star as soon as they stepped out of the doorway. The Donut depleted, it immediately started absorbing the energy of star Kepler-76. They clambered aboard the waiting tender. Jens tried to recognize the pilot, but his tinted faceplate made that impossible. The door closed behind them and the tender pressurized. The pilot took off his helmet, signaling to the others that it was safe.

"Louie!" Jens exclaimed.

"Good to see you, my friend," Louie said.

He lifted the tender off the surface of the Donut and turned it towards the *Cirrus*, flying on the dark side of the disc. The docking bay was open and welcoming, closing behind them and pressurizing.

Suzie and Jens stepped back on board their ship.

"Jens," Louie said. "We have a parcel for you." He climbed out of the pilot seat, and with Jie's help, maneuvered a large box out of the tender's hold.

"Wan gave you some homework for the trip to the Shack and back. Books to read, even assignments. I have no idea what you did to annoy him." Louie smiled. "There is a new Tang suit, so continue to practise. Zhang has made you some new clothes," Louie said. "And Genju has given you an old kitchen knife. He says you will know what to do with it, and Zhao agreed that it was completely out of balance. Do you know what that means?"

"Clearly," Jens said. "What's not to understand?"

"He said you would know. No need to be a smart ass," Louie said. "I've given you a dictionary, and some audio discs, so you can keep improving."

"I get to practise every visit to the *Xing*," Jens said.

"They will only teach you bad grammar," Louie said. "Practise daily with the discs I've given you."

"Yes, sir,' Jens said, saluting.

"Enough," Jie said. "It is time." Jie took Jens by the hand, pulled him close, and wrapped his arms around him. "Use your time well," he said. "We will see you at next Step."

"Shi guang liu shi, bu ke fu de," Jens said.

"Do your homework and work hard," Jie said. "And then you can use an appropriate proverb. Louie," he called. "It is time to go home. Is our passenger here?"

"Aye."

Jens turned to see Herschel. "Wait," he said. "Just wait a minute, okay, I'll be right back."

Jens ran to his quarters. He reached under his squab, shook out two of the mint shaped pills, and took the remainder with him back to the docking bay. When he reached Herschel, he pressed the bag into his hand.

"For Pani," he said. "So she knows."

"Are these Teal's drugs?" Herschel asked.

"Didn't you take one at Step, at her communion?"

"No," Herschel said. "I let her know I didn't want to be a part of it."

"You ... man, once you ..." Jens tried. "When you get a chance, just try it." He forced the bag into Herschel's palm. "Then, you'll understand. Herschel," Jens said. "Trust me. I felt like you at first, but then ... Just try it. Give yourself a couple of hours, keep your mind open. Afterward, you don't have to join them, but at least you'll understand what they're trying to do."

Herschel's hand closed on the bag.

"Good," Jens said. "I'll see you in eight months, my friend."

12

Jens and Lassen gazed at the planet filling the viewscreen. Shackleton. Deep greens and blacks patterned the surface. Bands of white cloud circled the hemispheres. Ice caps covered the poles. Each ship of the convoy fell into its individual orbit. The two men had spent most of the watch simply gazing at the screen, sometimes watching a freighter nearby drop its cargo, but mostly watching the planet beneath them slowly turn.

Jens was first to interrupt the silence on the bridge. "I haven't seen green for so long."

"That's what broke their hearts, man," Lassen said.

"What do you mean?"

"You know the story. There are other rocks that claim Shack status, but it was really this one. This is where humanity gave up."

"It's beautiful," Jens said.

"Which is why it hurt so much," Lassen said. "Imagine – almost a century searching for a ... who knows what they were looking for? Another Earth? And all they find is lifeless rock after lifeless rock. Air too thin or poisonous to breathe. Soil too poor. Nothing alive, not even a nanobe. Desperate suckers like those below would still take the chance, but it was here that ended all that for most. Where a planet of billions gave up hope and stopped looking. Come on," Lassen said. "You know the story."

"Yeah, who doesn't?" Jens said. "We finally admit that there is no Planet B. And we cleaned up what we had."

"That's funny, coming from you, Mr Garbage Man," Lassen said. "Take a look. This rock is why you lost your job. Or why you had one in the first place." He laughed at his joke. "Collecting garbage on a planet committed to no waste. Your days were numbered from the beginning."

"The pickings were getting slim out there," Jens admitted.

"It's because of this place," Lassen said.

They both lapsed into silence, watching the clouds shift in the currents of the upper atmosphere.

"Clouds, rain, an atmosphere that's almost breathable," Lassen said. "Put yourself in those guy's suits. They've probably been Stepping for over a decade. Rock after rock. Then they see green. They get into their flier and descend. The green gets closer. Closer. And the green turns out to be rock. Green rock. What kind of cosmic joke is that? There was a very high suicide rate on the Steps back to Earth. Those folks just gave up. Read *Stepping Out*, by the captain of one of the early exploratory ships. Teal has a copy. Reads like an extended suicide note, which I guess it was. But worth the read if you're going to stay out here."

"Thanks, I will," Jens said.

"You know the Shackleton story?" Lassen asked. Sharing long watches with the First Mate had led to a grudging yet mutual respect. But this was the first time Jens had heard his superior as talkative as this.

"Antarctic explorer. Ship stranded. Rescues his men," Jens offered.

"That's a hell of a story," Lassen said. "But not that one. You really need to read more."

"Go on, tell me the story," Jens invited, settling back into his chair.

"Get me a coffee first," Lassen said.

"Aye, aye sir!"

Jens returned in a few minutes with two mugs of coffee.

"Back in the day—"

"That's a great start," Jens interrupted.

"Quiet in the front," Lassen said. "Back in the day, nobody had reached the South Pole. It's hard to imagine now—no airlift, they walked! Across the ice for weeks, wearing waxed canvas, carrying everything, trudging across a frozen wasteland for weeks. Shackleton was an incredible leader. Wan's given you lots of books on that topic, but you need to read about Shackleton if you want to really understand about leading. He was well on his way to reaching the Pole, claiming the prize, being a national hero. Fame and glory. But somewhere along the way he listened to that small, quiet voice in the back of his head, and he did the math. He knew he could reach the Pole, be the first to reach it, knew the prize was his for the taking. But do you know what else he knew?"

Jens opened his hands and shrugged.

"He saw that, while he could reach the Pole, he wouldn't make it back. Not just him, but the men under his command," Lassen continued. "Think about the story you're familiar with. Ice crushes his ship, and his crew is stranded, so he takes five handpicked men and sails a dinghy hundreds of miles across treacherous seas, climbs mountains, finds another ship, and months later rescues the crew he left back on the ice.

"On that earlier expedition, Shackleton had the prize in his grasp. He would have been known forever as the man who conquered the South Pole. Know what he did? He turned around. His men tried to argue with him, but he would have expected that. So back they trudged across the ice, failures. But alive. Now, Amundsen was the first to reach the Pole, a few years later. Who was the second?" Lassen asked.

"Scott," Jens answered. "I grew up outside of Christchurch. Last stop to Antarctica."

"Good for you," Lassen said. "And correct. Scott was considered a hero. He reached the Pole. What else did Scott do, Jens?"

"He died."

"Exactly. Scott reached the same point as Shackleton. He even felt proud when he passed it, like it was some achievement. He beat Shackleton! Scott had a goal, and he was single-minded in wanting to reach it. Growth at all cost, the capitalists cheer. So, he carried on. He reached the Pole only to find that the Norwegian had beaten him by a month. Amundsen left him a nice note, too. Then, Scott turned around and walked himself and his men to death on the way back.

"This is it," Lassen said, gesturing to the view screen. "This the moment when we listened to the voice in our heads, the voice Scott ignored. The voice Shackleton listened to. People have come up with lots of reasons why Scott didn't make it back. Not enough protein for the walk, or not the right type of nourishment, to pull their sleds day after day after day, getting weaker and weaker. Through it all, they continued to drag sleds full of rock samples, too. Lots of analogies to draw from there, don't you think? And as a result, he lost his men and he lost his life. Scott was heralded as a hero at the time. But we know better now.

"And here we are," Lassen said. "The Shackleton Moment. When humanity chose to return while they still could, when they still had the chance, when they could salvage and clean up where they lived."

"The Shack," Jens said.

"That's right," Lassen said. "You ever see your grandparents again you can tell them about what you saw and say another thank you. That was a gutsy generation."

"As they like to tell us," Jens said.

"Believe them. They could have kept trashing and grasping, but instead, they became the generation that finally, *finally*, took responsibility. My oma was on the streets, stopping the tanks with her bare tits. I didn't believe her when I was a kid, and then she showed me the pictures. Standing in the street in with her shirt pulled up. She was a very pretty young woman. And very brave. But that was happening all over Europe and North America. Even in China."

Lassen leaned forward and peered into the view screen. "See that light down there?"

Jens searched the surface and saw a pinprick of light in a sea of green.

"Magnify," Lassen said.

The image on the screen increased in size. The light became a clear star on the green surface.

"Magnify and continue until command to stop," Lassen said to the computer. The light grew until what was a dome became blurrily apparent.

"Stop magnification," Lassen said. "Living under a dome. Their entire world, just a few miles in diameter—unless they suit up with an aspirator. And the settlers keep coming. Who would choose that kind of life?"

"You live in a lead-lined shoebox, Lassen, surrounded by the cold vacuum of space," Jens said. "I don't think you're one to criticize."

"True, true," Lassen said. "I'm not criticizing, just amazed. There are two more domes on the other side of the planet. McMurdo, mostly American, keeping with the theme of the Antarctic bases. And Vostok. This is probably like Siberia to the Russians, only much farther away from their worthless rulers. There are truckloads of Russians out here."

"I met some on Hat Pin."

"I bet they were very hospitable," Lassen said.

"Well, they pretended to be, but it wasn't a very relaxing situation. Very good vodka," Jens said.

"There's not a lot of Russians at Scott," Lassen said. "They're tending to stick to their part of the planet, like at Hat Pin. Laika vodka! You go to Laika and don't even bring back a bottle for the First Mate. Never mind. We'll sample the local brew at Scott tomorrow after we deliver the magic dirt we've hauled across the galaxy."

Teal banked the flier in a gentle spiral, slowly circling the green sphere as they descended. Folds in the landscape became visible, huge mountain ranges left from shifting tectonic plates, shaping the climate. Clouds battled on the windward side, dumping rain, creating rivers, appearing below as black ribbons on a green field. The lee shadow, the dry side of the ranges, although also green, was not dry plains like Otago, or Nevada, or Patagonia. Or like any place on Earth. That was the first indication to the *Fortitude's* survey party that something was amiss. Or at least it should have been.

Teal glided the flier closer to the surface, towards the Dome glistening below. As they descended, more signs of civilization appeared. Several smaller domes stood outside the main structure, dwarfed in comparison. Each was connected to the Dome by an access tube. At the next slow spiral, Jens could see the tubes were actually wide enough to permit large cargo pods to move between the main and smaller domes. As space inside the primary dome was re-prioritized, processing plants, reactors, mechanical services—all were moving 'outside' into the smaller domes.

The runway stood out as a thick scar cut into the stone. The last spiral of the flier was so gradual and slow that Jens thought he could step out and walk beside it. Teal was a good pilot. Touchdown wasn't even felt. The crew drew straws to see who would stay onboard the *Cirrus*. Lassen and Ed drew short, but they were promised shore leave before returning to the *Sukhavati* Convoy. On the flier, Suzie squeezed Jens hand. Stephan looked pleased. Even Baldy was smiling.

As the flier slowed to a stop, Teal followed directions given to her over the comms. The runway narrowed and branched into smaller lanes, like little rivers all flowing into the Dome looming over them. She folded the wings, and the craft no longer resembled something that rode the winds. The Dome rose ahead of them until the curving surface filled their entire view. The clear panels reflected their approach, translucent glass-like sheets that were stronger than steel.

A tall door began to rise as they approached, admitting them into the city. Once inside the door closed behind them. Four men approaching in a small transport indicated that the entry room had already re-pressurized.

"Looks like it's okay to get out," Teal said. "Once we unload, we celebrate. Time for some R and R."

"Aye, Captain," Stephan said.

"Fucking aye," Baldy agreed. "What they have here takes you wherever you want to go, and places you didn't even know existed."

The door lifted, and the four men lined up and made a welcome party. Jens patted his bare thigh, remembering it held no knife.

"No weapons allowed," Teal ordered before departing the *Cirrus*. "We're going among friends."

"It's always wise to be prepared for any contingency," Jens answered.

"Don't quote your Chinese philosophers at me, Jens. I said no weapons, and that's final," Teal said. "Stay aboard the *Cirrus* if you want to play with knives."

Jens rubbed his thumb into the palm of his open hand. He wouldn't leave that weapon behind. His whole body had become a weapon thanks to Zhang's tutelage.

"Really," Teal said, placing her hand gently on Jens' arm. "You can relax for a while. The Russians are on the other side of the planet, and they're just as ignorant about what we're doing as the ones on Hat Pin."

"They'll find out."

"Of course they will," she said. "Everybody will. But by that time, we'll be the ones controlling it. We'll need the Russians, especially at Laika, but they'll come in on our terms, not theirs. Business, Jens. Yuan taught you all this stuff."

"Consortia Chess, he called it."

"Exactly," Teal said. "But you have to shut off sometimes. Relax. That's an order."

The first in line grabbed Teal in his arms and lifted her off the floor. "Sandra! It is good to see you!"

"It's always good to see you, Peter," she replied.

At Jens' turn, Peter gripped his hand tightly. "Pleasure to meet you, man, a real pleasure. I want to hear your stories. Tell me all about that ocean you sailed."

Jens made his way down the line. He took the last man's hand, gripped his arm, and leaned into him. He let his nose touch the other's, breathing in as he did so.

"*Tena koe*," Jens said.

Jens stood back and watched as tears ran down the other man's cheeks. The tattoos on his cheeks glistened. He nodded to Jens. "*Tena koe*," he said. "*Kia ora*!"

"Alrighty, let's unpack and take our guests somewhere more comfortable," Peter said. The three with him fell to unpacking the flier. Teal glanced at her party, and they joined in, loading small carts that continued appearing until the flier was empty.

The crew walked to the exit of the loading bay and entered the Dome proper. The hardened glass panels arched away to their full two-kilometer height. The visitors were guided to hover pods. Peter motioned for Teal, Stephan and Baldy to enter one; Jens and Suzie followed two of the greeting party into another. As soon as the doors closed, the pod lifted. The settlement spread beneath them. Two older domes were in the process of being dismantled, now merely half-shells.

"The first settlers lived in something so small?" Suzie said, pointing.

"They weren't small until we built the grand Dome over them," the man next to her said. Suzie tried to remember his name from the greeting line. Paora.

"Look over there," Paora said. "That is Mount Erebus."

Jens and Suzie looked toward the center of the dome where a great pile of ground stone rose to a height of five hundred meters.

"It's just a baby, but there is a tree up there," Paora said. "It's a bristlecone pine, the oldest, toughest tree on Mother Earth. Resilient to bad weather, bad soils, thin air. It's like our flag. And I can tell you this, it's the most treasured living thing on the entire planet."

Jens and Suzie strained to see evidence of the plant but failed.

"We can hike up there later," Paora said. "Then you can see it. They live for thousands of years, and ours is just a baby. Literally." He pointed to open spaces in the distance. "Those fields will become fertile, growing our food in healthy soil, in good air—at least as good as we can provide. Everything used goes to building the soil if you get what I mean. Nothing is wasted." Paora smiled. He pointed to the center of the Dome where original stone buildings gave way to metal, stretching higher to the top of the Dome.

"Skyscrapers," Jens said. "They used to be called skyscrapers on Earth."

"They do that here," Paora said. "Right up to the top of the glass. Scraping the sky, I like that."

"It's beautiful," Suzie said.

"We think so," he said. "The panels of the dome harvest sunlight for energy as well as photosynthesis. Look at the rooftops, all gardens."

They gazed at the green of the top of each building, filled with plants, both edible and decorative.

"There," Paora pointed as the hover pod started to descend. Jens and Suzie followed his finger to a smaller skyscraper. "Beers await!"

"You've made me homesick," Paora said as he sipped his drink. "I haven't heard Māori in far too long."

"Is that what you spoke in line when you touched noses?" Suzie asked.

Jens stroked her back. "Don't mind her. She's from Kansas."

"Nebraska," Suzie corrected.

"Tell her where you're from, Paora," Jens said.

Paora cleared his throat. "*Ko Hikurangi toku maunga,*" he began.

Ko Waiapu toku awa

Ko Hourota toku waka,

Ko Ngati Porou toku iwi,

No Turanga nui a kiwa ahau,

Ko Paora Apirana toku ingoa.

Tēnā koutou, tēnā koutou,

Tēnā koutou katoa"

"What did you say?" Suzie asked.

"I told you where I was from," Paora said. "My mountain, my river, the waka—the ship—that my people took to come to our land, the place that is my home. We are *tangata whenua*, people of the land. I shared with you where I identify, the place that anchors me in every cell of my body."

"You're a long way from your mountain, my friend," Jens said.

"That I am," Paora said. "Something you reminded me about."

"Sorry, mate," Jens said.

"Not at all, brother. Out here, it is good to remember, and sometimes maybe a little too easy to forget. But we have ways to connect with home. Connect with everything. And I'm always busy." He shook his head, causing his dreadlocks to sway.

"The chemists will be busy now," Jens said.

"I will be, that's for sure," Paora said.

"You're a chemist?" Jens asked.

Paora smiled.

"He's *the* chemist," Peter said from farther up the table.

"That calls for another round," Jens said getting up.

"I love your work," Suzie said. "Jens and I ... we ..."

"Don't try to describe it," Paora said. "Just be it. When you come back and pick up the finished product, we'll all sit together. Do you know what I miss?" he asked as Jens set three glasses on the table.

"Mountains? Rivers? Trees?" Jens tried. "Air? Blue sky?"

"Close, but nah," Paora said. "Wood. Plain old wood. Look around. See any?"

Jens and Suzie looked around the room, metal tables, and chairs, metal benches softened with cushions. They shook their heads.

"Not a sliver," Paora said. "Maybe a little, a few very expensive pieces, out of my price range—"

"Not for long," Jens said. "From what I'm told, money won't be a worry."

"Not yet, though," Paora said. "Chickens hatching and all that. They had the same problem in Greenland."

"Who had a problem in Greenland?" Jens asked.

"The Vikings, man. A name like yours, you should know. Jensen. Son of Jens. That's a Viking name. They had a colony in Greenland for almost five hundred years. Vikings in Greenland. Wood was like gold, more than gold because you can't hold up your roof or fix your boat with a shiny metal. They even reached North America, hundreds of years before Columbus, probably looking for wood. But they all died out or left for somewhere else because the ships stopped coming. That's what it's like out here. If you stopped coming, I'm sure the colonies would slowly fade away and die out. Each one is trying to make itself needed by mother Earth, all trying to find special metals or minerals momma might need. But she won't have many needs in the future."

"But not The Shack," Suzie said. "Not with GLR."

"No, not The Shack," Paora agreed. "Say, you got any books, I'd be happy to trade. Books are like wood out here. You can't grow them out of rock. I like to hold what I read, and turn pages. I'm not a big fan of data readers. I look at screens all day."

"I brought a couple," Suzie said. "It pays to know what the natives need. Real dense classics that will take you hours and hours to finish."

"She's special, Jens," Paora said. "Hey, if you guys are ready to leave this party, I'd love to show you something I've been working on. I call it 'the sitting room.'"

Jens and Suzie looked up the table towards Teal. "I told you, you're off duty, do whatever you want," she answered before they could ask. "Those two are going to burn out," she said to Peter.

"Follow me," Paora said. "I'll take care of you." He scraped back his metal chair and started walking away from the table. Jens swigged the last of his beer and followed, catching up at the exit.

Paora led them to an e-car. As soon as the doors closed, he told it, "the lab," and it began to emit a soft purr as it moved away. The car drove through the center of the city, high rise buildings shading the outside sun. The buildings grew smaller as they continued towards the edge of the dome until only nondescript one-story warehouse blocks lined the street. The car doors opened when the e-car stopped in front of one.

"We're here," Paora said. "The epicenter of it all. Follow me."

Suzie and Jens walked side by side behind their guide. Paora looked into a retinal scan, and the front door clicked open. Sliding it wider he commanded the lights, and the space became illuminated. Rows of automated machines stood waiting – printers, centrifuges, evaporators. A fission reactor sat against the far wall, glowing blue lights giving it an air of sentience.

"This is where the final stages take place," Paora explained. "The minerals are processed off-site, and only the final ingredients brought here. It keeps me busy, but I get some time to create. Come this way."

They followed Paora upstairs to a room overlooking the floor equipment. Several large chairs and couches made it look and feel homey.

"I made a living room," Paora said. "It's my latest experiment. A living room for God's Living Room. Take a seat," he gestured.

Suzie and Jens sank into soft chairs beside each other.

"Synthetic leather," Paora said. "Disturbingly realistic. Comfortable, eh?"

"Very," Suzie said.

"In so many ways, GLR is a lonely trip," he said. "It always will be. It's all it can ever be. But we don't always have to be alone. So, I made a shared place. I think people will like it. I got the idea from an old picture of an opium den. People sat or lay together. The pipe would pass around and they would slump into their stupor. Recreationally blotting out their reality. That must have been comforting, as well as a bit safer."

He pulled a small remote out of his pocket and showed it to them. "With GLR, nothing is blotted out. It's enhanced. You know that," he said. "But it can still be experienced in a supportive way."

"We took it together," Suzie said. "In my quarters. I would have been too worried if I was alone."

"And you could both come out of it and share what you experienced," Paora said. "That's what I've tried to make here. Where we could sit together and touch the void, and then, well, try to understand it in company. Experience pure love, then share pure love."

Suzie looked at Jens and smiled. Jens nodded.

"Only here is the difference," Paora said, holding the remote up. "I press this, and the GLR infused in liquid-vapor is sprayed into the air of the room. All we have to do is sit back and breath. And then voyage."

Paora waited for a response. He watched as Suzie and Jens communicated to each other with their eyes.

"Okay?" Paora asked.

Without turning, they both nodded. Paora pressed his thumb down. A soft hiss came from a vent in the ceiling.

"Just inhale," Paora said. "See you on the other side."

Jens watched Suzie's face. The usual stress she carried between her eyes relaxed. Her cheeks became soft and flushed. Her smile deepened as she gazed back. He felt bathed in love. She closed her eyes and let her head rest on the back of the chair. Jens did the same.

A burst of color enveloped him, wrapping him in an embrace of warm pastels. Shades of pink, peach, orange, red. He heard distant drumming, a constant and slow beat. *Lub dub. Lub dub.* He let go of the sound and drifted into the color, fading and becoming the color itself. He let go of the perception of color, as color, and felt himself dissolve into molecules of light, each with a signature of its own. Pink, peach, orange, and red molecules, that then broke down into atoms, into electrons, protons, neutrons, which broke down into quarks, the Gluon force holding them together weakening until they separated into preons, into leptons. Those began to dissolve, and Jens dissolved with them, into even smaller pieces, into more made-up words, and even smaller until he became a universe of subatomic particles.

Jens looked within himself, inside each part of his being, which was a part of everything, and saw a dark center. He fell into the center, a blackness opening into countless universes, filled with countless galaxies, countless stars, countless beings.

Part 3: MisStep

13

Jens woke to red, flashing lights. Confused. This wasn't the *Sunrise*. That was months ago. He was on the *Cirrus*, four weeks out from Donut and Step to *Sukhavati*, weighed down by the gravity of Decel. And the lights weren't silent. There was a deafening alarm.

He got out of his bunk and got into his flight suit. He strapped his blade to his thigh, slipped a sounder into a pocket. After watching him pace for a week after leaving Shackleton and acceleration kicked in, Teal made him chief of security. A promotion, she chided. Full of routine checks in every crevice of the freighter, excuses to walk the hull, reasons to update (or, as he found, create) emergency procedures.

He had argued for drills for weeks. Now she decides to pull one. Without even telling him. *I should be leading this*, he grumbled to himself. Red flashing light, alarm of two prolonged bursts every two seconds. Collision. There's a lot a security officer can do in an impending collision, such as trying to limit any death or damage.

Teal interrupted his internal whining. "Jensen, get your ass up here!" she called over ship wide comms.

Jens pressed the comms button by his door. "On my way."

He entered the bridge to see Teal leaning over Suzie and Lassen, staring at the navigational monitor.

"Collision drill," Jens said. "Your choice. But I would have appreciated—"

"This is no drill, Jens," Teal snapped. "You wrote the plan, now do your job."

Jens tried to look at the monitor but couldn't see through their heads. "Bearing?" he asked.

"Position vector, Jens, not bearings. You're not at sea," Suzie said without looking up. "Never mind. The view screen is programmed."

"What are you looking for?" he asked.

"Small object, possibly small asteroid," Suzie answered. "Closing in fast."

Jens turned to the viewscreen and saw only empty space. "Magnify," he said. The screen increased the size of what was detected hurtling towards the ship. It was still too small to see. "Magnify, and continue until command to stop," he said.

The screen flicked several times before Jens stopped it. A small light stood out in the dark.

"Magnify," Jens said again. The light grew slightly larger. "Magnify," he said again. The small shape grew larger, the light brighter.

"That's not a rock," he said.

Teal walked over and stood beside him. "Why do you say that?" she asked.

"Look," he pointed. "The light. That's not reflection. It's ... a reactor. They're decelerating."

"They?"

"It's a ship. It has to be," Jens pointed. "It ..." But the light went out and the screen showed only dark space.

"Magnify," Jens said. "Continue magnifying." The screen flicked the darkness closer and closer until it lost clarity.

"Shit!" he said. "Time until impact? Suzie! Estimated time of impact?"

"At present velocity, eight minutes," she answered without looking up from her monitor.

"Can we evade?" he asked.

"Don't you think we would if we could?" she snapped.

"Teal," Jens said. "We need to shut down the reactor."

"Do what you have to," she said as she sat at the adjoining navigational monitor. "We'll need to try to deflect," she said to Lassen. She turned to Jens. "Go! Do what you need to do!" she ordered.

Jens pressed a control sequence and the alarm silenced, leaving only the pulsing red light. "Stephan, ready a tender for possible evac. Baldy and Ed, to the reactor, now! Initiate emergency shutdown protocol," he said into ship-wide comms.

"We're not shutting the reactor for drill," Baldy answered.

"Just fucking do it!" Jens said.

"Do as he says," Teal called from her console. "Jens is Security Officer. This is an emergency situation, so follow his fucking orders."

"I'll be at the reactor as soon as I can," Jens said into the comms. "Bring me a suit. All hands prepare for vacuum. That means you too," he said to the bridge. "Suit up. Time?" he asked Suzie.

"Seven minutes."

"Angle of approach?" Lassen asked her.

"Good thinking," Suzie said.

Teal shot Jens a glance. He ran out of the bridge. The increased gravity clung to his legs. His thighs burned as he drove each foot forward. By the time he reached the reactor, Baldy and Ed were at the control panel.

"Do it!" he shouted.

"We'll just hit the sun if we shut down," Baldy said.

"At least we'll have time to figure out how not to," Jens said. "If you don't shut down the reactor, we'll just be radioactive debris." He waved a hand at the control panel.

They grabbed onto the nearby handholds and hit the two switches simultaneously.

Jens floated off the deck as soon as the gravity failed. He attached a comms device to his flight suit.

"Reactor has been shut down," he said, directing his comment to Teal.

"No shit," she answered.

"All crew, brace for impact," he said to the others.

Baldy and Ed remained where they were, fixed to the handholds. Jens kicked off a wall and floated out of the reactor bay and into the corridor. He pushed off again and flew towards the loading bay.

"Stephan," he asked. "How is that tender?"

"Prepped and bay door open," he answered. "No time to prep the flier."

"Suzie," Jens asked. "Time?"

"Seconds," she answered.

"Fill me in," he said.

"We've altered the angle of impact. *Cirrus* is now at fifty-seven degrees to—" Her comms cut off and Jens was flung towards the starboard bulkhead. He fumbled for a handhold but was thrown across the room. He blinked in pain as he hit the ceiling, then saw the floor race to greet him. He reached out blindly and grasped a support, his movement stopping abruptly as his face smacked against the wall, leaving a patch of red where he hit.

"Bridge, talk to me!" he said.

He pushed himself towards the bridge, kicking off a wall and floating up the corridor.

"Bridge!" he repeated.

"We're okay," Lassen answered. "At least we will be."

"Where's Teal?" Jens asked.

"She's unconscious. I think. We don't have time to tend to her."

"The ship?"

"She deflected most of the force, but the hull took quite a blow," Lassen said. "We're blind outside. All vids are out."

"Suzie?"

"She's fine," Lassen answered. "What's the plan, Jens? Teal put you in command."

Jens turned in the air and hit the opposing bulkhead feet first, letting his knees absorb his momentum. He grabbed a handhold and stopped. He forced himself to breathe slowly through his nose, trying to slow the adrenalin coursing through his body.

"Jens?"

"Any readings of a breach?" he asked.

"Not on our monitors," Lassen said.

"Calculate thrust and trajectory to get us to Donut. Have your numbers ready, as well any additional fuel needs. Give us rolling data. We don't know when the reactor can restart. You've got to have an algorithm or something for that. And one of you, see to the captain. Baldy, Ed, respond," Jens said.

"Standing by," Baldy answered.

"Assess the reactor for any damage and prep for restart. The bridge will send the data. And prepare for additional mass. You're going to need it."

"Which one, Jens? Inspect or refuel?" Baldy answered.

"Just inspect the damn thing first," Jens snapped.

Jens pushed off the bulkhead, towards the loading bay. "Stephan, let's get ready to take a look outside. I'm almost to you."

As soon as Jens closed the loading bay airlock, Stephan opened the outer door. *Little Cloud* lifted from the deck and exited the ship. They followed the slant of the hull. Even though it made no sense in space, Jens couldn't help thinking of the *Cirrus* as 'listing to starboard'. *If she were at sea, she would be sinking*, he added to himself. *And we'd be abandoning ship.* Both sat silently, gazing at a huge dent across the surface. While hard to confirm without the reference of a horizon, the *Cirrus* looked off-course.

"What do you see?" Lassen asked.

"I'm not getting any thermal escape," Jens said.

"That is one tough hull," Stephan added.

"Evidence of impact from below midline all the way topside," Jens said. "Looks like your adjustment saved the ship. But it wasn't a rock that hit us."

"I see it too," Stephan added. "Scorching. Whatever it was exploded on contact. Bridge, I'm transmitting images through *Little Cloud* video."

They heard a gasp from the bridge as they slowly flew over the damage. "Are you suited? Can you walk it to inspect?" Suzie asked.

"There's no time," Jens answered. "We'll pass as low as we can and transmit to you visual and thermal data that should show any breach. Then we'll return and help with the reactor."

"Not good enough, Jens," Lassen radioed back. "Even the smallest crack could be catastrophic under Decel. I recommend a deck walk with sealant for anything that even looks like a crack. And I need to see everything."

"Okay," Jens said. "Stephan can set me down. I'll make my way to an airlock."

"No way, Jens. You heard Teal. You're in charge during this mess. You're needed back inside," Stephan said. "Set me down, fly back and get to the reactor. I'll transmit images to the bridge."

Jens took control of the tender and set it gently on the surface of the freighter. He depressurized the cabin. Stephan grabbed the emergency repair kit and climbed out of the cabin.

"Bridge, how are those numbers?" Jens said.

"Every minute we delay makes it that much more complicated," Suzie said.

"Okay," Jens said. "Give the reactor the fuel it needs for Decel. How's Teal?"

"Bad gash to the head, but she'll recover," Lassen said. "She's in her chair."

Jens entered the reactor room as Baldy and Ed were making adjustments at the base of the reactor. Baldy was strapped to the deck, while Ed hovered above. Jens tried to see what they were doing without distracting them from their work. He wasn't successful.

"She shifted on impact," Baldy said without turning. "We're making final corrections. It has to be precise, or Decel will tear us apart."

Ed read from the screen held in his hand, a soft murmuring of numbers.

"Shutting down was the right call," Baldy said to the instrument in his hand.

"How can I help?" Jens asked.

"There's going to be a shit load of fuel to move," Baldy answered.

"I'm kind of good at that," Jens said.

"Jens," Suzie said over comms. "We need a precise time for initiation of Decel."

Baldy paused his adjusting and turned to face Jens. He pointed to the base of the reactor and then at Ed. Ed nodded and pointed to the reactor without looking up. Adjustments, followed by restart. No time for a test run. Stephan on the surface. Hopefully finding minimal, or no, cracks in the inner hull.

"Three hours," he said for all to hear. "Three hours to Decel."

"Numbers for mass on their way," Suzie said.

Jens rolled up his sleeves, pushed off a bulkhead and floated towards the cargo bay.

Suzie started to count down as soon as they strapped in.

"This is going to hurt, boys," Lassen said from the helm. "And we'll be at 2.4 g's until we reach Donut."

"That's if the reactor actually fires," Ed said.

"And if the ship doesn't rip apart," Stephan added.

"Enough!" Jens said as acceleration kicked in and drove each of them into their seats.

They stared forward into the blackened view screen, waiting for something to happen, for an alarm to sound, for their lives to end. The weight continued to press into them, squeezing their lungs.

"Reactor?" Jens asked.

"Doing its job," Lassen said.

"Hull?" Jens asked. One word was enough effort.

"Secure," Suzie said.

"Course?"

"Course is good." Suzie didn't have the energy to protest against the insult. If she set it, it was correct. "It's good." She sucked in a breath.

Teal groaned as she regained consciousness. She gasped, trying to breathe. Jens unstrapped and moved his feet onto the deck. He felt his legs buckle as he stood. He sat back down, mustering his strength before trying to stand again. He took a step, then another. He was gasping by the time he reached Teal. Lassen plodded slowly to her and leaned on the chair for support.

"Report," she said through labored breaths.

Jens filled her in. Lassen added technical details about the course adjustment. She closed her eyes. Stephan rose from his chair and fell to the deck with a grunt. There was a sound like a pencil snapping.

Jens and Lassen thought Teal had fallen back into unconsciousness, but instead she spoke. "Fuck."

"Lassen," she continued. "You are now Acting Captain. Get us to Donut." He started to protest, but she cut him off.

"Jens, you are First Mate. Congratulations." She tried to laugh but concentrated instead on breathing. "I'll be too busy as lead medic ... trying to keep you lot ... alive ... to captain anything." She struggled to catch her breath.

"Ed," she called. "Get the medkit. Stephan broke something."

"My leg," Stephan said from the floor.

Teal knew it wouldn't be the last bone to snap. And bones would be the least of their worries. She glanced over to her now unusually quiet astrogator and saw that Suzie had blacked out as soon as she tried to rise from her chair. Increased blood pressure, internal organs under stress, nausea, fatigue, dizziness. Pressure sores. She would need everything from the medicine cabinet – cannabis, kava, and blue vervain for stress. Valerian, California poppy, and powdered reishi for sleep. Chai Hu Long and Gu Mu Li Tang for headaches. They'd all be crying for their 'gu mu' in no time. Cayenne capsules for circulation. That will be a big worry, keeping the blood flowing where it's needed.

"Get me up," she said. "Let's get Stephan to sickbay."

They levered her upright. "Thanks for saving my ship," she said. "I'll try to save you now." She stepped carefully to where Stephan lay, looking elderly as she slowly bent to join him on the floor.

Lassen followed each of the instructions Teal sent from sickbay. Watches were altered to an exhausting two hours on and two hours off, but duties were light and restricted to the bridge. Getting up for watch stopped blood pooling for too long, and they could spend the two hours off catnapping. They all began to resemble raccoons, with dark rings under their eyes. Bandages were turned into compression clothing. Blood thinners eased circulation. Ship life support provided higher levels of oxygen. Teal created a water pool crew could lay submerged in, breathing through a tube. She couldn't keep all their bones together. Or joints in place. Each of them wore a brace or sling of some sort. She issued GLR to reset the buttons on their nervous systems but rationed their dwindling supply.

Jens spent time during each of his watches studying the images prior to impact, as well as the video taken previously by Stephan outside. "There!" he said to those already tired of hearing. "The flare. It flickered, see?" *It flickered before it disappeared. They were trying to Decel. To do what? Board us? For what? Who were they? If they were trying to board the* Cirrus, *would others be at the Donut?* He slowed the images, and magnified until they became even more blurred than his vision, but couldn't find the answers he sought.

He took a drag from his vape pipe, which only slightly dulled the pain in his head. He looked at his watch, and his frown deepened. The varicose veins in Suzie's calves strained against the compression socks Teal printed for her. He knew how sensitive Suzie was about her legs. She would be scarred after this, if they made it. Jens tried to smile when she glanced over, though the dark rings under her eyes made him want to frown. But he was Officer of the Watch, and he had to set the example. He forced himself to stand, listening to every ache in every joint. His knee brace at least held the joint together. His lower back screamed in protest. He carefully made his way to the thermos Teal brought them, an awful and smelly concoction, the contents of which was better left a mystery. He poured three cups and brought them, one at a time, to his watch.

Ed looked at him as he sat the cup down on the console. Jens wasn't sure if it was thanks or resentment. A cup was, after all, something to lift.

"Almost there, buddy," Jens said.

Ed didn't respond. Jens made his way to Stephan. Teal had rigged a wheeled board to take his weight. Standing was out of the question with a fractured fibula. He dragged himself around the deck, lately with his left arm after a spill caused a fracture on his right. He insisted on maintaining watch, even though there was very little to see. He smiled at Jens, no doubt blissed out on the quantity of THC Teal prescribed him.

"Let me know if you see anything," Jens told him.

Stephan giggled.

Suzie placed her hand on Jens as he set the cup down. The fiber cast on her hand pressed into his flesh like a horse stepping on a foot. He had never had a horse step on his foot, but he guessed how it might feel. He smiled at her.

"Thank you, love," she said. She was on the verge of tears again.

Jens lifted her hand off of his and held it with the other.

"As soon as we're off watch," he said. "You're in the tank." He knew she would protest, claim she was okay, play the martyr. He knew she would unwittingly kill herself that way if he let her.

"I'll join you," he said. "I've been dreaming about that sexy body of yours. We can both get wet."

"Okay," she said. "But no sexy. Just floaty."

"Almost there, Suzie," he said. "We're gonna make it."

He almost believed it.

The time finally came when Lassen cut the reactor, and the weight on their bodies disappeared. Moments later a gentler gravity kicked in. They rose against their safety straps, exhaling and moaning in release, and then sank lightly back into their chairs before their bodies could go into shock from the sudden release from the pressure they had been under. Teal had given adrenalin pens' to Lassen and Jens before shut down, hoping they would stay conscious to use them on any crew who might need a jab. Jens clambered from his chair and pushed one into her thigh. Her eyes shot open, a panicked look on her face.

"Welcome back," he said. He stroked her face. "We're here. You did it. Thanks for saving your crew."

Lassen stood next to Baldy, patting his shoulder. An EpiPen stuck out of Baldy's thigh. His eyes looked as confused as his heart no doubt was. The Donut flickered on the screen, the jury-rigged camera link working, to a degree. Jens had to look up the term to remind himself of the meaning, as well as settle a bet with Lassen. Jury-rigged was makeshift and temporary. Jerry-rigged was cheap or flimsily built, slapped together by people who didn't know how, or didn't give a shit, to fix things properly. Jens spent enough time at sea to know the difference in practice. He doubted Lassen would ever produce the bottle of vodka he bet. Lassen navigated the freighter to its berth, guiding her slowly down and securing all clamps. They were in time for Step.

Suzie stood up, wincing. Jens moved towards her, but she held up a palm.

"I've got a ride to catch," she said.

He didn't try to argue. They had argued enough. You're not fit for it. You need to rest. You are injured. She would hear none of it. She hadn't missed a Step yet, and she wasn't going to shirk this one. It was her job, the only reason she was out here, she would fire back.

Jens supported her as she walked to the loading bay. He stopped when they were halfway there. "Let me at least give you this," he said. He and Teal had discussed this earlier. Suzie's stubbornness, and how to protect her from herself. Jens argued for a sedative, but Teal knew her astrogator better.

"It will perk you up," he said. "Give you some energy. So you can do your job." He showed her the hypodermic injector. "It's from Teal."

"Stimulant?"

"None but the best for our Donut Hole," Jens answered.

"Go on then," she said.

Jens stabbed it into her thigh, and her eyes widened. She shook her head. She still looked like death walking, but with a lighter step.

"Come on then," she said, continuing down the corridor. "Thanks."

Jens limped after her to the loading bay. The tender from the *Sunrise* was waiting. Jie sat inside, unseen, having left the co-pilot seat to Suzie. Louie waved from the pilot seat, his smile frozen as he saw the state of the pair. As the inner door opened, Herschel stepped out. He stood in front of Jens and Suzie, mouth open. Jens ignored him for the moment.

"Be careful," he said. "I'll see you on the other side."

Her mind was moving too fast to be sentimental. She kissed Jens and headed for the tender without saying goodbye. The door sealed behind her as she boarded the tender.

"What the hell?" Herschel said. He touched Jens' arm and pulled back when Jens flinched in pain.

"Good to see you, man," Jens said. "You're just what the doctor ordered." Jens laughed. "Literally."

"You got that right," Herschel said. "Teal said my coming back was non-negotiable." He continued to stare at Jens. "Comms said you guys had it rough, but I had no idea it was this bad." He pointed out the window as the tender left the bay. "How is she even walking?"

"Stims," Jens said. "Very powerful stims."

"And you? How are you still standing?"

"Adrenalin from a pen," Jens confessed. "And I'm running out." Jens pulled a second injector from his pocket and stabbed it into his thigh. "That's better." He shook his head. "Come on. We need to get to the bridge for Step. You're going to have to make sure we do what we're supposed to."

"What happened here..." Herschel's words trailed off as he followed Jens. He stepped over discarded bandages, fiber casts, empty food packages. The usually clinically clean walls were stained with body grease. At least, he hoped that was all it was. The inside of the ship looked as bad the outside he flew over.

"Fuck me," he said as he entered.

Stephan was already strapped into his seat and near unconscious. His casted leg was secured to his chair and his arm strapped to his chest. Baldy wore a brace to support his neck and what looked like a woman's corset. Teal had broken into her private collection to find support for her crewman's herniated disc. Lassen sat at the helm, slumped to one side. Ed's mouth hung open, head tilted back and his eyes gazing upward at nothing. Or at everything. Teal had clearly given them their dose of GLR to see them through the Step.

"Herschel," Teal said. "Welcome back. I'm really glad you're here."

"If I knew what ..." *If I knew what shape you were in, you wouldn't have had to order me back,* Herschel thought. "I'm here now, just tell me what to do." He looked at her hunched shoulders and deep-set eyes. The month under Decel added years to her tired face.

"I'm going to sit down now," she said. She took a white pill from her pocket and held it in front of her mouth. "Strap me in, okay? Then just look over us." She put the pill in her mouth as she fell back into her chair. She smiled absently at him as he secured her.

"Welcome home," Jens said as he sat down. "Did she have one of those for me?"

Herschel put his hand in Teal's pocket and pulled out another white pill. He handed it to Jens, who held it reverently. Jens smiled. He closed his hand around the pill and clenched his jaw as lights began to flash. Two red followed by a long yellow. The alarm sounded short blasts. He didn't have to count them to know what it meant.

"Sit down, Herschel," Jens said.

"What is it?" Herschel asked as he strapped himself in.

"Step. And something else. I can't remember that sequence of lights. Shit." Jens hit a comms switch connecting the bridge to the Donut Hole. "Guys, what's going on?" he said.

Screams from the comms filled the bridge. Shouting, too distorted to make out words. A crash, the sound of metal on metal, of metal breaking. The sound of flesh on metal, a dull wet smack. Screams. Male shouts. Female cries. *Suzie!*

Sound cut out as they sank into the gravity well. Jens felt his insides pulled down while his head and shoulders stretched upward as the convoy moved from Point A to a Point B, light-years away.

14

Flashing light illuminated the bridge. Two yellow flashes, followed by one green, followed by a long red. Jens shook his head, trying to register the message. *Yellow was bad*, he remembered. *Yellow was very bad*. The alarm was sounding. Two short, pause, one short, one long. *These signals are way too complicated,* he thought.

He shook his head again. There was a voice in the alarm. A loud, insistent voice, trying to tell him something.

"Emergency detachment in progress! Emergency detachment in progress!"

He unclipped from his chair and ran over to the helm. Lassen was immobile, a peaceful look on his face. Jens tried to read the data. The freighter was no longer secured to the Donut. It drifted in a slow spin. Jens used docking thrusters to correct the movement and stop the *Cirrus* from drifting farther away. He turned around to get Herschel and bumped into him.

"What the hell is going on?" Herschel asked.

"Just what it says!" Jens said. He tried turning on the outer feed and the Donut filled the screen. A freighter span slowly away from the disc.

"The *Ryk*," Herschel said. "Why is she drifting?"

Jens turned off the alarm and opened the link. "Suzie, what's happening?"

There was silence on the other end.

"Donut Hole, respond!" he shouted into the mic. "Suzie, respond!"

"This is *Sunrise Blossom* to *Cirrus*." Wan's voice cut in. Jens reflexively took a deep breath, calming herself.

"*Cirrus* here," he replied.

"Get me Teal," Wan said.

"She's ...ah ...incapacitated," Jens said. He glanced at the crew on the bridge. "I'm ranking officer," he said.

"Communications with Donut are down. You're the closest," Wan said. "Are you in condition to investigate?"

Herschel nodded to Jens. "Yes," Jens said.

"Go over and see what happened. A tender from the *Calderón* is on its way to *Ryk*."

"We heard ... it sounded like fighting prior to Step," Jens said.

"We also heard," Wan said. "Go prepared. Now waste no more time. Leave your comms open to report. Wan out."

"He's rather abrupt," Herschel said.

"Wan is just direct," Jens said. "Cold as ice when needed. Prep the tender, and suit up," Jens answered. "Now!"

Herschel hurried out the hatch, leaving Jens alone on the bridge. He turned on an automatic stabilization program, opened a screen on the helm and left a brief report for Teal, or whoever would come back to this reality first. He projected it onto the screen: *Emergency detach. Cause unknown. Investigating Donut. Comms open. Jensen and Folkes.*

Herschel was waiting in the tender, his helmet placed beside him. A suit sat on the co-pilot chair. Jens struggled into it as Herschel piloted the tender out of the loading bay. They flew over the freighter, the damage from impact looking as bad as it did during his first inspection. Herschel whistled as they passed but said nothing. He pointed the tender towards the disc that filled their entire field of vision and initiated thrust.

They watched the *Ryk* drifting off their starboard. As its stern spun slowly by, they could see flashes from the aft airlock. Herschel magnified the view screen.

"Look!" he said. "On the deck. Somebody is out there!"

He magnified the screen again and they made out a suited figure making his way to the airlock. His progress looked painfully slow, but he was jumping from handhold to handhold, without a tether. He leaped closer to the airlock, and a flash struck the deck near him. He stood up straight and let go of the deck, floating away from the ship.

The tender from the *Calderón* approached from the other side, oblivious.

"*Calderón* tender, this is *Little Cloud*, over," Jens said.

"*Aye, Pequeno Nubio, hablar con nosotros.*"

"Explosion from aft airlock of *Ryk*," Jens said. "Man on deck in trouble. Advise caution, over."

"*Claro*, Jens. Thanks for the heads up." Jens recognized the voice. Mateo, a capable officer. "Out," he added.

"Flashes continue aft," he said into the comms. "That is not an accident. You have a man adrift!"

"*No vemos a nadie*," Mateo answered. "We're coming in for a closer look."

"*Ryk*," Jens said into the comms, adjusting frequency. "This is *Cirrus—Little Cloud*. What is your status?"

"*Zur Luftschleuse! Alles zu den armen! Die reactor!*"

"What is that?" Herschel asked.

"*Armen*—arms!" Jens said.

In the total silence of space, the airlock door blew outwards. Flashes came from inside the lock.

"They're being boarded. That has to be a boarding!" Jens said.

"Do you want me to take us over?" Herschel asked.

Jens placed his hand on Herschel's, stopping him. He waited as seconds passed. Mateo maneuvered his tender closer to the *Ryk*. Then it disappeared as a blinding white flash engulfed it. Herschel and Jens shielded their eyes. The flash grew until *Little Cloud* was buffeted in the shock wave, spinning off course. Herschel grabbed the controls and stabilized the tender. Pieces of the *Ryk* floated off into space.

"Wan! Did you see that?" Jens called.

"Through your view screen, yes," he answered. "Proceed to Donut. With caution."

"The *Ryk* is gone," Jens said.

"Proceed to Donut, Jens," Wan replied. "You are needed there. Proceed with extreme caution."

"What does he mean, extreme caution? What the hell does that mean?" Herschel asked.

"Just what it sounds like," Jens said. "Take us in and keep your eyes open." Jens patted the pocket containing his sounder. He fingered the knife strapped to the outside of his suit.

Herschel exhaled slowly, taking the tender to the rim of the Donut. All of the docking bays were empty. He started to descend near the entrance to the Hole.

"Not yet," Jens said. "Let's look at some others."

They lifted several hundred meters above the docking bay and followed the curve of the rim.

"There!" Jens pointed to a docking bay left by the Hat Pin convoy. Only it wasn't empty. "Put us down next to that."

"What the ...?" Herschel guided the tender into the bay. The stars were lost to sight as they descended between the walls designed to hold a freighter. Occupying the bottom of the docking bay was a cylindrical vessel, smaller than the type of ship the bay was designed for, but filling at least half of the space.

"Investigate," Wan ordered over the comms.

Jens put his helmet on as the tender's magnetic clamps held onto the deck of the Donut. Herschel opened the tender hatches. They climbed out, turning on their boots as they touched the deck. Jens took the sounder out of his pocket and held it at the ready. He waved it towards the craft.

"Let's go," he said.

They approached the ship. Its metallic surface was scratched and dented, cratered with pockmarks. The metal appeared tarnished, even burnt.

"Are you seeing this?" Jens asked.

"We are seeing through your helmet camera," Wan said. "Resolution is poor. The docking bay is causing interference. Report."

Jens reached out and slowly touched the side of the vessel. "It looks old, like it's been out here a very long time. There is damage to the outer hull. Scratches. Marks from impacts—"

"Type of ship?" Wan cut in.

"I don't know," Jens said. "Herschel? Have you seen anything like this?"

"No," Herschel said.

"Report, Jens."

"It looks like a transport, but more ... I don't know. More advanced. More ... this thing is really old." Jens let his commentary trail off. Herschel gestured to him, pointing to a shadow on the port hull. An entrance.

"We're entering the ship," Jens said. He took a position in front of Herschel, letting his sounder lead the way. The spotlight in his helmet illuminated a dark passage, the rounded walls of a deserted corridor. He climbed through the doorway and helped Herschel board the craft.

"Did you feel that?" Herschel asked.

"Yeah," Jens said.

"Keep talking, Jens," Wan said into his ear. "Visibility is greatly reduced."

"We entered the ship," Jens said. "We have just walked through what felt like a pressure field, a force-field of some sort. It may be the airlock. We are proceeding down a corridor. There is a room at the end."

"Increase your luminosity," Wan said. "That's better. Proceed."

"Sir, we should be in the Hole," Jens said. "We—"

"You must know what may be in the Hole first, Jens," Wan said. "You know that. Patience and preparation."

"Yes, sir," Jens said. "The room appears empty. There are containers in the room. Eight. They have hatches that are open. Six of them do. Two are closed. They appear empty."

"No, they don't," Herschel said.

Jens peered through the clear glass that formed a lid. "I don't see anything," he said.

"Look!" Herschel said. "Wan, can you see this?"

"We see nothing," Wan said.

"There," Herschel pointed at the glass. "It's hard to focus. They seem to fade in and out. Try looking out of the corner of your eyes. Bones. With cloth. Old cloth. Something is inside. Something dead." He walked to the other closed container. "There! Another one," he said.

Jens peered into the container. "I don't see anything," he said. "This ship is empty, which means the Hole isn't. We're going there now."

"Then proceed," Wan said.

"Those things didn't look human, Jens," Herschel said as they made their way out of the ship.

Herschel sealed the tender and took it out of the docking bay. He applied thrust towards the entrance of the Donut, flipped and decelerated. He lowered the tender immediately in front of the elevator. They disembarked, paused a moment in front of the doorway, then cycled it open. Jens knelt before the inner door, sounder pointing towards it. Herschel pushed himself against the bulkhead as the seal released and the door slowly opened, feeling exposed, naked and very unarmed.

The entrance was empty. Jens turned off his boots once through the airlock and slipped out of his suit. He hung it up next to the eight already there. Jens strapped his knife to his thigh and detached the lens from his helmet, strapping it to his head like a flashlight. He pinned the comms onto his flight suit.

Jens kept the sounder in his hand. "Clear in here," he said at the elevator entrance, waving his weapon. Herschel hurried over.

"We're going down," Jens reported into the comms. "Do you have a weapon?" he asked Herschel.

Herschel held his hands palm up in lieu of an answer.

"Control room," he said to the elevator. The doors closed, and the compartment descended.

"Stop!" Herschel said. The elevator stopped moving. "We're defenseless in here. We don't even know who or what is waiting."

"We're not defenseless," Jens said. "And we're not trapped if we don't stay in here." He pointed to the back wall of the elevator and pointed towards the door. "You're not going to like this, but I need you to do it. The door opens into the control room. It's a big space. There is a large oval table, which is the monitor, in the middle. I need you to run across the room towards the other side. Run fast and keep low. Once you're at the table, dive down and use it for shelter. I'll cover you from the doorway, and be right behind you with this." Jens showed Herschel the sounder.

"If anybody's in there, I'll see them before they see us," Jens said. "Ignore any sounds behind you. Keep running for the table."

"That's not a plan, Jens," Herschel said.

"Yes, it is," Jens said. "You surprise, I shoot."

"But there were six pods in that ship."

"I know, but they can't all be here. The *Ryk* was attacked, which has to account for some. And what hit the *Cirrus* might have been some others."

"Folkes, let Jens do his job," Wan interrupted.

Herschel crouched against the back wall of the elevator as it continued to descend, ready to run out, while Jens took his place by the door. The elevator stopped moving, Herschel ran into the control room as soon as the doors slid open. His foot hit something slippery on the deck and he staggered forward, sliding into a chair. He slipped and fell to the deck, eyes wide and mouth open. Herschel's hand pointed towards the end of the table.

"There!" Herschel shouted. "Shoot!"

Jens couldn't see anything. Herschel continued to point. Jens fired his sounder in the direction Herschel's finger indicated. A pulse resounded, hitting an unseen target. Jens knew the sound from practice with sounders at a lower charge. Flesh. He fired again.

Herschel staggered to his feet, covered in blood. He stared across the monitor and began to point, but Herschel's body was lifted off the deck. It flew through the control room until it slammed into the opposite bulkhead.

Jens fired his sounder over the table and scrambled out of the lift. He backed against a wall and fired again. The pulse hammered against the opposite wall and ricocheted into a chair. Jens heard a boot land on the deck, followed by another. He ran across the deck towards a resting quarter, slipping and falling into the room. He rolled across the floor until his back hit a bunk. He heard steps coming closer, until they came into the room.

"Doors close!" he shouted, and the doors of the room slid shut.

Jens fired his sounder, again and again, as he curled into a ball on the floor. He buried his head in his arms with only the sounder pointing outward and pressed the trigger until the magazine was empty.

Pulses of sound ricocheted off the walls. Jens felt pain shoot up his leg as his foot was hit. He reached down and took out his knife, clutching it tightly. At the sound of the last impact, he stood up and slashed in a circle. He stepped forward, and his foot gave way. He fell forward and landed on a body. Jens brought the knife up and down, not seeing what it hit, but feeling it pierce flesh and slide between ribs.

The recognition made him push away from his target. He looked down at his hand holding the knife, coated in dark red blood that ran down his wrist. The deck in front of him was covered in a faint haze. He reached out a hand and touched a body that he couldn't see. He smeared his hand against it and an outline of a face appeared.

Jens pulled himself up using a bunk. He tried to put weight on his foot, and it held. Limping forward, he stood in front of the door. He gripped his knife tightly.

"Open door," he said.

The door slid open. Jens readied himself for the attack, but none came.

Herschel lay slumped against a wall, covered in blood. Jens limped towards him, knelt and saw that he was still breathing. He quickly checked for wounds but could see none. The deck around him was coated in blood that wasn't his. Jens' eyes scanned the room, and only then took in the carnage.

A woman's body lay face down under the table. Her black hair was matted with blood, a thick part showing bare skull. He had met her only once before, during the last Step. It was Ma Yun from the *General Xing*. A man slumped over a seat at the end of the table. His head hung limply to the side. A wide gash revealed the bones of his vertebra. Jens couldn't see his face but knew by his blond hair that it was Anton from the *Ryk*. Jens limped over to a body lying against the opposite wall. He knelt and gently touched the man's head, stroking his hair. He touched the man's neck, the cooling flesh telling him what he already knew. Jie was dead.

Jens felt a storm building within. He stood and took in more of the scene. Kawai Joe leaned against a bulkhead, his dead eyes wide open and staring at nothing. Chuck Young from the

Plymouth lay on his back nearby. Blood coated the floor and streaked the walls. He scanned the room again, looking for the others, for Suzie.

A movement caught his attention, and he stood, peering at a space in the floor. The blood on the floor seemed to move. Jens stepped over the body of Luciana from the *Calderón*, oblivious to the pain in his foot. He reached down when he was above the smear and felt a body. It moved away from his hand, but he gripped it. With his other hand, he brought his knife down. He heard a gasp, air being expelled. He pulled his arm back and stabbed down again. Jens pulled the blade up another time and felt his wrist grabbed. He swiveled and slashed backward. Herschel crawled backward, clutching his forearm.

"Easy man! It's me!"

Jens blinked at him. His gaze shifted from his frightened friend to his blood-soaked hand to the invisible form beneath him.

"Jens! Snap out of it!" Herschel still looked scared of him. "He's dead. You fucking killed him. It. Whatever it is."

Jens looked up and saw Herschel for the first time.

"Slow your breath, man, do whatever you do," Herschel said. "But we have a lot to deal with now, and I need you." He lifted his hand and looked at the cut on his arm, quickly wrapping his hand around his wound again.

"Where's Suzie?" Jens asked.

"I don't know," Herschel answered. "I don't see her. Jens, Wan is trying to call us."

He heard a muffled and broken voice in the resting quarters. Jens looked at where his comms used to be. All he could see was bloodstained flight suit.

"I have to find Suzie."

Herschel pushed himself up using the wall for support. "Okay," he said. "Let's go."

Jens scanned the room. He limped from resting quarter to resting quarter until reaching the only one with closed doors. He gripped the handle of his knife. His fingers felt sticky. He breathed in slowly and exhaled.

"Door open," he said.

The door slid open to a darkened room. Jens peered inside, crouched and ready. He heard movement, heavy breathing, a gasp. He readied himself for the attack.

"Lights on," he said.

Jens leaped into the room, blade first. He lunged towards a movement to his left, sliced downward, and stopped. Two terrified faces stared up at him. Suzie and Lena held each other, backed against the farthest bunk from the door. They screamed at the bloodied monster confronting them.

Jens' foot gave out, and he fell to his knees. He dropped his knife. The women screamed again. Herschel came up behind Jens and slowly placed a hand on his shoulder.

"You're safe now," he said. "It's Herschel. And Jens."

Herschel patted Jens' shoulder. "Take your flight suit off, buddy."

Jens turned a confused and blood-covered face towards Herschel. Tears had carved two canyons through the mess on his face. Herschel knelt and held Jens' head between his hands. "It's okay," he told him. "You did it. Suzie is safe. Now we still need you. Take off your flight suit. You're scaring the girls. Here."

Herschel carefully reached towards Jens' neck and pulled down the zipper of his suit. "That's good, mate," he coaxed. "Let's get you out of this thing."

Jens let him pull the soiled garment over his shoulders and down to his waist. "I need you to stand up now," he said. "Good, just like that." Herschel pulled Jens' flight suit off and used it to wipe his friend's face. He spat into his palm and cleaned it like his mother did when he was much younger.

Herschel stepped back and looked into Jens' vacant eyes. He pulled back a hand and slapped him across his stained face. Jens blinked. Herschel pulled back his hand and slapped him again, but Jens staggered back with his hands up.

"Stop it!" he begged. "Stop it!"

"Are you back?" Herschel asked.

"Yeah, I'm back," Jens lied. He looked at the two women clutching each other on the deck. Jens limped towards them and knelt in front of their terrified forms. He touched Suzie, and she flinched away.

"It's okay," he said, repeating something he heard somewhere. "You're safe now." He tried to touch Suzie again, and she shrunk into herself.

"Jens," Herschel said. "We have to let Wan know what's happening." He held out the comms. It crackled faintly in his palm.

Jens stood and backed away from Suzie and Lena. Turning slowly, he took the comms from Herschel, turning the device over and inspecting it. He put it in his pocket.

"There's comms in the monitor," Jens said. "Try to get them up, we need to get them out of here."

Jens left the room, stepping carefully across to the central table. He sat in a chair and studied the monitor in front of him. Mathematical figures danced across the screen. He touched the top right corner.

"Calling Wan in the *Sunrise Blossom*," he said. "This is Jens."

"Jens, this is Wan. Report," Wan answered.

"The Hole is secure," Jens said.

"Can you provide a visual?" Wan asked.

"No," Jens said. "No visual. We have two for urgent medical. We're returning to *Cirrus*."

"Wu Pen and Zhang are *en route*," Wan said. "They will relieve you and the others."

"There are no others," Jens said. "They're dead. All of them. I'm returning to the *Cirrus* with Suzie and Lena."

"Remain where you are until relieved," Wan repeated.

Herschel placed a hand over Jens'. "We'll be here," Herschel said to Wan. "The Hole was attacked by ... we don't know who they were. They're dead now. Jens killed whatever was in here."

"And how is Mr Jensen?" Wan asked.

"He'll be okay," Herschel said.

"Where are the astrogators, Mr Folkes?" Wan asked.

"They're dead. They're all dead. It's a mess in here," Herschel said. "We found astrogators Suzie Reynolds and Lena McGee hiding in a room. They're—"

"They're in pretty bad shape, sir," Jens interrupted.

"Injured?"

"More like traumatized," Jens said. "We need a med team."

"Wu Pen and Zhang are listening," Wan said. "They will arrive prepared."

"No," Jens said. "They won't be prepared. And they're not a med team."

"Mr Jensen," Wan said, "you are needed now. Focus. Tell me, what are the five cardinal virtues?"

Jens took a deep breath before answering. "You don't have to test me. I can do my job."

"Good," Wan said. "There is much do. There will be time to process later. After Wu Pen and Zhang relieve you, take Ms Reynolds and Ms McGee to the *Cirrus*. Teal will prepare for their arrival and see to their medical needs. Then come to the *Sunrise*."

"Lassen won't like me leaving the *Cirrus* again—"

"Lassen is Acting Captain. I outrank him. Follow my instructions. You have a lot to catch up on," Wan said.

"Mr Folkes," he added. "Assist Wu Pen and Zhang."

"No," Jens said. "I need Herschel to help get these two to the *Cirrus*. I can't do it without him. And I'll be over when I am certain the *Cirrus* is okay to leave."

There was a moment of silence. "Very well," Wan said.

Jens got up from the chair and started to walk towards the room where Suzie and Lena still hid.

"Jens," Herschel said. "Find somewhere to wash. You'll just scare them even more if you go in like that."

Jens looked at his stained hands and went to another resting quarter. He didn't recognize the face in the mirror under its mask of red. Most of it discolored the sink when he had finished. He entered the room where the astrogators still hid. Suzie had moved only to pick up Jens' knife, and held it firmly in her hand. She looked through him with wide and terrified eyes. Jens stood by the doorway and made a few reassuring comments, before returning to the control room. He made his way over to Jie's body, knelt and closed his friend's eyes. He moved Jie's hands so that they rested on his chest.

"Come over here, Jens," Herschel was kneeling over a figure on the floor on the other side of the room. His hands were moving over a form Jens couldn't see.

"See, they aren't too different from us," he said. "Two eyes, a nose, a mouth. But the resemblance stops there."

"Why can't I see anything?" Jens asked.

"I have no idea," Herschel said. "It's hard to focus on them. If I try to look directly at them, they seem to disappear. Try looking, but not at them. Let them go a bit blurry."

"Still nothing," Jens said. "Maybe a bit of a blur. Faint outline. He was tall."

"Maybe two and a half meters," Herschel agreed. "Ugly. Long narrow face. Chin looks like a pick-ax." Herschel's hands moved over the body. "This is an alien, man. What the hell did they want?"

15

Jens lifted the tender out of the docking bay and saw it for the first time. The sun that meant energy for the Donut for its next Step was not the blinding mass of erupting gasses filling their view screen, but merely a bright star in the distance. The screen was not even polarized. The sun was too far away. Much too far away.

Jens directed the tender to the *Cirrus* and froze. A planet filled the view screen. Not a sunbaked rock that they would typically shelter behind while the Donut charged, or a lifeless colony world. This planet had an atmosphere. Clouds swirled high above what looked like a blue ocean, surrounding archipelagos of hundreds of islands. It resembled no place he had heard or read about.

Suzie sat in the co-pilot chair, staring vacantly at the console, gripping the knife in her gloved hand. Jens glanced behind at Lena, seated beside Herschel. She looked back with vacant eyes, not seeing him. Jens brought the tender closer to the *Cirrus*, piloting it into the ship's docking bay. Teal and Stephan were waiting. Teal touched Suzie's face, stroking her cheek with the back of her hand.

"Why does she have your knife?" Teal asked Jens.

"It makes her feel safer, I think," Jens said.

Teal helped the younger woman out of her suit, and gently put her arm around Suzie's shoulders. Jens and Herschel helped them limp to the sickbay, where Teal coaxed Suzie onto a bed. Stephan and Herschel laid Lena on the bed next to her. Teal prepared a damp cloth and moving very slowly wiped Suzie's face, passing the cloth over her nose and mouth. Suzie's eyes closed, and her body relaxed. Her hand let go of the knife, and Jens caught it before it fell off the bed. Teal turned to Lena and gently wiped the other woman's face, pausing over her nose and mouth.

As soon as Lena went limp Teal deposited the cloth in a disposal chute and washed her hands. She prepared a saline solution and hung it on the stands Stephan had moved into place. Inserting a cannula into each of their hands, she opened the valve that let the fluid into their bodies.

"What are you doing?" Jens asked.

"Buying time," Teal said. "They're in shock. I let them go to a better place until we're able to care for them."

"A better place?"

Teal gestured to the bag containing the saline. "Micro-dosing of GLR," she said. "They'll sit on the edge of a universe of love for now. I think that's a much better place, don't you?"

"Yeah," Jens said. "It sounds a lot better."

"What happened to them?" Teal asked.

"Not now, okay?" Jens asked. "I don't think I can go there again."

Teal nodded.

He returned to his quarters to wash and change before flying the tender to the *Sunrise*. He put on his grey suit. He looked at his knife lying on his bunk. He delicately lifted it and put it in the pocket of his jacket.

Wan gestured towards the screen when Jens entered the bridge.

"Magnify," he said. The planet grew larger. "Magnify," he said again.

Jens gazed at a large island, covered in green.

"That's not rock," Jens said.

"It most certainly is not," Wan said.

"It's alive?"

"It most certainly is." Wan sat in his chair and motioned Jens to take the one next to it.

"Where are we?" Jens asked.

"We are getting a better fix. First estimates seemed too outrageous. Ten thousand light-years. Give or take a few," Wan said. "We are not here by accident."

"No," Jens said. "That was no accident."

"Wu Pen has filled me in," Wan said. "The computer in the Hole was hacked. Somehow. We think they tried to take over the *Ryk* as well."

"And tried to board the *Cirrus*," Jens said.

"That appears more likely now. You have seen Genjo, and he has given you what you need?" Wan asked.

"I did. He did," Jens said. "I have been numbed. And he says I'll be awake for a while more."

"There will be time to process later. I promise you that."

"I don't know if I look forward to that," Jens said.

Wan laid his hand on Jens' shoulder and squeezed it for a moment.

"Look." Wan pointed to the monitor. "Magnify," he said. The island grew. "What does that look like to you?" he asked.

Jens studied a valley on the island, dense jungle following straight contours. "Ruins?" he said.

"We think so," Wan said. "Most of the larger islands show similar signs. Ancient cities. There was definitely a population here at some time. Colonists from the *Xing* are surveying the surface, seeing if anybody is home. There has been no response to any of our attempts to communicate. It certainly looks empty." Wan leaned back. "You said the beds in their ship looked like some kind of cryo-chamber?"

"I've only seen them in science fiction movies."

"And it looked old?"

"Very old. You saw the vid link."

"I am just trying to figure out the puzzle," Wan said. "They hi-jack a Donut, try to board a fuel transport and a medical ship. Maybe that's what they were sent out to find. If they were from here. Whoever they were. Wherever we are."

Jens shifted in his chair. "You wanted me here. Why?"

"We will hold *shou ling* for Jie. You will like to be a part of this," Wan said. "You will take a shift watching over him."

"Thank you," Jens said.

"And events need to be managed before they get out of hand. They are already starting to unravel. I do not think the Colonists on the *General Xing* will leave this planet. They've secured the Donut. A team arrived shortly after you left. They've already boarded the *Calderón* and taken control of the fliers. Alvarez has been confined to his quarters. As you can imagine, he is not very happy about that. I need you to go over and stabilize the situation. It is very delicate at the moment."

Jens waited.

"The Colonists are in negotiations with the *Cooper*. They argue that the cargo is theirs, whether they are at *Sukhavati* or here. And after seeing this place, that cold rock does not appeal to them anymore."

"And the *Plymouth?*" Jens asked. Seed and fertilizer from the *Cooper*, building supplies and prefabs from the *Avarua*, fliers and technology from the *Calderón*. Machinery carried by the *Plymouth* would be next.

"If they do not agree, you'll find a way," he said. "And we'll need Herschel to go to the *Avarua* and negotiate," Wan continued.

"You don't sound like you are going to go anywhere either," Jens said.

"The colonists are forcing my hand. I intend to claim *Terra Nullius* on behalf of the Consortium," Wan said. "If it is uninhabited, then we will claim it. And all other Consortia will have to negotiate with us to participate in developing it."

"Can you do that?" Jens asked.

"Out here," Wan said. "I am the Consortium. In fact, on Earth, I am as well."

"If that's true, then what are you doing out here?"

"It pays to keep an eye on business, especially business partners, as you saw at Laika," Wan said. "And with this new venture—"

"GLR?"

"Yes," Wan said. "With GLR and all it promises, we needed to ensure all pieces and players were in place."

Wan waved a hand at the screen. "But this adds a whole new dimension. You still do not realize what it means, do you, Mr Jensen?"

"I'm obviously missing something," Jens said.

"This means, Mr Jensen, that you are now a ridiculously wealthy and powerful individual," Wan said. "The Consortium will claim its rightly share of fifty-one percent. The remainder falls to those who discover and settle it. That's why the colonists are so excited. You don't look very excited, Mr Jensen."

"I think what Genjo gave was a little too strong to let me feel excitement," Jens said. "And I've had a pretty shitty few days."

"You have done well," Wan said. "There is one more thing I have to ask."

"Go on," Jens said.

"It appears that Captain Hui Yin has abandoned his command and is joining his cargo in exploring the planet," Wan said. "Most, if not all, of the crew have joined him. After two years in that box I don't fault the colonists, but Hui Yin ... well, it means somebody needs to assess the situation and take charge of the *Xing*. It is probably rather chaotic over there at the moment."

Jens took off his atmosphere suit and made a show of dusting off his tailored grey suit, pretending to stroke out non-existent wrinkles in the fabric and ignoring the action around him. Once the docking bay airlock was secured, colonists continued loading the tenders in the bay. He was sure the port docking bay was similarly busy.

Jens slowly took his knife out of his jacket pocket, studied the blood on the sheath, and strapped it onto his thigh. Pure drama. It had the desired effect. The colonist sent to greet his tender stepped back.

"*Take me to Alvarez,*" he said in Mandarin.

"*I am to confine you to—*" the colonist stammered. The young man's hand was shaking. Jens took advantage of his fear.

"*You know who I am, and what I want,*" Jens said. "*Take me to Alvarez. Now.*"

"*Yes, sir, Mr Jensen,*" he said.

The loading bay went quiet as Jens spoke, and remained that way until he had left. The young man led Jens down several corridors until reaching the Captain's quarters. He opened the door, and Jens entered. Turning around, he said, "Wait outside," and closed the door in the colonist's face.

"You look like shit, Jensen," Alvarez said.

"I feel like shit," Jens said. "*Mierda*, isn't it?"

"It is. *Mierda* describes much at the moment," Alvarez said.

"I am sorry about Luciana," Jens offered. "And Mateo and Bayardo."

"And you killed the thing that killed her?" he asked.

"I did," Jens said. "Both of them. With this." Jens touched the knife on his leg.

"Then I owe you," Alvarez said.

"A drink will do." Jens sat down on the nearest chair, soft and made of real leather.

Alvarez nodded, took a bottle of wine from a cupboard, and poured two glasses. He handed one to Jens. They took a sip at the same time.

"So, your lot have taken my ship," Alvarez said, "and are no doubt busy ransacking it at the moment. Why, if I may now ask, are you here, Mr Jensen?"

"They're not my lot," Jens said. "They're a little over-excited at their good fortune, and a little out of control. Wan has sent me to calm the situation."

"And yet my remaining crew are held hostage while my holds are emptied," Alvarez said.

"The colonists feel they have paid for the goods, and want to collect them," Jens said.

"Those 'goods' are for the colony on *Sukhavati*. We are not at *Sukhavati*."

Jens took a sip of his wine. "No, we're not," he said. "You've seen where we are, and you know what that means. Your cargo is paid for. You and your crew are now shareholders in the only known habitable planet outside of Earth."

"My crew are prisoners," Alvarez said.

"They will be released," Jens said.

"And this planet is worth nothing if Earth is not aware of us."

"True," Jens said. "Some of us will have to go back and tell them about what we found. To represent the new holding."

"So you are part of this rabble," Alvarez said.

"Just as much you are," Jens said. "Evidently, we're both now very wealthy men." Jens took another drink, enjoying the feeling of alcohol mixing with Genjo's meds. "Today you lose your cargo, but you keep your ship, and become rich beyond your wildest dreams."

"My ship?" Alvarez asked. "I am a prisoner."

"Not for long," Jens said. "I'll ensure that you are given back command."

Alvarez put his hands together as if in prayer and touched his lips. "I want my crew released and empowered to over-see removal and assembling of cargo," he said. "Immediately, so they can prevent these yokels from killing themselves or damaging equipment."

"Consider it done," Jens said.

"You seem rather confident in your abilities, Mr Jensen," Alvarez observed.

"Something about the clothes," Jens returned.

"No." Alvarez shook his head. "It's not your clothes." Alvarez picked up the bottle. "Another drink, Mr Jensen?"

Jens put a hand over his glass. "I'd better not," he said. "I have a couple of other stops to make." Jens rose from his chair and pounded on the door. It slid open, and he issued orders. The young man looked doubtful at first, but a glower from Jens sent him dashing up the corridor, leaving the door open. Jens turned and gestured to Alvarez.

"Captain," he said. "Your ship."

"*Gracias, Señor Jensen*," Alvarez responded.

Jens guided the tender towards the *Plymouth*. He let it drift slowly, taking in the scene. He was almost impressed with the colonists tactics. Almost. They had positioned a tender directly in front of the *Plymouth's* reactor. If the ship accelerated away to a safe distance, they would destroy the tender, and kill anyone crewing the small ship. Several colonists were attempting to enter the stern airlock. Jens watched as one worked at the hatch with metal tools, as he jerked violently and then floated limply away from the hull. Others tried to reach out to grab him but missed. They backed away from the airlock. Electrified. Clever defensive move on the part of *Plymouth's* crew.

Closing his helmet, Jens switched off life support in the tender. He manipulated thrusters to turn the craft side on to the colonists. *No different than a man overboard*, he thought. Put the body to windward and let it drift to the ship. Only there is no windward in space. Jens applied a light thrust and opened the portside door. Another small adjustment and the colonist floated inside. Jens pushed the man into the co-pilot seat and strapped him in. The vitals on his suit showed that he was still alive.

"*I'd stay away from the airlock*," Jens said in Mandarin.

"How is Li Wei?"

"Li Wei is alive," Jens said. *"Have you disabled the video links on the hull?"*

The delay in response told him that they hadn't, that they had no experience or plan for what they were doing and probably weren't even aware those in the *Plymouth* were watching their every move.

"I suggest you do that now," Jens said. *"And I'll need one man to accompany me. One that is conscious."*

"Who are you to give orders?" the same voice asked.

"That is Jensen," another said, trying to whisper over the open comms.

"You'll do," Jens said to the whisperer. *"I'm setting down now. Get those cameras covered. Do not damage anything."* Jens lowered the tender and saw helmeted faces looking up at him. *"Move!"* he said.

"Yes, Mr Jensen!" Jens recognized the first voice. Soon colonists were spreading over the hull.

Once the tender touched down, he opened the door. *"Take him out and secure him to the hull. And get in here,"* Jens said.

The colonists moved clumsily but got the job done. As soon as the whisperer was in the co-pilot chair, Jens lifted the tender and floated just above the hull until he was close to the bow. He applied a side thrust and drifted over the edge. A small blow from the compressed air of his top thruster brought them down the port side. He set the tender down and applied its magnetic lock.

He got out of the tender and walked to a circular hatch. On the *Sunrise* he was tasked with securing the ship in the case of a boarding. Part of that study was finding any and all possible entries. He was pleased that the *Plymouth* wasn't that different from the *Sunrise.* The emergency airlock was near where he expected it, its circular hatch probably never used, and hopefully not electrified.

"I'll need you to lift the cover plate and pull the lever to release the lock," Jens said. *"Clip on first."*

The colonist stood looking at Jens for a moment before tethering himself to the deck and reaching for the cover plate. He slowly reached out and jerked it open as quickly as could.

"Phew, not electrified," Jens said, *"That's good. As soon as we open the hatch, they'll be alerted. We won't have much time. We need to crawl in, close the hatch behind us and open the internal hatch as soon as we can. What is your name?"*

"Yuan," the colonist said.

"Yuan, good work," Jens said. *"We have to move fast now. We do not have much time."*

Jens slipped into the narrow chamber, turned and pulled Yuan in after him. As soon as Yuan closed the hatch and sealed it behind them, they crawled through the two-meter thick hull of the ship. At the end of the chamber, they squeezed past the waiting escape pod and opened the airlock behind it, gaining entrance into the ship. Jens stood upright, feeling gravity again. He helped Yuan out of the chamber and walked down a corridor, stopping at a cover plate on the bulkhead.

"Give me the tools," Jens said.

Yuan was quick to hand over the pouch. He watched as Jens pulled out a long screwdriver and pried open the panel.

"We just set off another alarm," Jens said. *"This will get their attention. See those wires?"*

Yuan nodded as Jens pointed the screwdriver at the clear wires inserted into what he thought was a relay switch.

"Those are a relay for their life support," Jens said. *"Whatever you do, do not severe them. Is that clear?"*

Yuan nodded again.

"Cut any other wires you want, but do not touch those," Jens said. *"All I want you to do is buy me some time. They'll come, and when they do, drop whatever you have in your hands, and raise your arms. Okay?"*

Another nod.

"And Yuan," Jens added. *"Don't take your helmet off. I am going to need you once we take care of the crew."*

Jens turned and hurried down another corridor, looking upward. He turned a corner and continued down it. Turning down another, he saw what he was looking for, or at least what he had hoped was there. It was another potential weak spot in the *Sunrise*, mirrored on the *Plymouth*. The air circulation system has intake valves, where a boarding party, so inclined, could poison the ship's air supply.

Jens pried off the system's protective covering and exposed the intake. He reached into the pocket of his suit and withdrew a small bag of finely ground powder, a parting gift from Paora, to use as Jens saw fit. Snorting. Mixing into a cake. Smoking. Creating a mist to inhale. Jens held the bag up to the vent and opened it. The bag soon emptied as the powder was sucked into the system. He carefully closed and secured the vent. Jens waited several minutes before returning to Yuan.

Yuan was standing by the opened panel where Jens had left him. At his feet lay two crew members from the *Plymouth*.

"They just lay down," Yuan said. *"I do not know why. Are they dead?"* he asked.

"They're fine," Jens said. *"They're better than fine. Come with me."*

Jens led Yuan towards the bridge. On the way, they passed two other crew, slumped against the wall. Kneeling, Jens could see they were breathing. He moved their bodies to make them more comfortable, knowing they were very far from the physical realm. Evans was slumped in the Captain's chair. Jens felt a tinge of guilt for usurping his command. But he would give it back, Jens silently promised. Jens accessed the ship's life support from Evans' monitor and purified the air. He used the comms to contact the boarding party waiting in the vacuum outside.

"The ship is now secured," Jens said, *"and you may board. You are to confine the crew to their quarters, but you must*

treat them with the utmost respect. If you do not, you will not only have me to deal with. Is that clear?"

"Yes, Mr Jensen." Jens recognized the voice of the colonist outside.

"And you are to treat the ship with similar respect. You will cause no damage whatsoever," he said.

"Yes, Mr Jensen."

Jens opened his helmet and looked at Yuan. The young man opened his helmet. Jens smiled.

"And one more thing," he said to the party outside. *"Yuan is now Acting Captain of the Plymouth. You will obey his orders as you would mine."*

Jens turned off the comms. *"Well done, son,"* he said. *"Evans will want his ship back in good condition when he regains consciousness, so make sure it is."*

"But I am not a Captain," Yuan said. *"I do not know what to do!"*

"You will do well," Jens said. *"You won't let me down. Wu Pen will be by to speak with Captain Evans. See that he is comfortable in his quarters. And make sure his ship is not damaged. Wan will thank you for your work."*

Jens patted the young man's shoulder before leaving him alone on the bridge.

Jens piloted the tender into an empty docking bay. He didn't have to radio for access—the door was left open by the colonists eager to board the *Plymouth* and confiscate its cargo. He exited the small craft and manually shut the outer lock. After the room pressurized, he took off his helmet and outer suit, stowing them in the rear of *Little Cloud.* His tailor-made suit was getting wrinkled, looking more and more like he felt. He uselessly smoothed the worse creases and ran a hand through his hair.

The inner lock opened, and Fran Lu entered, followed by a crew member dressed in his white uniform and looking even younger than she. They drew to a halt in front of him and saluted.

"Thank you for coming, Captain Jensen. Wan said you would come. We are very glad you are here," Fran Lu said. Her English was improving.

"I am sorry for your loss, Third Mate Lu," Jens answered in Mandarin. *"Ma Yun was a superb astrogator."*

"And she was a very dear friend," Fran Lu said, bowing. *"Thank you, Captain Jensen."* She gestured at the crewman next to her. *"I introduce Able Crewman Chen."*

Jens nodded towards the man. *"Chen."*

"Sir!" he said sharply, standing straight.

"At ease," Jens said. Captain, he thought. Wan's plan all along. Fran Lu didn't use the pre-fix 'acting'.

"Where is the remainder of the crew, and what is the current situation?" Jens asked.

"Able Crewman Shinje is on the bridge, keeping watch," Fran Lu said.

"And? Where are the others?"

"Able Crewman Shinje is on the bridge," she repeated. *"The others—"*

"I understand," Jens said. *"I think you have both been promoted. So, tell me, First Mate Lu, what is the current state of the ship?"*

"Sir, thank you," she said blushing. *"If you will follow, I will brief you as we go to the bridge."*

She led Jens through the lock, sealing it after her. They continued down the corridor until reaching the main hold. Jens scanned the area. Stalls stood empty; goods removed. There were more empty gaps in the once-bustling rows of stalls. He stepped forward and walked into the market, feeling like it was a winter day in his home town, rain and cold doing its seasonal job of chasing away the usual crowds. He followed a familiar smell.

"Why haven't you joined the others?" he asked the woman roasting cavy.

"There is plenty of time for that," she answered. *"And there is plenty of planet to go around from the images I've seen."* She wiped her hands on her apron and prepared a serving. *"Besides, people still have to eat. Here, Captain Jensen,"* she said, offering the meat. *"You look very hungry."*

Jens took the food and bowed. *"Thank you."*

"If it were not for vendors like Mrs Liu, many colonists would go hungry," Fran Lu said.

"They are behaving like excited children," Mrs Liu said. *"They journeyed with hope, but not expectation. Now they think they have found a world beyond any expectation."*

"Maybe they have," Jens said.

"The initial surveys are very favorable," Fran Lu agreed. *"Atmosphere, temperature, gravity near Earth."*

Jens took a bite of the cavy and chewed slowly. *"Who is tending the cavy?"* he asked Mrs Lui.

"Those ranchers!" she said. *"They wanted to leave the herd, pack up, and go. But I put some sense into them. At least a couple of them were too scared of a small woman to follow their worthless mates. They are tending the animals before they are shipped down. Everything is falling apart. I am so happy you are here to fix this."*

"Fix this," Jens said, closing his eyes.

Other colonists started to gather around, listening and murmuring in agreement. Jens heard the word 'Captain' again and looked around at expectant eyes. He bent to return a bow, placed a hand on his knee, and held on until the ship stopped spinning. He straightened himself and glanced at his First Mate.

Fran Lu briefly placed a hand on Jens' arm. *"Captain,"* she said, trying to be discreet in her concern. *"Let us go to the bridge where you can sit, and we may brief you."*

"Yes," Jens finally said. *"Yes. Thank you for the meal, Mrs Liu. Very delicious."*

"The Captain will address the ship after he has been briefed," Fran Lu said crisply. *"Now continue your activities."*

She led the way before the crowd grew any larger. As soon as they reached the bridge, she sat him in the chair that belonged to Hui Yin before he deserted his post.

"May I have some water?" he asked. As soon as Fran Lu returned, he placed the last of Genjo's pills on his tongue and swallowed. After a moment, he felt more alive. Fran Lu, Chen and the one he assumed was Shinje stood stiffly, waiting.

"Report," Jens said.

"All systems operational," Shinje said. *"We are in a stable orbit above the planet."*

"That seems to be the only thing that is stable," Jens said, immediately regretting it. *"Thank you, Officer of the Watch, Shinje. You have behaved commendably. You all have,"* he said, looking at each in turn. *"You have stayed at your post when that is what duty required,"* he added.

"First Mate Lu, what do you identify as the primary task of the crew?" he asked.

"Sir?" she asked.

"I am asking your opinion, First Mate Lu."

She shifted uncomfortably. *"We must calm the colonists,"* she said after a pause. *"They, too, must do their duty. Disembarkation must be as organized as it was planned for at* Sukhavati, *for their safety and the safety of the ship."*

"Well said," Jens agreed. *"Do you also concur?"* he asked Chen and Shinje.

They looked uncertainly at Fran Lu, who nodded slightly.

"Yes," they said.

"Good," Jens said, feeling the chemical energy strengthen his body. He didn't know how long that would last. *"So, we stop the colonists from packing up and demand they return to*

their quarters until an orderly process can be restored. There are lots of ways to achieve that. Ideas?" he asked.

The three looked at their feet, then around the bridge searching for the right answer. Hui Yin's leadership style was becoming apparent. Crew members weren't asked their opinion. Jens put them out of their misery.

"A disaster," he said. *"Something bad. Like a hull breach. Those are bad. What is out there shouldn't come in. What is in here shouldn't be made to go out there. Right? Have you ever been in a ship that has suffered a breach?"* he asked.

"No, sir," they said.

"Not a pleasant experience." He let them believe he had. *"Which is why we train for that eventuality. You have trained for breach, as part of your safety protocols?"*

"Captain Hui Yin did not prioritize such training," Fran Lu said.

Jens tried to hide his anger at his predecessor. *"But you know the protocol?"* he asked.

"Yes sir," Shinje said. Jens opened his hand towards the young man.

"In the case of a hull breach, the alarm will sound—"

"Be precise, Able Crewman Shinje. Color and sound?"

"Yes, sir," Shinje said. He cleared his throat. *"When the ship senses that its hull has been breached, or that a breach is imminent, the alarm will sound for a prolonged period of two seconds, repeated every two seconds. A red light will flash quickly."* Shinje's eyes darted to the left as he recalled the information. *"Quick flashing for a period of six seconds, repeated every three seconds. Ship's airlocks, inner and outer, will close and seal. Emergency bulkheads throughout the ship will close. All passages between decks will seal. Reinforced bulkheads will enclose the reactor, which will, if operating, begin shut down. All colonists are to assemble at the nearest muster station. Crew are to assess the situation and report all—"*

"That is enough," Jens said. *"Very good, indeed. That will do perfectly. Able Crewman Shinje, in addition to your other duties, you are now Ship's Safety Officer. I am sure you will take this responsibility with the utmost seriousness."* He continued, addressing all three crew. *"Now, it appears we are about to suffer a catastrophic mishap. During the period of the emergency, you are to follow the orders of Safety Officer Shinje as you would follow my orders. Once the situation has been contained, summon the leaders of the colonists to the mess hall where I will speak with them and give them the opportunity to behave in a more orderly manner. All other colonists are to remain confined in their muster stations until then."*

Jens watched as the three stood unmoving in front of him, like deer in headlights.

"Take some time," he said. *"Study the protocol and plan your action. You will do fine. I know you will. Begin the drill when you are ready. You have already proved your ability. Being here, on your ship, right now, you have proved your ability."*

They stood in their white uniforms, slight smiles forming on their faces. He noticed his crumpled clothes for the first time, and how out of place they were. This was neither the time nor place for silk or woollen suits.

"One thing though," he said. *"Can you please find me a uniform? I must be dressed suitably."*

"Yes, sir," Fran Lu said. *"It is on your bunk in the Captain's quarters. I guessed your size."*

"Thank you," Jens said.

He sat back in his chair as they left, and turned on the viewscreen. The new planet lay below him. He stared at the blue ocean dotted with islands, large and small, north and south of the equator. It would be a planet for sailors. He found familiar shapes in the islands as if he were viewing clouds from the deck of a ship floating below. A boot. A bull's head. A bitch suckling her pups. Jens smiled and pressed ship to ship comms.

"Teal, it's Jens, here on the *Xing*."

"Greetings, Captain," Teal said.

"Can we have visual?"

An image of Teal replaced the planet. She sat in her chair, trying to make a slump look like a recline. Her face was lined with exhaustion. Dark rings framed her eyes. Her back was hunched at the shoulders, the tension gathered at the base of her neck, forcing her head to bow.

"You look like shit, Jens," she said. "Seriously, I don't know how you are still conscious."

"It's better this way," Jens said. "I don't want to face what I'll see when I close my eyes."

"What did Genjo give you?"

"Something called Modafin or ... I can't remember the name. Stuff that works."

"That stuff will kill you, Jens," she said. "You're going to crash really hard. Don't take more than one."

"I don't care about that at the moment," Jens said.

"Please do," she said, trying to smile.

They sat staring at each other in silence as a minute passed.

"How is our girl?" he asked.

"She's fine, they're both fine, physically at least." Teal shifted uncomfortably. "They're still sedated. I experimented with reviving them, but it was too much for them. Deep trauma. They're better off where they are. I'll gradually reduce the dose."

"They're in good hands," Jens said.

Teal didn't look convinced.

"I'd like to have my hands on you," Jens said. "Do you know what I'd do, with my hands on you?" he asked.

Teal gave him a faint smile and shook her head.

"I'd rub those shoulders of yours. Knead those muscles and make them relax," he said. "I'd work my way all down your body, down your spine, and around your ass. Your ass would know real pleasure. Then I'd hit the top of those luscious thighs and knead my way down to the tips of your toes. No part will be spared."

Teal breathed out slowly in a way Jens knew well. "You've been well trained, Captain Jensen," she said.

The bridge filled with quickly flashing red light and an alarm sounding a prolonged blast of three seconds. Jens smiled.

"It seems our hull has been breached," he said. "I'm going to have to get ready to speak with the colonists. They'll soon figure out that I've locked them in until they can behave."

16

Jens woke to a scream that he knew was his own. And hands, shaking him.

"*Ma fan ni, chuan zhang, qi lai!*" The voice sounded frightened. Female. She spoke in a foreign language, but somehow Jens knew what it was. *Who* it was. He had asked her to do this.

"*Chuan zhang, qi lai!*"

The dream was not the same. He was on the scow, sure, but it wasn't at sea. It was in open space, buffeted by non-existent winds and waves. He wore a spacesuit but had no helmet. His eyes didn't freeze or implode. They stared ahead at the creature he held by a fist full of oxygen cables. Skipper got ugly. His face was elongated. His chin pointy and mouth a small beak-like and terrifying opening.

Jens hated the creature. He hated it in a way that knew no redemption. His hate came from every injustice and jealousy, and inadequacy, and ... He hated it all. He held his knife in his hand, cold Japanese steel handcrafted by a master who traced his lineage back to Gorō Nyūdō Masamune, Japan's greatest swordsmith. The maker of Jens' knife won the Masamune prize. Not for this knife, but that didn't matter. What he held in hand, what was gifted him by Wan, was worth a fortune, because the winner of the Masamune Prize made it. The greatest swordsmith of his time.

Jens knew all this already. In the dream, he knew it in an instant. He knew he carried the knife all the time. It was a symbol and a badge. It had meaning that nobody around him realized.

Jens hated that knife. But it was now a part of him.

As he grabbed the creature's suit, and as the ship rocked on non-existent waves, Jens stabbed and stabbed and stabbed. As much as he hated the knife, he hated the creature.

"All I want is to save my people," the creature said calmly.

Jens stabbed again.

"You're a fucking worthless murderer, Jensen." The creature's tone was not calm any more. It sounded a lot like Skipper's. The face morphed from long and slender to round and angry and back again to long and slender. Jens tried to push the creature overboard, but he was stuck fast. His hand was glued to the knife, the knife was fixed to the creature, the creature was fixed to Jens. They fell and fell and fell into the bottomless emptiness of space, bound together. Forever.

"Please, Captain sir, wake up!" Fran Lu shouted. She shook him fruitlessly, finally raising a hand and slapping his face. He had told her to do that if needed. She didn't like doing it. But it was needed.

Jens opened his eyes and took in his surroundings. He smiled at the face above him. He regretted putting her in this situation. But she was his First Mate, and she would be discreet. There was nobody else on this ship he trusted as much as her.

"Thank you, First Mate," he said. *"Thank you. I am awake now."*

"Yes, Captain sir," she said, stepping back from his bunk.

"You can call me Jens," he said, knowing she never would. At least not for a while.

"Your flier to the planet will be docking soon," Fran Lu said. *"I have your uniform ready."*

"Thank you, First Mate," Jens said.

"You should take the medicine Mister Genjo has given you," she said.

"I don't trust his chemicals." Jens had been out for three cycles once the stimulant wore off. He had a vague memory, or dream, of crew standing over his bed with defibrillator handles during that long sleep.

"In that case, I do wish you would take what Doctor Captain Teal has given for your sleep," she said in a moment of daring. She was getting used to voicing her opinion, but it wasn't something she did naturally.

Jens sat up, letting his feet touch the cool deck. The young woman in front of him looked taller. She was growing in confidence.

"You are being quite forward, First Mate," he said.

"I am doing my job, Captain Sir," she fired back. *"A ship is only as healthy as its Captain. It would be a dereliction of duty for me to watch the ship's Captain become an emotional wreck."*

"You are right, First Mate," he said. *"I promise I will do that as soon as I return—take my medicine. And First Mate—"*

"Sir?"

"I am in my underwear. You may stand at ease," he teased.

A faint smile played across her face before she could catch it and hide it away. *"Sir!"* she said and turned sharply. Jens wondered if he should feel guilty for watching her bottom as she exited the room.

The planet grew closer, spiral by slow spiral. The flier reduced speed each time around. It was a comfortable descent. Larger, seating over one hundred and fifty and filled with colonists on their first trip to the surface, all that it lacked was drinks service. All the large fliers for the *Sukhavati* colony had been taken from the *Plymouth* and assembled. All the equipment from the other freighters had been sent to the chosen landing site below.

By the time the flier reached the hastily constructed landing strip, the craft was practically at a standstill. The pilot literally *touched* down.

Teal looked younger. Jens knew it wasn't the massage. The sun on her skin did much more than his amateur fingers could have. She was slightly bronzed from her first trip to the surface. But it was more than hands or sun. Jens didn't know what it was.

"Straighten your tie, this is important," she said. "I like your gangster suit better. You look like you work on a cruise ship."

Teal adjusted his necktie and dusted his shoulders. The black epaulets and gold braid didn't have any dust on them. He felt awkward wearing them, but Fran Lu insisted, and his crew expected it. He put his hat under his arm and followed Teal out of the flier. An un-manned hover pod was waiting for them, and they boarded. It lifted, propellers whirling, and he got another view of the emerging settlement. They had certainly been busy. Being cooped up in a lead-lined box for months on end paid dividends in pent up energy. Prefabs spread out in a semblance of streets along the edge of a deep water harbor. Larger complexes were taking shape outside the ring of shelters.

"These people work fast," Teal said.

"*Zhongren shichai huoyan gao*," Jens said. "When many people work together, the job gets done faster, and it is easier for everyone."

Teal looked at Jens, lips pursed.

"You know," he said. "Many hands make light work, and all that."

"I get it, Jens," she said. "Now shut up."

"The ideal communist is the first to worry and the last to enjoy himself," Jens quoted. "I forget who said that."

"And I don't care," Teal finished. "I'm serious Jens, shut up."

She led him away from the emerging town center, to a squat structure, no different to that under Shackleton's Dome, except for the clear sky and bright sun that shone above. They entered the building and passed an un-manned reception desk. Teal opened the door to a large room and took her seat at a table next to Wan.

Jens looked at those gathered. Some were colonists he had met on the *Xing*, after he had locked them in. Xian, the eldest, and the one he gave most respect. Han, who was more popular among the colonists. Jens couldn't remember the others names. They weren't worth remembering. Jens had power-mapped the group assembled in the mess hall during the hull breach drill. It only took a moment, and he dealt with those who had the power. He had seen that it was Han and Xian whom he needed to win over. It was easier than he expected.

Todds from the *Cooper* sat next to Rangi. Jens smiled at her. He nodded to Alvarez, who returned the gesture. Hui Yin sat at the end of the table. Jens ignored him. *Once a general was appointed, it was his duty to carry out his mission,* Sun Tzu echoed in Jens' mind. Hui Yin didn't fight a war or a battle. He saw a glittering prize and grabbed for it. Now Jens was sleeping in his cabin and wearing an uncomfortable shirt.

He walked to the table and stopped in front of Evans.

"Sir," he said. "I apologize for boarding your ship."

"Thank you, Captain Jensen," Evans said. "We'll speak about your methods another time. About the *experience*. When we are alone."

"Captain Jensen," Xian said. *"Thank you for joining us. Please take a seat."*

A young colonist moved forward and placed a chair in front of the tables.

Jens ignored it. He bowed towards Xian. *"Thank you, Elder Xian, but I will stand."*

"As you wish," Xian said. *"As the Captains around the table do not all speak Mandarin, I will hand the chair to Representative Wan."*

"As you wish," Jens said.

"As Representative Xian has said, thank you for coming," Wan said.

"I didn't get the impression that I had much of a choice," Jens said.

"Everybody here has a choice," Wan said. "And they are exercising it." Wan glanced at Hui Yin.

"We have an opportunity to build a new world, a second Earth," Wan said. "We want to offer you a role in that building. If you will hear us."

"How do you know this world is even free for your taking?" Jens asked.

"We have found no sentient life, only faint remains," Wan said. "The planet is not inhabited."

"By anything you can see," Jens said.

"We have found no inhabitants. Glimpses of life, yes—" Maia, a colonist from the *Xing*, was an ethnobiologist.

"So, you just take what you want."

"Jens!" Wan's tone was sharp. A slap in the face.

Jens bowed. *"Apologies, Sensei,"* he said.

"We are here to ask you a favor. A very important favor," Wan continued in English. "We want to ask you to return to Earth as our representative. As our ambassador, to negotiate for us all."

Jens stood, waiting.

"You will represent us, and you will represent the Consortium," Wan said. "We now have what billions on Earth sought for decades. They will be very interested in what we have to offer. And we will be in great need of what they have."

"Supplies, settlers, technology," Han added. "Most of all settlers."

"It is an onerous task, what we are asking you do," Wan said. "It will mean years of travel, to Earth and then back. But when you return you will be rewarded handsomely. The

Consortium is now more powerful than any other. We have what they need."

"I don't think I can return to Earth," Jens said. "I'm not sure what will greet me if I do." *And I don't care about your god-damned Consortium,* he thought.

"As our ambassador, you will have nothing to worry about," Wan said. "Right now, we only ask you to think about it."

"We have no astrogators," Jens said.

"You will have trainees," Wan said.

"Not the same," Jens said. "Trainees can't direct a Donut. And I have a crew of three. They are very loyal," he said, glancing briefly at Hui Yin, "but they only have so many hands."

"There will be no shortage of volunteers," Han said. "They, too, will be rewarded handsomely."

"With parts of a planet that isn't ours?"

"Jens, we have settled that," Wan said. "We have found no trace of sentient life. All scans have shown the same. There may have been such life here in the past, but for some reason, it is no longer here."

"How can you be certain when we can't even see them?"

"Their skin seemed to emit a phenome that clouds vision, or rather how the brain interprets what is seen," Maia said. *"It may be an evolutionary development, a means of protection against predators."*

"English, please," Wan reminded.

"We are scanning the islands using infrared and have discovered only small reptilian and amphibian type life forms. No creatures like the ones you met on the Donut."

"That I met," Jens repeated. "It seems this meeting is a mere formality," he said. He sat down and placed his hat on his lap. "You already knew what my answer would be. Why don't you tell me what you have decided to do?"

"Good," Wan said. "Let us begin."

As the hover pod lifted, Teal placed her hand on top Jens's. "Relax, this is a treat," she said.

He leaned back next to her and gazed out the window. The landing pad disappeared beneath them, and the shoreline was replaced by the open sea.

"I love the blue of deep water," he said.

"I bet you miss it."

"Not as much as I expected," he replied. "But it's nice to see it again."

"Can you take us a little lower," Teal said to the pilot.

The young woman in front of them nodded, and the hover pod slowly descended. Jens watched the gentle swell.

"Such a calm sea," he observed.

"No moon, no tide," Teal said.

"That's not entirely correct," the pilot said. "If I may?"

"Of course," Teal said. "Jens, meet Xiu."

The young woman swivelled in her seat and turned to face the pair. She reached out her hand, and Jens took it. "It's an honor, Ambassador Jensen," she said in almost accent-free English.

"Just call me Jens," he said.

She smiled before swivelling back to the controls.

"The planet's rotations, as well as the sun, create small, regular tides," she said. "And the winds affect the swell and waves. The landmasses seem to break up larger storms. We haven't seen any of those yet, but there is evidence of strong winds. Nothing like the typhoons on earth, though."

"Did you pilot there?" Jens asked.

"Oh no," she said. "I learned on the *Xing*, in a simulator. For smaller pods. We never knew we would have such nice machines."

"The *Calderón* was well stocked," Teal added.

They sat in silence as the hover pod flew north. An almost hypnotizing blue water passed beneath them. Teal finally broke the spell.

"What do you think of the name?" she asked. "The colonists seem to like it."

"*Pemako*," Jens said. "What does it mean?"

"It's a place in Tibet—"

"If I may, Captain Teal?" Xiu interrupted.

"Of course," Teal said.

"*Pemako* is a region in the far west, in *Xizang*, in Tibet," Xiu said. "It is a very remote land, in the Himalayan mountains, where India and China meet. Very difficult to get to, and very difficult to travel in. It is considered the supreme of all hidden lands."

"So far, pretty close to here," Jens said.

"Yes," Xiu said. "It is very difficult to reach. But it is also considered a magical place, a very spiritual place. By enduring great hardship to reach it, the traveler is purified, and prepared to receive its gifts."

"What kind of gifts?" Jens asked.

"Well, look," Xiu said. "Everything we have dreamed about is below. But to get here we had to give up all hope, all expectation, all ideas and preconceptions. We had to sacrifice a great deal." Jens watched her profile as she spoke. Her eyes were closed as her mind traveled to a distant, ancestral land.

"I was very pleased when this name was proposed," she said.

Jens started to open his mouth to comment, but Xiu continued. "In the Buddhism of the Tibetans," she said, opening her eyes, "Pemako is the center of the universe. It is a sacred place, where the physical and the spiritual worlds overlap. It is a place to enter into a deeper reality. It is a place of pilgrimage. Oh! Look! There they are," Xiu said, pointing out the window. She slowly took the pod over a disturbed area of water. Bubbles rose on the sea, and a glint of silver broke the surface, followed by more. The sea seemed to boil as fins emerged and disappeared. The mass moved through the water like a flock of birds through the air, veering sharply in different directions. Xiu increased altitude so her passengers could appreciate the size of the flock.

"We don't know if they're fish or mammals, or if those categories even make sense here," Xiu said. "Land animals might be hard to find, but from what we've seen, the sea is full."

"Life, Jens," Teal said, grabbing Jens' hand. "We found life!"

"Amazing." He stared out the window, following the flock with his eyes.

"The biggest creature we've seen was over one hundred meters long. That is three times larger than a blue whale," Xiu said. "But we don't know if they are like whales. I will keep an eye out for one. We have so much to learn."

"Maybe you can figure out how to ask them," Jens said.

"I hope so," she said.

"Let's show him the mountains," Teal said.

"Yes, Captain Teal," Xiu said. "They should come into view in about thirty minutes on the left."

"Mountains?" Jens asked.

"You said you grew up next to mountains," Teal said. "The Southern Alps on your horizon, I remember you wistfully saying."

Jens kept his gaze to the left, waiting. As the minutes passed, he began to see a dark ridge grow on the horizon. Rocky peaks emerged. Slopes covered in green rose out of the water.

"There is no snow at this latitude," Xiu said. "But islands towards the poles have colder winters."

"That could be your home, Jens," Teal said. "It's not as big as New Zealand, but it's close. We'll have to bring back lots of houses."

"And sailboats," Jens said without taking his eyes off the land. "I miss sailing."

"Xiu," Teal said. "Ambassador Jensen hasn't mentioned it yet, but he's looking for good pilots for the Steps back."

"Go ahead and get in, Jens," Herschel said. "You look hot."

"Go on, Ambassador, the water is fine." Suzie sat cross-legged in the sand, smiling at him.

"There are some awfully big creatures in there," Jens said. "We don't know what they eat."

"Sissy."

"And please don't call me that," Jens said.

"Sissy?" Herschel asked.

"No."

"Ah, Mr Ambassador," Herschel said. "I'm sure if you stuck around for another couple months, it would be President. Or King. What is it with this guy?" he asked Suzie. "He seems to jump all those steps between promotions."

Suzie closed her eyes and giggled. "He's a tin-ass."

"A what?" Herschel asked.

"It means 'lucky' where he's from." She lay down on her towel, resting her face on a hand.

"I'm not a tin-ass," Jens said. Lucky was the last thing he felt.

He stood and walked into the warm water, lifting his arms as the water rose past his waist and to his chest. He bent his knees and let the water cover his face. He sat on the bottom, submerging his entire body, and listened to the silence of the water. Such a calm sea, lapping passively at the shore of the island. He opened his eyes and looked into the blue. Such blissful silence, such comforting wet arms.

Jens rose and wiped the dripping sea from his face. He walked back to his friends on the beach. Their beach. They didn't question his choice, to leave this new world and spend years in space, making his way back to Earth. To let Earth know what they found and where it was. To deal for their future.

He sat back down on his towel and smiled at Suzie. Her skin was pink. She would need lots of moisturizer or she would be quite sore in the morning. He glanced at the aloe-like plants up the bank and thought of the gooey healing interior of the leaves he could rub over her skin. If she would let him touch her. He would have to be very gentle. Reaching near her, he lifted the lava lava next to her and draped it slowly over her shoulders.

"You'll burn," he said.

"It feels too good to care," Suzie said. She inhaled on a glow stick, held her breath, and then exhaled.

Jens looked into her eyes, searching for the woman he knew. She was in there, somewhere, but not ready to come out. She blinked slowly. Jens let her stay where she was.

"What's in the pipe, sugar pie?" he asked.

"Micro-dosing, Teal calls it," she said.

He reached over and ran his fingers through her hair. She tilted towards his hand, purring.

"How can you leave this, Jens?" Pani asked. Her skin glowed in the light, sucking in the warm rays and turning them brown. She looked at Suzie and smiled sadly.

"You know, duty," he joked.

"You can step off, mate," Herschel said. "Grab your island and settle down."

"No, he can't," Rangi said. "He thinks he has a debt to pay. Or some sort of duty to perform." She wiped sand off her hands. "But he'll be back."

"That I will," Jens agreed.

"Mr Ambassador," Pani said.

"Tell me, Jens, really," Herschel asked. "What's in it for you?"

"Diplomatic immunity," Jens said.

An uneasy silence settled among the friends. Guilt? Remorse? What's the word when you think you don't deserve or aren't entitled to ...?

"Unworthy," Jie said.

"Yeah, that's it," Jens agreed. *"Maybe my greatest weakness, eh?"*

"No," Jie said. *"Not quite as simple as that. Keep searching."*

"Hey," Rangi said. "Snap out of it Jens, answer the question."

"It's only ten years," Jens said. "Earth and back. Let you guys do all the hard work. I'll have lots of time to study and train. Consortia negotiations. Property law. Maybe another language. I always wanted to learn Spanish. Twenty new crew to teach the ropes. Pick up Teal's tickets to heaven, enough for a small continent. Slip by the Russians. Try to avoid Stepping into a star with untrained astrogators. Then bring back supplies and colonists and anything else we might want. Maybe a Donut or two. Piece of cake. I expect lots of nieces and nephews to spoil when I get back."

"Maybe you'll bring some of your own," Pani teased. "Herschel tells me that First Mate of yours has quite the crush on you."

Jens smiled at Suzie and took her hand. He squeezed it gently. She was already sitting outside God's living room.

"She can't even bring herself to use my name. 'Captain sir' is as close as she dares."

"Oh, knowing your charms, you'll break her down," he said.

"Stop it, you two!" Rangi said. "Teal was keen to join your convoy—"

"She wants to finish her big drug deal," Jens said.

"Partly," Rangi corrected. "She really believes it can change people. And I agree. But she only knows one life. Settling down isn't part of it. I'm surprised so many wanted to sign up for the return."

"It's a hell of a pay packet," Jens said.

"Ora, bring the man a beer," Rangi called.

"Is this like your home islands?" Suzie asked her sleepily.

"Nothing is like the home islands," Pani said. "But this can be a new home. We've named this island Rarotonga. It is nothing like its namesake, but it's going to be home." Pani placed a hand on Jens'. "It won't be as easy as you think. You'll have to be prepared."

"I know," Jens said.

"Enjoy this, man. It's from the last crate," Ora said, handing Jens a beer.

"Maybe you should keep it," Jens said.

"Don't cause a cultural scene, bro," Ora said. "Take the gift. This *umu* is for you."

"Thanks for the beer." Jens took a long draft from the bottle. "I'll bring some back."

"Too right, you will," Ora said. "Maybe by then we'll know what happened to the originals."

"Let the Ambassador relax," Rangi said. "His time is fleeting."

Jens looked at Herschel. "How about showing me that *umu* pit?" he said.

"That's a good idea," Pani agreed. "You boys show him around. I'll look after our girl here."

"Come on, man," Ora said. "Bring your drink."

Jens followed him up the beach and into the trees. In a small clearing, he saw smoke rising from overturned soil. It smelled of home, or a place that had been his home.

"I know a man on Shackleton that would love a bit of this," Jens said. "They call it a *hāngi* back home."

"Bring him back with you," Ora said. "And thanks for the meat, bro. I was looking forward to prepping it myself, but skinned and ready was cool, too."

"I am not about to introduce a live rodent to a new ecosystem," Jens said.

"So that means you're not going to leave us any?" Ora said. "Harsh."

"He's right, and you know it, Ora," Herschel said.

"We'll freeze-dry you enough until you can find your own meat if that's what you'd want to eat. The colonists have brought enough plants to keep you healthy."

"Healthy, maybe," Ora conceded. "I wouldn't necessarily say happy. A man needs his meat."

"You could come back with us," Jens said. "I could use some more experienced crew. And I can always use another cavy rancher."

"Not on your life," Ora said. "I'm done with living in a box." He closed his eyes and turned his face to the sun. "Hemi, how's that food?" he called without moving.

"Almost ready," Hemi answered.

"How's Lena?" Herschel asked.

"Still unconscious," Jens said. "Teal said she should be awake, but it seems like she doesn't want to wake. Teal's having her brought down to the hospital that's being erected. Her mates from the *Cooper* will take care of her, and hopefully bring her back. The *Ryk* had all the pharma printers, but they're cannibalizing the sickbays of the ships not coming with us."

"Fucking monsters," Herschel said.

"Or very desperate monsters. Maybe. God knows how long they were out there. Or why they ... ah, fuck it," Jens said. "Are you serious about this being the last of your beer?"

"For you, bro, there's always another," Ora said.

The four freighters tethered to the Donut, two on each side. The *General Xing* positioned above the *Calderón* on one side and the *Cirrus* took her place above the *Sunrise Blossom* on the opposite. They would accelerate for months towards the sun before swivelling to decelerate. Jens would have to introduce some sort of celebration for First Flip. More months spent waiting for the Donut to power for Step. Months to train astrogators, or to learn to trust the quantum computer whose calculations held their fate. Months to train a new crew. To learn about the Consortia, and how to get what he wanted out of them.

Dark years exploring the artifact they carried back, an ancient ship with its silent crew. There had to be a way to pry their story out of those dead lips.

"Qianli zhi xing, shivu zu xia," Jens read from the book in his hand. "A journey of a thousand miles starts with a single Step." The bridge crew listened, waiting. "A beautiful sentiment, from the master, Lao Tse, reduced over time to cliché," he said to them. "But we're going to give it new meaning."

Fran Lu sat in the chair next to Jens, smiling. He looked into her brown eyes for a long moment.

"First Officer, you do the honors," he said to her.

Fran Lu sat up straighter, if that were possible.

"Communications," she said. "Open ship to ship comms. All ships acknowledge."

"Cirrus standing by," they heard. "Reactor synchronized."

"Calderón esta lista. Reactor sincronizado."

"Sunrise Blossom awaits your command," Wu Pen answered.

"Helm," Fran Lu said. "Prepare for acceleration. Three-two-one-Accelerate! Accelerate! Accelerate!"

They felt the gravity increase, pushing them into their chairs. They were going home.

One Step at a time.

Part 4: Stepping Back

17

"Chuan zhang, qing xing xing!"

Jens felt shaken. A firm hand on his shoulder.

"Captain, please wake up," Fran Lu said. Jens feigned sleep, making her say it again. He listened closely.

"Please, Captain Sir. The crew is assembling."

She still wouldn't bring herself to use the name everybody else called him, but there was something in the way she ...

He heard her step back and plant her feet at attention once she realized he was awake. "Was I shouting?" Jens said.

"No, Captain Sir, you were sleeping quietly," she said. "I regret waking you. I know how busy you have been. But it is time to address the crew."

Jens waited for Fran Lu to leave his quarters before getting up. His uniform was laid out, the white pants and shirt ironed by an enthusiast. No wrinkle survived. The fit was perfect. Zhang had done a wonderful job on the tailoring, as usual. The black epaulets sat stiffly on his shoulders, their four gold strips a nod towards tradition. Four represented Captain. Fran Lu's epaulets bore three stripes.

Jens straightened his black silk tie and adjusted his cap. White top, black hood. Gold embroidered rope formed a near circle on the front of the cap. Instead of the traditional anchor, Zhang had stitched an old-fashioned rocket, probably giggling as he did so. Wearing a hat on a spaceship struck Jens as pointless, but it was all about image and playing the part.

Fran Lu stood waiting. "The crew is ready, sir," she said, turning on a heel and leading him to what used to be the village square.

It still was, of a sort. The crew waited, standing to attention in two rows of ten. Second Officer Chen stood at the end of one row, while Third Officer Shinje stood beside the other. Jens smiled briefly at Yuan where he stood in the first row, pleased that he decided to sign on. Jens had met with each of the crew standing before him, interviewed them, assigned them roles, even had to barter with Alvarez and Teal to get who he wanted, but he wouldn't tell the crew about those negotiations. Each crew member had their reasons for shipping. A few said it was because he was captain. Others said that they needed more skill to make life a success on *Pemako*. Many said that they wanted to collect family and friends from Earth. That was a sentiment of many including those not making the return voyage. No one mentioned reward.

Jens stopped in front of the first of the crew, a young woman. She wore three gold stripes on her epaulets, banded by purple. Chief Engineer Baolin. Jens nodded to her. She assisted in the reactor room as a colonist and was now the most experienced, which meant she was now in charge of the engines. He walked down the line stopping in front of Nima, their trainee Donut Hole, prepared to spend the coming months secluded with the other three studying astrophysics. He put out his hand. She held out hers, and he grasped it briefly, gently. He moved to the next, Han, their cavy rancher, as well as several other roles. They all had several other roles, not only in keeping the ship on course, but feeding the convoy in years to come.

Next to Han stood Liao, hydroponics, maintenance, communications, et cetera, et cetera, et cetera.

Jens made sure he acknowledged each member of the crew before speaking. They all had so much to learn. Some of that learning would be on the *Xing,* and some would be on the other ships, especially the *Sunrise*. Genjo was, no doubt, preparing his library, and Zhang his dojo. Jens wanted competent crew that could think as well as defend the ship. Preferably at the same time, if the need arose. Wan may have chosen to hand his ship over to Wu Pen and to stay on *Pemako*, but he was still a mentor in many ways. The crew's collective inexperience made Jens' hands slightly shake. He clasped them behind his back and tried unsuccessfully not to think about it.

The last person he acknowledged resented being at the ceremony and didn't hide her resentment at wasting time she could have been spending on the artifact. Jens didn't care how she felt. He agreed to take responsibility for her and let her utilize the resources of the *Xing* for her research. Their relationship had yet to warm, partly due to the scientist's typical absence from the ship, partly due to personality, and no doubt due to plain dislike.

"Dr Lin," Jens said, bowing.

"Captain Jensen," she replied.

Jens stepped back and faced the crew. He had thought more about what not to say than what he would. He smiled.

"I'd like to thank you, once again, for signing on to the journey ahead of us," he began in Mandarin, the lingua franca of the ship. *"We have a long way to go, and a great deal of work to get there, but together, I am sure we will accomplish what we set out to do."*

Jens stopped, out of words. The crew continued to look at him expectantly. Jens glanced at Fran Lu, who did her best not to laugh.

"So, crew of the General Xing, *"* Jens said. *"Are you ready to Step across space?"*

"Yes, Captain Sir!" they called back in unison.

"Good," he replied. *"Good. We have prepared a shared meal, a tradition I would like to see established, times when*

we can come together as one crew. My thanks to those who have prepared our food, from tank or pen to our table."

They stood still, watching him. *"Come, follow me, let's eat,"* he said, walking towards the mess hall.

"How's the crew working out?" Teal asked.

"Fine," Jens answered. "So many new faces. And so young. But they're getting used to training."

"You are hopefully giving them more time to rest than we gave you," Wu Pen said. "We were trying to find your breaking point."

"And point taken," Jens said. "No, they get to rest. I have to make them sometimes. They are very keen." He held out a glass towards Alvarez, who filled it with wine.

"Unless you're growing grapes in the *Xing,* we'll have to start rationing this," Alvarez said. "As for this maneuver, my team sent over a plan. Have you received it?"

The other three captains nodded. Swiveling the entire Donut so that the reactors of the combined freighters faced the star and could decelerate.

"That's a lot of force on one point of the Donut," Teal said. "It's not designed for that."

"It's how they move Donuts towards the sun from Earth," Alvarez said.

"Not with the combined thrust of four freighters," Teal said.

"Our calculations show a very little risk factor," Alvarez said.

"A little risk is already too much," Jens said, "we could do it with three."

"Which would increase gravity and increase the risk, Jens," Wu Pen said. "Alvarez's team has it worked out. The numbers look good."

The fortnightly Captain's meeting. When Jens suggested it, he thought it was a good idea. But he usually left strongly reminded that he was the junior member of their impromptu Consortia. He pushed the feeling aside.

"If we increase the time to full thrust," he said. "We could monitor the stress on the Donut superstructure. It would mean an increase of gravity by 0.2, but allow us to minimize the risk of damage. I've had Nima run various scenarios."

"She's supposed to be focusing on astrophysics, not—"

"It was their idea to do it, Captain Teal," Wu Pen interrupted. "All four were concerned about the stress on the Donut."

"Very well, then," Alvarez said before Teal could argue. "A slower Decel, with continued monitoring of the superstructure. Thoughts about our rotation?"

"Managed by a team of tenders, it should only take a few days," Wu Pen said.

"I'd like my pilots to manage that," Jens said before another Captain could volunteer. "The *Xing* has the most tenders, and the pilots have been training for it."

"Agreed?" Alvarez asked.

Wu Pen nodded.

"I'll send over some fuel," Teal said.

"Wait ... wait ..." Billi said. She was new to these drills, they all were, but she enjoyed them. She was good at them. It wasn't just self-opinion, Captain Jensen himself had complimented her. He told her, "well done," after an early exercise. It was probably just an encouraging verbal pat on the back as they passed in the corridor, but she felt herself grow a couple centimeters with each of his words. They made her want to do better, to be better. The captain made each of the new crew feel that way.

Disun took his hands off the controls and quickly rubbed his palms together before taking the stick again.

Billi turned her head to Disun and mouthed the word, "Now!"

The pilot smiled and lifted the tender out of the empty docking bay. He accelerated forward, hit a side thruster to turn the craft one hundred and eighty degrees, and sank into the next bay. The vacant space dwarfed the tender. He settled lower into it, disappearing in shadow.

"Any sighting?" he said.

"No," Billi said. "They're laying low. Now's our chance."

"Are you sure?"

"We're not going to get it by hiding," she said. "It has to be in Bay 12. It's the only place it can be. That's just across the lower side of the Donut."

"It doesn't have to be," Disun said. "There are a lot of bays it can be hiding in."

"You know that isn't true," she said. "*In war, victory should be swift*. Run fast, in an evasive pattern, just like we've practised."

"I am so tired of that book," Disun said. "Okay. Fast and loose."

"Exactly," Billi said. A smile crept across her face. Disun caught it, and both sat grinning at each other before closing their helmets.

"They can't hit what they can't aim at," he said, rubbing his palms together. He placed them back on the controls. As soon as Billi nodded, she was pressed back in her chair. Stars replaced shadow and swung across the viewscreen as Disun banked to port.

Billi grabbed the arms of her chair as her body shifted to the side. "We have a contact!" she said.

Her body shifted to the other side of her chair before slamming harder against the port side. Her head jerked forward as Disun brought the tender closer to the surface of the Donut, then hit the back cushion when he leveled out and accelerated even more. She tried to focus on the monitor, to warn the pilot of any possible tags, but her vision was blurred by his erratic turns, dips, rises. All she could do was hold on.

At the rim of Bay 12, he spun the tender around and hit all aft thrusters. Their seat straps strained as their bodies tried to shoot forward, and the tender stopped a meter from the docking bay wall. He descended to the bottom. Billi jumped from the tender before it had halted and pushed herself away from the craft to the center of the bay. She reached forward and grabbed the orange flag Jens had attached to the deck. She raised it above her head and waved it, shouting and laughing as the pursuing tenders flew over.

Jens called out as he entered the Artifact, as if a bear might be lumbering around the next bend. It's never a good idea to surprise a bear.

"Dr Lin," he called. "It's Jensen. I've brought supplies for you."

"There's no need to shout, Captain Jensen," he heard from an intercom in bulkhead. "And I can see you too. I am on the bridge."

"She did it," he said to himself.

"I have done nothing," she said over the intercom.

Jens walked deeper into the ship, down the same corridor he and Herschel had walked months earlier. Marks on the walls showed where Dr Lin had been at work, either buffed smooth and exposing symbols, or pried open and showing luminescent wires. He paused as he walked past the cryo-beds. Dr Lin had clearly worked on the two desiccated skeletons. Sections of bone and any remaining fabric were missing.

Jens leaned over the two cryo-beds that contained the corpses retrieved from the Donut Hole. Dr Lin had sprayed a fine paint over them so they were visible. Jens looked at a mutilated face. One eye remained open, its large pupil making the entire orb look black. He clenched his hands into fists as he remembered an interaction with Dr Lin.

"You mutilated these specimens," she charged. "How am I to study these?" she demanded, throwing her hands into the air. "What a mess!"

Jens clenched his fist, ready to punch the woman. His mind turned and twisted, almost out of control, a wave too large breaking on an unknown shore, as images of the blood-drenched Donut Hole, of Jie, of Luciana, Lena, Suzie, of Skipper, tumbled past.

He had no response that time. Back on the *Xing*, he confided to Fran Lu. He told her how he had felt at that moment, with his fist and jaw clenched shut. He told her about the Hole and what had happened. She was the first person, besides Herschel, that he spoke to about that day. She was such a good listener that Jens almost talked about Earth. He wanted to. Instead, he closed his eyes and his mouth, and Fran Lu let him keep his secrets. She asked him not to make this visit, but Dr Lin was his responsibility.

"They are dead, Captain Jensen," he heard.

"I am very aware of that," he said without turning.

Jens straightened and continued to the bridge of the ship. Dr Lin sat hunched over a control panel. Jens set down the food he had brought and walked over to where she worked.

"I would appreciate it if you do not let your crew play in this docking bay," she said, still staring at the monitor in front of her.

"They are not playing, Dr Lin, they are training," Jens said.

"Training! Bah!" she spat.

"They are participating in an important drill," Jens said. "It is called 'Capture the Flag'. But I will make this bay off-limits in the future."

"Thank you," she said. Jens paused, trying to recall if that was the first time he had heard those words come out of her mouth.

"These controls are not too dissimilar to what you might find on one of our ships," she said. "These here operate ship comms and video links." She pointed to symbols inlaid into the console. "An alphabet, just like on Earth. They are all I can make sense of at the moment."

Still not turning toward Jens, she walked to another control panel. "I am starting to translate some of the symbols, but many are still too difficult. You are mentioned here," she said.

Dr Lin pressed a control, and the alien symbols appeared on a monitor. "They were way ahead of us in some ways," she said. "But they didn't know how to Step. Look here." Dr Lin pointed to some symbols on the screen.

"They knew what each freighter carried. Their technological ability is very impressive. They knew the *Cirrus* carried fuel. They knew the *Ryk* carried medical technology. Look," she pointed at a symbol on the screen. "That means something like 'great value,' I think. They really wanted what was inside the *Ryk*."

"They wanted to board the *Cirrus*," Jens said. "I saw the flash of their reactor."

"It no doubt failed," Dr Lin said. "I still have no idea how old this ship is. *Very*, is as close as I can get at the moment. Maybe a thousand years, maybe more. They definitely realized how important the Donut was. See?" She pointed at more symbols.

"They were dying," she said, before Jens could answer. "They were traveling in space, obviously, but not faster than light, and certainly not *through* space, as we know it. So, they froze these guys and cast them out, hoping they would find what they needed. When an advanced technology showed itself, they were woken."

"What did they need?" Jens asked.

"Help," she said. "I think."

"They had a hell of a way of asking for it," Jens said.

"They were desperate."

"They don't need excuses," Jens said.

"According to this, their entire species was dying, Captain Jensen. A type of illness, or plague."

"I don't care," Jens said.

Dr Lin turned and faced him for the first time since he boarded. "I can understand your feelings, Captain Jensen," she said. "Much as you might want to think, I am not unfeeling. I am sorry you lost friends."

Jens stared at her, unable to answer.

"Look here," she said, turning back to the monitor screen. "I think this is a type of a journal or log. It tells a story, as far as I can decipher. There are many words and phrases I cannot translate. Their planet was dying, at least what lived on the surface. I don't know why, yet. But they were so desperate they cast ships like this out into space, looking and hoping for a technology that might help. Here," she said, pointing. "Do you see those markings?"

"They look like the others," Jens said.

"But they aren't," Dr Lin said. "This is more recent writing. I think this was when they realized how long they had been adrift. These here," she said. "Must be names, maybe the skeletons in the cryo-beds. I think what we are looking at is the anguish of whoever wrote this."

She turned and looked at Jens again. "But I know, Captain Jensen. You do not care," she said. "And you have good reasons not to care. But I must find out what these beings were doing in space, and maybe what happened to them on their planet."

"I understand that, Dr Lin," Jens said. "We all value the work you are doing."

"Thank you, Captain," she said. "Which leads me to my next question: why are you here, and not one of the children you call crew?"

Jens smiled. "We are going to Step soon," he said. "I would like you to be on the *General Xing* when that happens."

"What you would like, and what will happen, are not always the same thing," she answered. "Isn't that what some of those books you make your crew study say?"

"You have already been exposed to unhealthy doses of solar radiation," Jens said.

"Not on this ship," she said. "Their technology is far beyond ours in that regard. I am very protected where I am."

"That may be so—"

"It *is* so, Captain Jensen," Dr Lin said. "This ship is far safer to be in than your freighters, even if it is anchored in a Donut next to a star."

"That may be so," Jens tried again. "But I would appreciate it if you joined us on the *Xing* for Step."

"And I must again disappoint you, Captain Jensen," she said.

"Very well," Jens acquiesced. "Is there anything I can get you to ... make your work easier here?"

She looked at him and shook her head. Jens could see she was smiling. "You continue to surprise me, Captain Jensen," she said. "I don't suppose you have a neurologist or a xenobiologist you could lend me?"

"I'm afraid I don't have any of those to spare," he said. "But Alvarez sent over a bottle of merlot if you're interested."

Dr Lin laughed. "Very well, Captain Jensen," she said. "But drinking alone is a bad habit. I hope you brought glasses."

18

Step.

Again.

Pulled up and down. Ripped through space and time. Jens sat up in his chair. Time to act the Captain. He watched the red numbers counting down. Words. He needed words.

"Qianli zhi xing, shivu zu xia," he said. "A thousand miles, a single Step, you know the speech. Today we do it. Prepare yourselves for Step. Spare a thought for our Astrogators, and those in the Hole sent to guard them. Thank you all for getting us this far. I will see you on the other side. This is Captain Jensen. Out."

Red numbers ticking down. Jens adjusted himself in his seat, not that it would do any good. At this moment, he envied those on the *Cirrus*. But he would have to feel it all sober and in-the-moment, as that moment stretched over thousands of light-years. Jens turned and smiled at Fran Lu, and felt himself being stretched in different directions.

Fran Lu coughed, undid her straps and fell to the floor. She gasped for breath. Pulling herself up she released Jens straps. He fell to the floor, gasping. The bridge was filled with smoke.

"Visual," he said. The bridge remained in darkness.

"Visual!" he repeated.

Light flickered and the viewscreen came to life. Bright orange light flooded the bridge. Jens looked around the bridge and noticed other lights, pulsing yellow and red. It wasn't a single light, but two, three, four combinations. Multiple alarms, multiple system failures. The viewscreen brightened with the pulsing orange light of the nearby star. He tried to focus on the image but it danced.

"Jens! We are too close!" Fran Lu shouted in his ear and shook him.

He lurched to the helm and shook the pilot. "What do you see?" he shouted at Xiu.

"Nothing!" she answered. "It's just all—"

The view screen flickered and went out.

"It's all sun," Xiu said.

Jens listened to the alarms, trying to separate the different codes. Atmospheric. Hull breach. Imminent reactor meltdown.

"Emergency detach!" he ordered. "Now! Now! Detach the ship!"

Bridge crew looked at him blankly, gasping for breath.

"Detach the ship now!" Jens staggered to the helm and accessed the control panel. Bingyun pulled himself up and accessed the other.

"Sir?" he asked.

"Now!" Jens called.

The ship lurched as the clamps holding to the docking bay blew loose. Jens fell to the floor as thrusters lifted the freighter away from the Donut. Smoke continued to fill the bridge.

"Eyes! I need eyes! What is happening out there?" Jens demanded. "Report!"

"Hull temperature at critical!"

"Life support failing!"

"Reactor room!" Jens called into ship wide comms. He coughed. "Chief Engineer Baolin! Report!"

"Sir, comms are down," Xiu said.

"Then come with me," Jens said. "Suit up, everybody. I need pilots at Docking Bay One, now!" He staggered to the door. "Fran Lu, take the bridge!" he called over his shoulder.

Jens grabbed Bingyun and pulled him down the corridor. Disun leaned against a bulkhead, gasping and they pulled him after them. By the time they reached the tenders, they had two other pilots.

Jens closed the inner airlock as the four powered their tenders. "Assess the situation. We need to know what is happening," he said. He operated the outer loading bay, but nothing happened.

"Door won't open," he told the pilots. "One of you use a tender."

Disun lifted off the floor and slowly advanced to the loading bay door. He nosed his tender against it and the door began to buckle. He applied more thrust and it blew outward. His tender scraped the frame of the door as it slid out of the freighter.

"It's melting, sir!" Disun said. "We are too close!" The other pilots flew out into the blazing light.

"Move us if you can," Jens said. "We have to move the Donut!"

"Yes, sir, but—" static replaced their voices.

Jens left the loading bay and headed for engineering. The freighter lurched to its port side and gravity failed. He pulled himself along the handrails. All crew he saw were busy repairing or keeping systems together. The freighter lurched again from the other side. Jens saw Baolin at the reactor controls, initiating an emergency re-start. Her team was busy around the reactor. Jens felt both proud and superfluous.

The freighter lurched forward, sending any crew not holding on to something sailing against the nearest wall or ceiling. Jens fumbled for something to hold onto and a hand grabbed his wrist.

"We must have just hit the Donut," he called. "Initiate thrust."

Baolin sent a command and programmed in the desired power. The freighter lurched again and weight began to return, a gentle force that lowered Jens slowly to the floor and kept him there.

The comms crackled. "Comms operational. Life support stabilized, Captain," Fran Lu said.

"What is happening out here?" Jens asked.

"The ship is moving the Donut away from the star," she said. "Hull temperatures are decreasing."

"Put me through to the pilots," Jens said.

"We have not established contact with tender pilots."

"Visuals?"

"Visuals are out, Captain Sir," Fran Lu said. "We have no eyes."

"Then we'll have to get some out there," Jens said. "Where is Disun?"

"He's in Bay One. His tender is damaged and there's no way to get in with the outer door open," she said.

"No more problems, First Mate. Give me solutions."

"Pilots are on their way to Bay Two," she said. "Crew are cutting the outer door open as we speak."

"Cutting the door open, First Mate?"

"Solutions, Captain Sir," she said. "The door will be operational by the time you arrive."

"Good," Jens said. "I'm on my way. I need to see what's happened."

Jens followed the tender out of the loading bay and slowly spun his craft around towards the ship. He exhaled and forgot to breathe. The outside of the ship resembled a melted candle. Lead flowed over the loading bay door, frozen in place like cooled lava. He directed the craft towards the bow, aiming for a tender embedded in the side of the freighter. Jens hovered next to it and peered into the cabin. He turned off his comms so nobody could hear.

Bingyun sat at the controls of his tender. His head leaned back, mouth open. His blank eyes stared through the viewscreen at Jens.

Wiping his eyes, Jens turned his comms back on. "Get visual back up and plant those antennas. We need to be able to contact the convoy," he said. "And let's focus on our work. There will be a time to talk about …"

"Understood, Captain," he heard a tender on the other side of the ship.

"We'll have time to talk about our friends later," he said. "Finish your work and get out of this radiation. I am checking on Dr Lin."

"Sir," he heard. Billi. "The bodies?"

"There is nothing we can do about them at the moment," he said. "Get those comms up."

Jens lifted away from the embedded tender and damaged hull. Another tender was embedded in the top of the hull. Nothing had survived the heat, cameras, communications, his crew. The reactor functioned, as the *General Xing* pushed the Donut to a safe distance. He pointed the nose of the craft towards the rim of the Donut over half a kilometer away and accelerated.

The artifact was filled with smoke. Jens made his way to the bridge and found it empty. He retraced his steps, pausing at the cryo-beds. He peered into each one. Four held corpses. He looked into the fifth, at another body.

Dr Lin opened her eyes. Her mouthed moved. She pounded a fist against the inside of the lid.

"I can't hear you," Jens said looking down at her. "Which, unfortunately, means you can't hear me. Not that you would listen, anyway."

He searched the room for Dr Lin's suit and brought it over to the bed. She coughed as he opened the lid. He lifted her out and she climbed into the suit. Jens tapped his helmet and she turned on her comms.

"Follow me," he said. "I've got astrogators, and their guards, to collect in what has to be my least favorite place in the entire god damned galaxy. And I've got a ship to see to. Then you'll come with me to the *Xing* where you'll do whatever you're told to do." He turned and walked back to the tender.

Dr Lin followed without speaking. They boarded the tender and flew to the elevator.

"What happened?" she tried as the elevator began to descend.

Jens ignored her. She placed a gloved hand on his suit. "Please, Jens."

"I don't know," he answered without looking at her. "We came out of Step close to the star and almost all cooked. Three crew died saving us."

The elevator came to a halt at the center of the Donut. "I have no idea what to expect when these doors open," he said, taking off his gloves. He reached into a pocket and withdrew a sounder. From the other, he withdrew his knife. He crouched low.

"Open the door and step back," he ordered.

The doors slid open and two sounders pointed at Jens's face. He raised his hands.

"Captain Jensen!" one of the men said. *"We felt a jolt and didn't know what was happening."*

"Well," Jens said. *"Now that you know who it is, Wang Jing, would you mind lowering your weapons?"*

Jens and Dr Lin entered the control room. The four astrogators sat at the table housing the quantum computer. "Is the computer damaged?" he asked.

"No, Captain Jensen," Li Na, from the *Cirrus*, answered.

"Then what happened?" Jens asked.

"We are exactly as programmed, sir," Nima said.

"Then you don't know?"

"Communications with the ships failed," she said. "Is everything okay?"

"Donut integrity," Jen said. "Speak to me."

"Everything is fine, Captain," Nima said.

Jens looked around the room. Clean, polished even. He stared at the floor at the end of the table, looking at something that was no longer there. The air was a perfect twenty-two degrees, but he felt sweat trickle down his temple. Dr Lin placed a hand gently on his shoulder and he faced the four young women.

"There will be plenty of time to figure out what happened," he said. "Let's get you to the *Cirrus*, where you can rest. I need to return to the *Xing* as soon as possible."

"Sir?" Nima asked.

"Of course," he said. "You will return with me and Dr Lin."

Nima sat silently as the tender returned to the damaged *Xing*. Dr Lin tried asking questions but Jens only gave her silence as an answer. Nima knew from the size of the sun they had Stepped to that they were far too close, or had underestimated the size of the star. Something, somehow, had gone drastically wrong, that was obvious. When she saw the freighter, she put her hand over her mouth to stifle a gasp. She saw suited crew cutting into the hull where airlocks used to be. The protective lead covering on the ship resembled melted black ice cream. What kind of temperatures did it take to do that? Just how badly had she and her novice Donut Holes screwed up?

Jens took the tender low over the ship. Crew were erecting video links and communication antennas. Others were running cables over the surface. Nima looked over her shoulder and saw the immensity of the Donut behind the tender. It dwarfed the freighter, and yet the freighter was pushing it through space, away from the star filling the entire viewscreen. Even at full tint, she had to look away.

"This is Jens, returning with Dr Lin and Nima," Jens said. "Please advise us where to go."

"Docking Bay Two, sir," he was answered. "Welcome home. We're happy you're all back."

Jens turned the tender towards the bay. He hovered briefly above an empty tender embedded in the top of the hull, before directing the craft to the opening.

"Leave your helmets on," they were directed. "We are using corridor doors seven and eight as our inner airlock."

"Thank you, Xiu," Jens said. "We are exiting tender." He checked his companions' helmets were sealed before opening the doors. They walked through the inner docking bay door and stood aside as four suited crew passed them. Recognizing their captain, they stopped briefly and saluted. Jens raised his hand and returned the gesture. He shook his head inside his helmet and breathed out slowly. He would have to talk to Fran Lu about how that started. But that could wait.

"First Mate, this is Captain Jens," he said into his comms. "I'd like an update. Where are you?"

"You can find me in the ranch, Captain," she said.

Fran Lu had blood to her elbows. She grabbed another Cavy, stretched its carcass on the table, and cut off its hind feet. She pinched its back, slit the skin, and twisted and pulled the fur off the carcass. She tossed the fur in a large bucket, returned to the head of the animal and sliced it off with one flick of her wrist. She turned the naked creature on its back and made a small incision on its belly. She cut into the chest cavity. Reaching in, she pressed her fingers all the way to the spine and pulling downward removed the intestines and internal organs in one motion.

She tossed the gutted carcass onto a waiting tray where several others lay. Wiping away sweat, she left a red smear across her forehead.

"They are all dead, Captain," she said, glancing his way for the first time since he entered. "The smoke and the heat killed the entire herd. We must preserve the meat for future rations."

Jens stood still as she continued, staring at her, transfixed. She looked absolutely beautiful.

"Hydroponics has survived; although our fungi have been damaged, Hou assures me they will revive." She grabbed another cavy and started to skin it. "These crew have just finished work outside. I have them on two-hour rotations, and continued doses of chelators to counteract the radiation we've all been exposed to."

"Hull damage?" Jens asked.

"As you've seen," she said. "It did its job, but all communications and sensors melted with the lead. We've re-established contact with the other ships. They were protected in the Donut's docking bays."

"And our pilots?" Jens asked.

"I have placed them in sickbay, Captain," she said. "They are ... comfortable."

"Thank you, Fran Lu," Jens said.

Fran Lu looked up from her work. Her eyes met Jens' and she touched his face gently, wiping away a tear and leaving a red smudge. She turned back toward the others.

"Nima, I very happy to see you. And you, Dr Lin," she said.

Jens watched the handful of tired crew skinning cavy. One came and took the bucket containing skinned carcasses. "And the bridge?" he asked.

"Chen is on watch. He is directing repairs at the moment."

Rolling up his sleeves, he stood beside her. "Show me what you're doing, so we can get this done," he said.

"It is okay, sir. You have duties to perform," she said.

"And the first is to help you here," he said. "I am sure Chen is doing fine." Jens held out a hand. Fran Lu smiled at him and placed the handle of a knife in his palm.

"Dr Lin, you can be helpful in here," Jens said.

"That's why I'm still here, Captain Jensen," she said from beside him. "If I can please have a knife, First Mate."

"Nima, go get some rest," Jens said over his shoulder. "That's an order. There will still be plenty to do later." He turned to make sure she left. When the doorway was empty, he picked up the cavy that was in front of him and copied Fran Lu.

19

"Your ship looks terrible, Jens," Teal said.

"She still works," Jens replied.

"Which is quite the achievement," she said. "Well done."

"Thanks," he said. "I'm glad yours escaped the worst of it."

"We were busy, but not like you."

"I have saved this wine, Captain Jensen, for a special occasion." Alvarez held up a bottle. "It is a pinot noir from the Casablanca region of Chile. I think it is time to drink it." He twisted a corkscrew into the top and pulled. The captains smiled at the pop. Alvarez filled Jens' glass first.

"I thought Casablanca was in Morocco," Jens said.

"No, think Spanish. Casa means house, blanca is white. It is a beautiful valley near my birth place of Valparaiso. I must show you when we return. It is a city of artists and anarchists."

"I want to drink," Teal said.

"To the *Xing*, and her Captain and crew," Alvarez said, raising his glass. "Risking themselves to save the Donut and the convoy."

He waited as Jens slowly raised his glass. "To Pilots Bingyun, Kueng, and Jonah, who gave their lives, so that we could live," Jens said. He looked at each Captain before taking a sip. There was a shift in these meetings. Gone were the little jokes, or the pecks to remind him of any order. They waited for him to speak, and valued what he had to say. Most of the time. Teal even acquiesced when he requested her crew remain sober during future Steps. He sat silently for several moments, staring into his wine.

"To *Shackleton*," Wu Pen said.

"Are you confident in the astrogators' calculations?" Alvarez asked.

"They will get us there," Wu Pen said. "Maybe a little farther away to play it safe, but we can maneuver the Donut into range as before. Their confidence has taken quite a hit." He gave Jens a sympathetic smile and took a drink. The others followed.

"Very well," Jens said. "It's not like we can stay here. Once the Donut is in position, we'll convoy to the *Shack*, and Teal can pick up her cargo."

"Our cargo," Teal corrected.

"Our cargo," Jens consented. "I agree that it is important to bring it to others."

Wu Pen and Alvarez nodded. Jens tried to read their thoughts, but they remained elusive.

"I'd like to continue our training regime," Jens added. "They've been through hell and they've proved themselves, but my crew still have a lot to learn. And they have to get through a couple more Steps."

"We all have new crew that need training," Wu Pen said. "I concur with Jens."

"Then it's settled," Alvarez said. "We convoy to the *Shack*, using the time to train and repair."

"Dr Lin will no doubt be unhappy about that," Jens said.

"You'll convince her it's for the best," Teal said. "You seem to be the only person she likes."

Jens laughed. He finished his drink and set his glass down. The other captains got up.

"Thank you, Captains," Alvarez said. "Next meeting will be on the *Xing*, if I am not mistaken. Don't forget your First Mates on the way out."

Teal laughed as she looked at Jens. "I am sure that won't happen," she said. As they left Alvarez's room she turned to him. "Jens, let's talk as we walk."

Jens nodded and clasped his hands behind his back as they walked towards the docking bay and their waiting tenders. They watched the First Mates leave Enrique's office ahead of them.

"This was a good idea, your executive officer meetings," she said. "Lassen's enjoying himself as senior First Mate." She smiled at him. "Speaking of First Mates, when are you going to make an honest woman of yours?"

"Excuse me?" Jens asked.

"Come on, Jens, everybody can see it," she said. "And we're going to be out here a very long time. Why don't you take the opportunity to be happy?"

Jens walked beside her without speaking, watching Fran Lu in front of him.

"She is a good First Mate," Jens said.

"She is a good woman," Teal said. "And she is in love with you." She hit Jens on the shoulder. "And you're in love with her."

"Sandra—"

"Even if you're not ready to admit it," Teal said.

"Besides," she added. "You shouldn't be so selfish. You need to think about your crew."

"My crew?"

"They're looking at you as an example," she said. "After all that time with Wan, he didn't teach you that?"

"Of course he did," Jens said.

"Well, from where I'm standing it doesn't look like it. On the *Cirrus* I let the crew know they could play around when they were off duty," she smiled at Jens. "And the crew were happy for it. But I think your crew is a little more conservative. They're probably getting extremely frustrated, watching and waiting for you two to finally start the pairing."

Jens stared at her, knowing she was right. Fran Lu turned at the docking bay door and noticed Jens for the first time. She frowned briefly when she saw who was next to him, but it wasn't lost on the other woman.

"And one piece of advice, Jens," Teal said. "Do not ask me to officiate. Your First Mate would not appreciate it."

She stopped and placed her hands on her hips. "I'll try to help you," she said to Jens. "Let her know she has nothing to worry about from me."

"Once again," she said loudly, "you get your way, *Captain* Jensen." The First Mates all turned to listen. "Here's where you shout back at me," she whispered.

"Thank you, Captain Teal," he said loudly. "Will that be all?"

"I hope that it will, *Captain* Jensen," she said. Even Jens flinched from her condescending tone. "Now if you will excuse me, I have a tender waiting." Teal marched down the corridor and past Fran Lu without a glance.

Fran Lu waited at the lock for Jens. "Tough meeting?" she asked.

He smiled at her. "They usually are," he said.

Jens turned his head and gazed at the green below. It was dead rock, but it was still beautiful, like an impressionist painting. It always would be. A storm raged over the southern hemisphere, adding white to the picture. The edges of the viewscreen made a poor frame, but who ever notices the frame? He smiled at Fran Lu. This was her fault. Or maybe Teal's. She said this would happen. As soon as he admitted how he felt about Fran, and they made it official, crew became more open about their own affections.

Jens faced the two crew members opposite him. The man was wearing his ceremonial whites, buttons shining, buckle polished. His epaulets were new. They no longer marked him as a cadet. Jens had promoted the entire crew after Step. One stripe, bound in purple. The woman wore a red dress, slightly altered to fit her shape. Fran Lu was both taller and thinner, but Zhang had no trouble altering it. He enjoyed the challenge of tailoring for a woman.

"*Li Jun,*" Jens began. "*Ni yuan yi qu Pang fua zuo wei ni de qi zi ma, yu ta zai shen sheng de hun yue zhong gong tong sheng huo?*"

Li Jun, you are willing to marry Pangfua as your wife, in sacred marriage together for life? They were traditional words, probably not said on Earth for a hundred years. But they weren't on Earth.

"*Wu lun shi ji bing huo jian kang, pin qiong huo fu yu,*" Jens continued. "*Shun li huo shi yi, ni dou yuan yi ai ta, an wei ta, zun jing ta, bao hu ta? Bing yuan yi zai ni men yi sheng zhi zhong dui ta yong yuan zhong xin bu bian?*"

Whether she has sickness or health, poverty or wealth, in good times and in bad, you are willing to love her, to comfort her, to respect her, and protect her? And willing to be forever loyal to her?

Li Jun swallowed. "*Wo yuan yi,*" he answered.

"*Pang fua,*" Jens said to the bride. "*Ni yuan yi jia Li Jun zuo wei ni de zhang fu ma, yu ta zai shen sheng de hun yue zhong gong tong sheng huo? Wu lun shi ji bing huo jian kang?*"

Are you willing to marry Li Jun as your husband, in sacred marriage together for life?

"*Wo yuan yi,*" she answered.

"*May this ring be blessed so he who gives it and she who wears it may live joyously together, and continue in love all their lives,*" Jens said.

Li Jun placed a golden band on Pangfua's finger. "*With this ring, I thee wed,*" he said.

Jens faced Pangfua. "*And may this ring be blessed so she who gives it and he who wears it may live joyously together, and continue in love all their lives,*" he said.

"*With this ring, I thee wed,*" Pangfua said, placing a golden band on Li Jun's finger. "*Wear it as a symbol of our love and commitment.*"

"May this couple continue to live and grow, be able to forgive and learn together, to be better together than they were apart," Jens said. *"With the authority vested in me, as Captain of the* General Xing, *I now pronounce you husband and wife. Li Jun and Pang fua now begin their married life together."* Jens opened his hands and presented the couple to the crew clustered in the bridge. They clapped and came forward to congratulate the couple.

"Cute couples," Paora said.

"They wanted to honeymoon on the Shack," Jens said. "They think it's romantic, for some reason."

"This is a very romantic place," Paora said. "They'll have a good time. And congratulations, man. You should be honeymooning too, I hear."

"My lady said absolutely not. She's minding the ship so the children can play," Jens said.

"Minding the ship?"

"She's the First Mate, it's her job. She takes her work very seriously."

Jens walked slowly around the room, fingering small items on the shelves. He picked up a piece of greenstone, carved and polished to resembled a *toki*, a tool for cutting and digging, representative of mana. Jens liked the concept of *mana*, a Māori word that wasn't easy to translate into English, or any language, for that matter. It meant self-image, self-worth, self-respect. But those were just words that tried to describe it. *Mana* was something that was earned through action, and it was something that could be lost the same way. Maybe it had to do with values, as well. Living up to your values. No compromise.

Jens let a wayward visitor enter his mind for the first time in months. Skipper had talked about *mana*, though he never understood it. Not that Skipper would admit it, know it, or that Jens ever let that thought escape his mouth. Skipper understood ego, that was true. But he confused ego and *mana*, which made an understanding of *mana* impossible. Part of having *mana* was enhancing the mana of others. Giving them a chance to grow and shine. Maybe mana is also all about leadership. Good leadership.

Jens carefully set the stone back on the shelf and sat in a large chair across from Paora.

"So, is it true?" Paora asked.

Jens relaxed into the faux leather chair, letting months of tension seep out of his muscles. Paora watched and smiled. He handed Jens a small cigarette and he inhaled. Jens blew out the smoke and held it up.

"Nothing like traditional medicine, man," he said. "I've always loved this smell."

"You didn't answer my question," Paora said, taking the joint from Jens' hand.

Jens shook his head. "Your medicine is going to be the new tradition. This is just a pleasant diversion." Smoked floated to the low ceiling and hung there.

"You've grown into a very serious man, Captain Jensen," Paora said. "But seriously, relax. And answer my question."

"Suzie stayed behind," Jens said, still evading. "She'll probably never be the same again. It's your medicine that's keeping her ... alive. Or at least giving her a chance to heal."

"What happened, Jens? Tell me. I don't like rumors," Paora said.

"I don't know exactly what you heard. But it's true," Jens said.

"I don't know what that means."

"Okay. The Shack's not the end of the road," Jens said. "Not anymore."

Paora sat across from him, waiting. Jens closed his eyes.

"It has islands, thousands of islands," he said. "Some are as big as New Zealand. Or Japan. Archipelagos stretching for thousands of miles. Room for millions. Even more. It's beautiful."

"So that bit about you being an ambassador?"

"It's true. All of it," Jens said. "We're going to Earth to—"

"Hand it over to the Consortia," Paora finished.

"That's the plan."

"You find a planet—"

"We didn't find it," Jens interrupted.

"As I was saying, you find a planet and all you can think about doing is giving it away." Paora licked his fingers and pinched the tip of the joint, putting it out. He placed it on the table between them.

"I represent the Consortium," Jens said. "They sent me to do a job."

"From what you've told me, you don't owe them anything," Paora said. "Can I speak ... nah, I'm not going to ask if you mind or not, I'm just going to tell you what I think, and then you can tell me to fuck off if you want, no hard feelings."

Paora leaned forward and put his hand on Jens' knee. "You're being used and you don't owe the Consortium shit."

"Good start," Jens said.

"But true. And I'm telling you this because if it's true there's another planet out there, we have a chance of doing things better, doing it for something bigger than money."

"There is another planet out there," Jens said.

"So, let's not just give it to the richest group of pricks earthside," Paora said. "Let's blow the people's minds open, and then give it to *them*. Give them the whole planet."

"Sounds simple enough," Jens said. "There might be a few armies of Consortia strong men that would want to stop us just giving it away."

"We'll have plenty of time to figure out how to get around them," Paora said.

"So, you're coming back?"

Paora sat back in his chair. "Teal invited me. I'd like to see this through to the end," he said. "And I'd like to see home. I've trained all the chemists here. They can keep things going."

"You are welcome to travel on the *Xing*," Jens said.

"I was hoping you'd ask. Besides, I think you could use my help."

"What kind of help?" Jens asked.

"We've still got to get past the Russians," Paora said.

"I met them on the way through," Jens said. "Not a very trusting lot."

"And now you have a very lucrative cargo, as well as an incredible secret. They'll try to take the first, and surely kill for the second."

"And you already have ideas?"

"Of course," Paora said. "For what it's worth, I'd give them the first, or at least a large stake in it. They'll be distracted by the money. And you won't be able to work in Laika without them."

"And the second?" Jens asked.

"Ah, that one." Paora held another joint in his fingers, paper opened and dried green leaf inside. "Do you want some GLR sprinkled inside?"

"Not at the moment," Jens said. "I'm still trying to process what happened the last time I took it."

"Which is exactly what you should do. It's not the experience, per se, but thinking about the experience. I forget who said that." Paora licked the paper and rolled it into a tight cigarette.

"And the second?" Jens repeated.

"As for the second, if they tried to take it, I'd kill every one of them." The tip of the joint glowed bright orange as he inhaled. He handed it to Jens as he exhaled. "But I don't think that will be necessary if we do things right."

"Pull your foot in," Shinje whispered. "It can get hit like that."

Li Jun sat up against the bulkhead, moving his foot. Worry flashed across his face.

"This will be exactly as we trained," Shinje said. "They will come down this corridor, and we will delay them until time to fall back."

"I wondered why we always trained, why Captain Jens made us study," Li Jun said. "How did he know what would happen?"

"He didn't," Shinje said. "But because of training, we are ready. Is your sounder loaded?"

Li Jun lifted the weapon for Shinje to see.

"Try it. We have a little time. Make sure it works," Shinje said. "Go ahead. Just like you practiced. One round." Shinje nodded and smiled, pointing at the corridor.

Li Jun reached around the small wall he hid behind. He squeezed the trigger. The gun made a hollow *fmmmp* as the pulse of sound was discharged. The pulse ricocheted twice before the corridor grew quiet. Li Jun smiled.

"Feels good, doesn't it?" Shinje asked. "Hear that? They have entered the corridor."

Li Jun answered with a nod. "Do you think the tender is out?" he asked.

"If Yuan is doing what he should."

"Then it is out," Li Jun said. "He always knows what to do."

"Yes, he is a good student," Shinje agreed. "After he sees them enter the airlock, he will disable or steal their tender. Hey, finish this: *First on the battlefield waits for the enemy fresh—*"

"*Last on the battlefield charges into the fray exhausted.*"

"Well done. All part of the plan. See—all those months of studying Sun Tzu had a purpose. Feeling fresh? They aren't. Take a quick look. Are they still wearing helmets?"

Li Jun took a deep breath and looked quickly up the corridor before pulling his head back and pushing himself against the bulkhead.

"Their helmets are off," he said.

"Good, that will make this easier," Shinje said.

Li Jun allowed himself a small smile. "Your turn: *The skillful warrior stirs and is not stirred—*"

"Too easy," Shinje said. "*He lures his enemy into coming or obstructs him from coming.* Mind that foot."

Li Jun moved closer against the wall, pulling his foot back again.

"What is the form of this terrain?" Shinje asked, keeping the younger man's mind off the coming fight.

"Ummm," Li Jun said, thinking. "*Enclosed* terrain. We occupy it first, and we block it and wait for the enemy.'

"Not *precipitous* terrain? We hold and wait for the enemy. We entice him by retreating," Shinje said.

"But you are ahead of yourself," Li Jun said excitedly. "The plan is—"

Shinje raised a palm, and Li Jun grew silent. They listened as the invaders grew closer. Li Jun raised his sounder.

"Wait," Shinje whispered. "They must all enter this section of corridor. How would you describe this ground?"

"Are you serious? Terrain and ground—now?"

"Of course I am serious, Able Crewman Li Jun," Shinje whispered. "Answer the question. Tell me what kind of ground you see here."

Shinje watched Li Jun try to concentrate, fidgeting as the sounds down the corridor grew louder.

"*Light* ground?"

"That sounds like a question, not an answer," Shinje whispered. The sounds in the corridor were growing louder. He tried to count the boarding party by their boots. At least five, he thought.

"Bridge," he said into his comms. "I estimate five, possibly six."

"Copy," the bridge answered.

"Why *light* ground?" he asked Li Jun.

"Mmm, ummm ..." Li Jun stammered. "When an army enters enemy territory, but not deeply ..."

"No," Shinje said slowly and quietly. "I would say this is *intractable* ground. They are not going to get through. Are they?"

"No, sir," Li Jun said.

"Good," Shinje said. "They are almost in place." He spoke into the comms pinned to the collar of his shirt. "Bridge, close corridor door one. The Russians are coming." They heard a thick door slide shut behind the boarding party. Shouts came from the corridor.

Shinje held his fist up to Li Jun. He raised one finger, then two. At the third finger, they reached around the corridor and fired their sounders, three times each. *Fmmmp, fmmmp, fmmmp.* More shouts came from the corridor as the Russians tried to seek cover where there was none. Pulses ricocheted off bulkheads, but not all. A scream of pain echoed in the corridor.

"Fire again, you high, me low," Shinje instructed.

They reached around the small walls and fired, Li Jun at chest height, Shinje at knee. *Fmmmp, fmmmp, fmmmp.* They emptied their magazines and snapped fully loaded ones in place.

The bulkhead above Li Jun's head sparked, and the air near them whined. "They are using projectile weapons!" Li Jun said. "That is crazy! It is banned!"

"Captain Jens said to expect it," Shinje said. "They don't play by the rules. Now, again. Empty them." Pulses bounced down the corridor as they discharged all the charges in their magazines.

"Okay, fall back," Shinje said. He ejected the spent magazine and clicked another in place.

Li Jun reloaded as he backed down the corridor. Shinje fired a round and followed, backing away low, but letting the Russians know they were fleeing. Safely around the corner, he spoke into his comms. "Time to close corridor door two."

"Consider it done," the bridge replied. "Wish our guests a good night." Shinje grinned at Xiu's sense of humor. GLR infused air would send them someplace nice for a long time.

A heavy door slammed shut. Shinje glanced around the corner, then holstered his sounder and relaxed. He patted Li Jun on the shoulder, then took the other man's hand and shook it.

"Well done, Li Jun," he said. "Very well done. Did you think you would be fighting off Russians when you signed on?"

"No. Did you?"

"Absolutely not," Shinje said.

"Jens didn't say anything," Paora said. "I take it you haven't told him?"

Fran Lu tried to hide her surprise. She didn't succeed. "If he knew he would have tried to stop me from coming down. And we would have had a fight, and he would have lost and had a big sulk until something distracted him. But of course, I told him. We fought and he sulked."

"You know your husband well," Paora said. "I bet you call drills just to keep him busy, don't you?"

"Sometimes," she admitted. "But the crew also needs them."

"Like hell they do," he said. "They need a break from you two, is what they need."

"They are happy," she said.

Paora heard the defensiveness in her voice and regretted pushing. She was still getting used to his accent, let alone his sense of humor.

"So," he said after an uncomfortable silence. "Have you met Mr Smith?"

"No," she said. "But Jens said he would know us."

She walked down the stone street. She marvelled at all the stone, above and underfoot. The road itself was carved from the cave's floor, scraped and polished. She squinted upward at mirrors mimicking daylight, channelling the alien sun deep into the cavern. The prefab buildings they walked beside were a welcome contrast. E-cars humming by became rarer the farther they walked into the district.

"I don't get why we're wearing these clothes," Fran Lu said. "Anybody who sees us will know we're not from here."

"Anybody watching a surveillance camera won't," Paora said. "We'll look just like other workers. Smith is no doubt under surveillance."

She nodded but kept her face down. She hoped looking up at the mirrors hadn't been noticed. A large door on a prefab slid open in the building beside them. They looked into the dark interior before walking into it. The door slid shut behind them and a light flickered. Mr Smith was just as Jens described. Dignified bordering on dangerous.

"I apologize for the welcome, but things have been rather tense since your ships returned," Mr Smith said. He approached Fran Lu, bent and kissed her cheek. "Welcome to Laika."

Smith offered his hand to Paora. "Jens told me I was to rub your nose, but I think I'd rather not."

"Good choice," Paora said.

"I'd like to offer you a drink or something," Smith said. "But I fear time is becoming short."

"Have you heard anything?" Fran Lu asked.

"The *General Xing* is under attack," Smith said. "But the Russians sound angry, which means their plan probably isn't working the way they hoped."

"And Captain Jensen?" she asked.

"He and Yuan entered the Pistolety," he said. "That's all I can say. We don't have any ears there. Total comms block. But that was to be expected." He led them to the cargo trucks waiting in the warehouse. He opened the back of the nearest truck and pointed to the stacks of sacks.

"That's as much of the supplies as we could spare. You must have taken a beating," he said.

"Steps have proved more difficult and time-consuming," Fran Lu said.

"The Russians have a large presence outside. You didn't see them, because they didn't know where you were. We'll make sure they see the trucks and divert as many as we can towards them. As far as they're concerned, you're here to pick up a consignment."

"How are we going to get these to the fliers?" Fran Lu asked.

"A parade, of course," Mr Smith said. "I reckon on Earth it must be around May, so we'll have a good old-fashioned May Day Parade. Workers of the world, unite! They'll escort you to the loading bay where you can get back on your flier, and others will surround the Pistolety. We can't match them gun for gun, but we have something they don't, which makes us a lot stronger."

"Brilliant," Paora said. "People power."

"Indeed," Smith said. "It's good to remind management who has the real power. There are always more of us than them. I think with the Pistolety surrounded, our comrades inside will come to an agreement."

He patted the side of the truck. "Charge 'em up boys!" he called. "And get on the horn. It's time to get out the banners and march."

The trucks began to hum and he turned and faced them. "I have heard things," he said. "Are those things true?"

Paora bit his bottom lip and avoided the man's eyes, but Fran Lu smiled at him.

"That's all I need to hear," Smith said. He hugged Fran Lu. "And congratulations," he added, glancing at her flat belly. "To both you and your new husband. Tell Jens I think he has made some very good choices since the last time we met. And help him reflect on what happened here. Or what's going to happen, very soon. Laika is no different from Earth in lots of ways. Powerful people needing reminding about where the *real* power lies."

He helped her into the cab. Before Paora climbed in, Smith offered his hand. Paora took it firmly.

"It's an honor and a privilege," Smith said. "I admire your work. I wish I could go with you and take the product back."

"The feeling is mutual, man," Paora said. "There is plenty of space on the *Xing* if you want to come."

Smith shook his head and laughed. "We all have our reasons for being out here, and sometimes going back just isn't an option. Besides, I think I'm going to have my hands full as soon as you folks leave."

Paora climbed into the truck and sat beside Fran Lu. Smith closed the door, slapped the side of the vehicle and the truck moved away.

The Pistolety was exactly as Jens remembered. He and Yuan entered the stone building, as arranged. He let his eyes adjust to the dim light. Two thugs posing as drinkers sat at the bar. Their drinks barely touched, no evidence of empty glasses, their weapons obvious to the trained eye. Amateurs? That could be good. Or it could make the entire situation more volatile. Professionals knew when to hold, when the inexperienced might panic.

A busboy entered and cleared a table. One of Jens' first jobs had been washing dishes at a cheap café. The pay was so low he actually enjoyed it until he could find something better. When the pay is low, you don't have care. This busboy was either paid very well, or he wasn't an actual busboy. And the lovers in the corner, half touched plates in front of them. They looked well trained.

Natasha sat at the head of a table set against the wall. From her position, she could see the entire restaurant. She smiled as they entered, warm, yet hard. Very hard. She wore a red dress, which made her fair skin look even whiter.

The hulk sat next to her. Just as Jens remembered. He didn't seem to care that his back was to the door, no doubt choosing that position as a statement. He couldn't see the Japanese blade strapped to Jens' thigh, nor the bulge of the sounder in his left pocket. Or the unmistakeable fold in the fabric of his pant legs that gave away the presence of another sounder concealed by his ankle.

Vladimir was playing this well. He sat at the table with both of his tattooed hands in front of him, turning vulnerability into a malignant statement. He was the reason Jens had spent so much of his time in the dojo. Much as he wanted, he just couldn't see a scenario where their differences were not settled.

"The principle on which to manage an army is to set up one standard of courage which all must reach." Jens copied that into his personal log. It was his duty as a leader. At this very moment, he expected others to show courage, including his wife. Only Fran Lu knew how tiring he found it, carrying that responsibility. She was the only person he dared show, and he was grateful there was at least one person he didn't have to pretend to. That made her far stronger than he. The others saw a competent leader, what sometimes still felt to Jens like

an elaborate act. But it was time to play the part. Jens stood a bit straighter and dusted off his clean epaulet, even if Vladimir wasn't watching.

Jens let Yuan greet Dimitri, who stood before them in his crisp black suit. It gave Jens the seconds needed to assess the situation and a couple more to regret they hadn't brought another crew member with them.

"Yuan," Dimitri said. "*Vsegda priyatno, moy drug.* Always a pleasure, my friend! Come in, come in! We have ordered a meal." He grabbed Yuan in a bear hug and kissed his cheeks three times. "It has been too long!"

He faced Jens. "Mister Jensen, no, I insult you," he said. "*Kapitan* Jensen! You have not only learned well, you have risen in the ranks." Jens waited for the pat-down. He returned Dimitri's hug, letting the man feel each weapon that he carried. He let his foot brush Dimitri's leg in case the man missed that sounder.

They walked to the table and Natasha and Vladimir stood. Jens kissed the woman's cheeks. He greeted the man with an outstretched hand. Let him guess what he carried. Vladimir grabbed Jens' hand and squeezed. Jens was ready for the macho display.

"Enough, boys," Natasha said. "Let us enjoy our meal. You may have time to play after."

Jens and Yuan moved around the table, taking their seats. Their backs were to the wall. The Russians could read into that whatever they wanted. Waiters came and placed dishes in front of them (real waiters, Jens noticed), but he continued to stare at Vladimir despite the pull of the food. Jens smiled at the man opposite, then ignored him and breathed in the dish.

"This smells wonderful," Jens said to Natasha.

"I remembered how much you enjoyed your last meal with us, Mr Jensen," she said. "I am sorry," she added. "I have addressed you incorrectly, Captain Jensen."

He looked at his epaulet. "No offense taken," he said.

"You have risen since we last met," she said. "You have your own ship now."

"Yes," Jens answered. "The *General Xing*. We've had to make some improvements, but she is a fine ship, with a fine crew."

"Didn't she already have a captain?" Vladimir growled.

"She did indeed," Jens said, smiling. "But once the colonists were discharged, he lost his usefulness." Jens made a show of examining the knife in his hand, then cut a piece of cavy and placed it in his mouth, chewing slowly. "This is absolutely delicious," he said, ignoring the man opposite.

"Did you not keep some after dropping off the colonists?" Natasha asked.

"We did, but they were lost during a Step," he admitted.

"That is unfortunate," she said, although Jens thought he heard 'unusual.' Yuan glanced over at him. Good. *They know we are hiding something,* Jens thought, *just as we know they are hiding something. It's the first principle of business, as Yuan would lecture.*

"Fresh greens," Yuan said, admiring his plate.

"You left me haunted, Captain Jensen," Natasha said. "After you left, I could think of nothing more than the sunrise. I have even suited up and gone to the surface to view one. But it is not as you describe. Here there are no colors. Only rock and light."

Jens cut another piece of cavy and held it on his fork. "Perhaps you should come with us back to Earth, and I can show you one from the sea."

Natasha laughed. "Are you sure your wife would not mind, *Captain* Jensen?"

"She is very understanding," Jens said. "But perhaps you are right." *Why is it so hard to keep a secret in space?* Jens wondered. He smiled at Natasha and set down his cutlery.

"I thank you for the meal," Jens said. "But we do have business to conduct."

Natasha pushed her plate away from herself and smiled at Jens. "And I thought you had merely risen in rank," she said. "You have risen to your reputation. Dare I ask what has become of Captains Teal or Wan?"

"That depends on the type of answer you seek," he said. Jens stared at Vladimir as he spoke. The larger man returned a glare. *Good*, Jens thought. *With a fork and a knife in your hands, how can you draw a sounder? Must be driving you mad.*

"We don't need to know or care about who is captain of what," Dimitri cut in. "What we do need to know is why you are trying to make deals that do not involve us."

"Your wife will not leave Laika," Vladimir said. "Until we say she can."

She was the shiny lure, which was exactly why Jens didn't want her to come. But that, as she pointed out, was why she would be perfect. Jens pursed his lips. "We may be finished with dinner, but is it too late for drinks?" he asked.

"Not too late yet," Natasha said. She raised a hand and snapped her fingers. Waiters (real) quickly cleared the table. Another brought a tray with shot glasses and a bottle of Laika vodka. He poured the clear liquid into the glasses.

Natasha raised hers.

"To an open and honest business arrangement," she said. She downed the shot and slammed the empty glass on the table. The others still held their full shots. Jens carefully set his down on the table.

"We do not tolerate secret deals like that which you are trying to conduct," she said. "We consider that a breach of goodwill, a breach of contract."

"I was not aware that we have signed a contract," Jens said.

She looked past him for the first time. "Yuan, what the hell is going on?"

"You need to speak with Captain Jensen," he said, raising his palms.

Natasha laughed. "Very well," she said, shaking her head. "Captain Jensen, your ship is being boarded and the shipment you hoped to collect will not leave the surface."

Jens never fished from the scow. He never understood the attraction, and if he were honest, which he never was about this subject, he didn't like fish. The smell, the taste or the texture. But he would watch other crew cast out when they were off duty, standing by their rods and waiting for that pull or snap that meant a fish had taken the bait.

"Natasha," he said. "I must apologize if it appears we are trying to cheat you." He pushed his chair back from the table. He showed his hands to Vladimir and winked at the brute. Jens turned to Natasha. "Although it may *appear* that we are trying to cheat you, we have come here today to do the opposite."

"You have nothing to bargain with, Captain Jensen," she said.

Captain. Good. She still had no idea. Time to flash more shiny things in front of her. The drinker from the bar came over and whispered into Natasha's ear.

"I am guessing that I still have the ability to bargain?" Jens asked.

She leaned back in her chair and waited, frowning. Jens tilted his head and listened to the singing from outside the building. The couple from the corner table stopped pretending to date and went to the door.

"I am also guessing," Jens said, "that your men at the loading bay are letting *my wife* get into her flier, with her cargo, and exit the loading bay." He watched as Vladimir clenched his jaw muscles. Yuan pretended to ignore the scene and sipped his vodka. Dimitri appeared amused.

"And I am guessing," Jens continued, "that your boarding party has failed, and that your fliers have been disabled."

No color entered Natasha's face, but her eyes glowed.

"Your men will be well cared for and returned," Jens said. "There is no need for this to become any more unpleasant.

We'll need to talk about the fliers later, though. Those are hard to come by, and my crew may not want to give them back. You will be reimbursed."

The drinker from the bar returned to the table and bent to Natasha's ear.

"*Prosto skazat' eto!*" she snapped. Just say it!

The man stood. "There is a large crowd surrounding the building, ma'am," he said. "Hundreds of workers."

Jens remembered his crewmates grinning at this point, as they began to reel in their catch. Jens didn't grin. He exhaled slowly and smiled as pleasantly as he could at Natasha. He made his crew study ground and terrain. This was ground and terrain dissolving, right beneath her feet. Jens almost felt sympathy for her position.

"I am being genuine when I offer you passage to Earth," he said. "And I am certain my wife would not mind me showing you a sunrise. They are as beautiful as I have described. Every morning, every day. But we are not here to discuss the sunrise." Jens lifted his shot glass and drained it, then raised a hand and snapped his fingers. The bartender glanced at Natasha, and then rushed over and filled the empty glasses with more vodka.

"We are here to conduct business, so let us do that," Jens said. "Yuan says that dinner is the sunrise of the deal, and the sun is now up. So, let's make a deal."

"It seems that you hold most of the cards," Natasha said.

"Only at this moment," Jens conceded. "Any business done on Hat Pin must involve you, and we would rather you were a partner than an adversary."

"Go on," she said.

"Partners, by definition, are equals. Is that not right, Yuan?"

Yuan looked at Jens but didn't speak. "That's what I've been taught, anyway," Jens said. "Partners have to be equal. I am offering you fifty percent of any trade in GLR passing through Hat Pin. Which will be, as you no doubt realize, a lot of trade."

Jens tried to read Natasha's face. For a moment it was indecipherable. But then she made it easy. She relaxed into her chair and smiled.

"Yuan," she said, "*Ty sukin syn.* You have taught Captain Jensen too well." She clapped her hands. "Leave us," she said. The drinker at the bar and the couple dining stood and left. Two others that Jens had not noticed left a table in a darkened corner of the restaurant. Yuan winked at him. Yuan hadn't missed them.

Natasha snapped her fingers and the waiter appeared beside her. "Take this away and bring the good stuff. And prepare a case for our ... partners ... to take with them. I like how you do business, Captain Jensen. Very entertaining. And that American, Smith, has turned out to be a rather sly fox."

She raised her shot glass towards his. He touched hers and they downed them at the same time. She snapped her fingers again and the glasses were refilled.

"Fifty percent," she said. "Very well, I accept your offer. And you can keep the fliers. They are old anyway."

Jens smiled and lifted his glass. The vodka burned as it flowed down his throat, but he liked it. "Mr Smith will represent us on Hat Pin," he said.

"Of course, he will," Natasha said. She snapped her fingers again. Glasses were refilled.

"When the freighters return, they will bring your share. I would like to give you this," Jens said. He reached towards a pocket and Vladimir tensed. Natasha placed a hand on the big man's arm.

Jens pulled out a bag full of white pills and placed them in front of her. "We'll send more down with your men. If you open comms, I can contact the *Xing* and make arrangements."

"Done," she said.

Jens pushed his chair back and stood. Natasha stood and placed her hands on Jens' shoulders. She leaned forward and kissed his cheeks.

"And congratulations," she said. "You will make a wonderful father."

21

Jens stood at the door of the creche. There were only four little crewmates so far, but that was bound to change. The youngest was a month old. He slept soundly despite the noise of his crewmates playing nearby. Lijuan cried angrily as Supervisor Boatswain Billi walked with her back and forth across the room. Jens had created a new rank for Billi. A boatswain supervised deck crew, and as such Billi supervised the *Xing's* youngest crew ... Her young charge, Lijuan, may be a first in her own right—Step induced labor, being born at the end of an Einstein-Rosen bridge. *If I had come into the world after that experience*, Jens thought, *I'd be angry as well.*

He walked to the eldest junior crew in the room. The little girl smiled and reached out her arms as soon as she saw him.

"Ba!" she shouted.

Jens scooped her up and gave her a hug. "Hello, little princess!" he said, kissing her cheek. "Shall we go see Captain Mommy?"

The little girl nodded. "Say 'bye to your crewmates," he told her. "Billi, I'm taking Ling to the bridge. It's time."

"Good luck, sir," Billi called over Lijuan's cries.

Jens could hear Ling gasp as the door to the bridge opened and she saw the blue-green planet on the viewscreen. "That's where your mama and ba were born," he whispered to her.

"Hello, Captain Mommy," Jens said to Fran Lu. "Permission to enter the bridge?"

"Permission granted, Ambassador Daddy," she said. "Bring me our daughter."

"Aye, aye, Captain." Jens walked across the room and brought Ling close for Fran Lu to kiss. He placed a hand on her swelling belly where their second child grew.

"Are you ready?" she asked.

"I guess I have to be," he said. "Daddy made a video, my little jinga-Ling, and he's going to show it to everybody down there!"

"Ugh," Fran Lu said. "Don't talk to her in that baby voice!"

She stroked his arm. "Wu Pen's flier descended this morning."

"I know," Jens said. "He is going to have a tough meeting."

"He'll be fine," Fran Lu said. "The Consortium will see why we're doing this, and that they'll still gain."

The Consortia poison life on Earth, we don't have to let it poison Pemako! That was Alvarez, bringing an already heated argument to full boil. Wu Pen looked at the captains around the table, his face an unreadable mask. Finally, it softened and they knew he would agree. His expression haunted Jens. He couldn't decide if it was one of relief, that weeks of deliberation were over. Or if was the look of the condemned accepting their fate. In the convoy they were their own bosses, making their own Consortium of sorts. The bosses Wu Pen had to face were very different.

"Jens, he'll be fine," Fran Lu said again.

"They'll view him as a traitor," Jens said. "This convoy was theirs, so they'll want a claim to everything."

Ling used the shoulder of Jens' shirt to wipe her nose. "This will be the first time I see your film," Fran Lu said. "Imagine, I thought I married a Captain, but it turns out he's a movie star."

"Yeah, well, he had to give up being a captain when he got promoted," Jens said. "You'll like this one. It's got everything a good film needs. Good guys," he pointed his thumb at his chest. "That's me, by the way. It's got bad guys, which Dr Lin will talk about, and a bug that wiped them out, a bug our medicine could have killed. But they were too late, or too early. And it's got great scenery."

"And demands, no doubt," Fran Lu teased.

"Plenty of those," Jens said. "Donuts, technology, settlers, open access for all, distribution and sales of GLR—"

"Sir, it's time to broadcast," Xiu said from the helm. "All channels are open."

All channels. Governments, Consortia, unions, ships and hubs. Media outlets. Social networks. All soon very keen to acquire the coordinates of *Pemako*, which would be released as soon as everybody agreed to play and pay by their rules.

"I was thinking," Jens said. "I mean, technically, we're like visiting aliens, aren't we? I'm just saying that to warn you about the beginning. I couldn't help myself."

Jens carried Ling over to the helm. Xiu indicated to the transmission icon on the monitor. "Why don't you do this, my little jinga-Ling," he said in a baby voice, and with her little hand he pressed send.

The image of Earth was replaced by the image of Jens, dressed in a suit specially tailored by Cheung for the occasion.

"Greetings, people of Earth," his image said. "My name is Andrew Jensen, and I stand before you as Ambassador representing the planet of *Pemako*. The sister planet of our own Earth, which for years we have dreamed of and searched for.

"I am here to tell you that such a place has been found ..."

Also by Christopher McMaster

SEEDERS

The exciting sequel to MisStep:

They tried to hide from certain death. Now it's time to find them

A pandemic spread over their planet and swept them from history. In a desperate act to save their species they launched a remnant of survivors into the depths of space, frozen in cryo-sleep, to be awakened only when their ship detected a habitable planet. But there were no planets and the ship continued into the cold and dark.

Thousands of years later humans have settled the ocean world. Earth's dream of finding her sister planet has come true, and it was free for the taking. They gave it their own name, Pemako, and lived beside the ruins of what was once a mighty civilization. Picking through the artifacts, xeno-linguist Peter Taylor and a small research team find evidence of the Original's desperate mission. Plotting the probable course of the ship, the team locate where it might be, if it really exists, and if it is still operational.

The promised technology of the Originals outweighs any 'ifs'. But they need the help of a powerful earth-based consortia, as well as from Andrew Jensen, the only man to ever survive a confrontation with those whose planet they now call their own.

Find it HERE